P9-DXE-526

INFESTATION

ALSO BY HEIDI LANG
& KATI BARTKOWSKI

Whispering Pines

The Mystic Cooking Chronicles:

A Dash of Dragon

A Hint of Hydra

A Pinch of Phoenix

Whispering Pines

Infestation

Heidi Lang & Kati Bartkowski

MARGARET K. McELDERRY BOOKS

NEW YORK LONDON TORONTO SYDNEY NEW DELHI

MARGARET K. McELDERRY BOOKS
An imprint of Simon & Schuster Children's Publishing Division
1230 Avenue of the Americas, New York, New York 10020

For information about special discounts for bulk purchases, please contact Simon & Schuster Special Sales at 1-866-506-1949 or business@simonandschuster.com.
The Simon & Schuster Speakers Bureau can bring authors to your live event. For more information or to book an event, contact the Simon & Schuster Speakers Bureau at 1-866-248-3049 or visit our website at www.simonspeakers.com.
Jacket designed by Tiara Iandiorio
Interior designed by Mike Rosamilia
The text of this book was set in Adobe Caslon Pro.
Manufactured in the United States of America
0821 FFG
First Edition
2 4 6 8 10 9 7 5 3 1
Library of Congress Cataloging-in-Publication Data
Names: Lang, Heidi, author. | Bartkowski, Kati, author.
Title: Infestation / Heidi Lang & Kati Bartkowski.
Description: First edition. | New York : Margaret K. McElderry Books, [2021] | Series: Whispering Pines; 2 | Summary: "Rae discovers that killer alien centipedes have overrun the town of Whispering Pines, while Caden deals with the fallout of his brother Aiden's return from the Other Place"—Provided by publisher.
Identifiers: LCCN 2020054461 (print) | LCCN 2020054462 (ebook) |
ISBN 9781534460508 (hardcover) | ISBN 9781534460522 (ebook)
Subjects: CYAC: Supernatural—Fiction. | Extraterrestrial beings—Fiction. | Monsters—Fiction. | Secrets—Fiction.
Classification: LCC PZ7.1.L3436 Inf 2021 (print) | LCC PZ7.1.L3436 (ebook) | DDC [Fic]—dc23
LC record available at https://lccn.loc.gov/2020054461
LC ebook record available at https://lccn.loc.gov/2020054462

For Alan, who has helped dig us out of a few plot holes over the years and will undoubtedly do so again in the stories still to come.
Thank you.

PROLOGUE

{ THREE DAYS EARLIER }

Blake woke to the most horrible screaming he'd ever heard. He lay frozen on his cot as it went on and on, high-pitched and awful.

Heed the warning cry of the banshee, his grandmother used to say. *They wail when someone you love is about to die.* Eyes red and swollen from endless weeping, long streaming hair, and bony hands extending with nails curved and dirty. Blake could picture it perfectly.

He hadn't been there the night his grandmother finally passed away, but his father had told him stories about it. About the spirits that had surrounded the house, their sorrow loud and keening, and how his own father had run outside with a shovel in one hand, a cross in the other, trying to keep them away. It hadn't worked, of course. And in the end, the banshees had taken him, too.

Blake clutched at his thin blanket as if it might protect him. But gradually he realized it wasn't banshees at all. The *goats* were shrieking.

His uncle kept nine of them in a large pen outside his yurt, and every evening he took them out for a hike to settle them down before bed. Blake had been staying with him for the past three weeks, and they had been peacefully quiet every night before this. Why would they be so agitated now?

"Uncle Gary?" he whispered. His uncle was lying on his own bed on the other side of the yurt. Blake could see the gleaming white of his wide-open eyes, but he didn't answer.

Another goat bleated, high-pitched and terrified. Blake recognized that voice: Waffles. His favorite. Every morning the goat would trot up to him and put his little goat head against Blake's shoulder until he scratched him behind the ears.

Blake sat up and swung his legs over the side of his cot. He couldn't stay here and do nothing. Not if Waffles was in danger.

"Wait," his uncle croaked, and Blake froze, his hand on the door latch. "I can't protect you if you go out into the night. When the sun sets, the forest belongs to *them*."

"Them, who?"

"The other things that live here."

Blake's heart pounded, his mouth dry. He thought of his nice, safe, solid house with its thick walls and firmly locked doors, and wished he'd never run away. Tomorrow he was going back home. Immediately. "What other things?" he asked.

His uncle didn't answer.

Waffles shrieked once more. Blake couldn't take it. "We have to help the goats." He pulled open the door and slipped outside, half hoping his uncle would try to stop him again.

But he didn't.

It was dark here in the middle of the Watchful Woods. His uncle didn't like people—he barely tolerated *Blake*—so he'd set up his yurt as far from the streets and houses of Whispering Pines as he could. The tall pines loomed overhead, patches of brilliant starlight visible between each treetop. They gave off just enough light to see the outline of the goat pen a few yards away, but not enough to see the goats in it. Blake could hear them, though, bleating in sharp, anguished tones.

He hesitated, the cool night wrapping around him. There were no crickets chirping, no owls hooting, nothing but the goats. It felt wrong, like the rest of the night had been artificially muted by something that didn't belong here. An unnatural force worse than any banshee.

Blake shivered, wishing he had grabbed a jacket and a flashlight, and maybe a weapon. He thought of his friend Jeremy and what had happened to him just weeks ago, and almost sprinted back to the yurt. But in the end, it was just a glorified tent. If there were something truly dangerous out here, he doubted its walls would protect him, no matter what deals his uncle had made. So he forced himself to walk toward the goat pen, the grass whispering against his bare feet.

When he reached the gate, he could just make out the goats all huddled together in the nearest corner like one trembling mass.

All except one.

Waffles lay motionless on his side in the middle of the pen, the white star-shaped fur on the top of his head almost glowing against the dark. The night breeze picked up, and beneath the ever-present smell of goats Blake caught a whiff of fresh-turned earth and the metallic tang of blood. The scent of new death.

He made a small involuntary sound, his fingers trembling as he yanked back the lock on the gate and pulled it open. He stepped inside, careful to shut the gate behind him, and moved closer, still staring at that sad crumpled form lying in the starlight like one of his baby sister's abandoned toys. Closer still, and he noticed the scuff marks in the dirt, like the goat had been dragged.

And then something moved next to Waffles. Quick, furtive movement, like a spider scuttling out of the light, only with way too many legs—hundreds of legs—and a long body a few feet in length and thick as his waist, all of it the same color as the night-washed grass. As it crawled around the goat, it made little clicking noises like a dog's nails against a hardwood floor.

Terror trickled down Blake's spine, icy and numb. He put a hand over his mouth, choking down a scream.

The thing stopped moving abruptly, all of those legs still. Two long stalks on the top of its head trembled in the breeze, flicking forward and back and then pointing right at him.

Blake was very aware of the beating of his heart, the hitching sound of his breath, the noise of the other goats. He could feel a lock of hair sliding against the side of his face, the rough texture of the cropped grass under his feet, his pajama bottoms, baggy and comfortable. And the absolute silence of that impossibly large insect, the weight of its full attention bearing down on him.

Abruptly its torso bunched, and it sprang forward, all of its legs moving furiously fast as it sprinted right at him.

Blake screamed and ran blindly across the pen, scrabbling at the gate, dragging it open.

He wasn't fast enough.

It hit him in the back of the knees, knocking him sideways into the grass, its tiny legs already moving over him, pinning him down. It reared up, half its body lifting like the striking head of a cobra, and Blake glimpsed something underneath that looked almost like a face, with dark, soulless eyes and slits for a nose, and where a mouth should have been, a pair of serrated mandibles dripping some strange yellowish liquid that gleamed in the starlight.

He realized he was still screaming but couldn't stop, the sound of his own terror echoing in his ears, sharper and more desperate than any goat cry as that insectlike head lowered over him, those mandibles clicking, extending—

Crack!

The creature flew off him and landed on the ground with a sickening crunch. Blake looked up. His uncle stood over him, panting, the blade of his axe glittering. Blake swallowed. "Is it dead?"

"I think—"

The thing shuddered suddenly and twisted around, sinewy as a snake, those tiny legs quivering, the torso bunching.

Uncle Gary leaped forward and brought the axe back down,

cutting it in half. The legs kicked a few more times and then went still. "Now it is," he said.

Blake nodded, unable to look away as more of that strange yellowish liquid oozed out of the neck cavity to puddle against the ground. His stomach roiled in sickening waves, and he could still feel the scuttling of all those legs up and down his body. "Is that one of them?" he gasped. "One of the things that live in the forest?"

His uncle pulled his axe up and wiped it on the grass. "Nope. That is something else. Something that has no business being here." He looked past the corpse. The lines of his face trembled, then hardened, and he lifted his axe and slung it over his shoulder. "The things that live here know better than to mess with my goats."

Blake tore his gaze from the corpse and glanced back at Waffles. He wanted to cry, but he felt too drained inside, like a wrung-out sponge.

His uncle sighed. "We should probably tell someone about this."

"Like who?" Blake knew his uncle didn't like talking to anyone who wasn't family. And even then, he wasn't thrilled about it.

"I'll have to think on that," his uncle said at last. "But this thing, whatever it is and whatever it means, is beyond my pay grade." He scrubbed a hand over his face, suddenly looking as exhausted as Blake felt. "I'll have to get myself another goat too."

Blake felt like it wasn't the time to talk about that. Not now, not when Waffles was still right there. He climbed to his feet and walked over to the small animal, then knelt and ran his hands down his soft, warm fur.

The chest rose and fell beneath his trembling fingers.

Blake caught his breath, then leaned in closer. Hope beat inside him like a second heart. "Uncle Gary? I think . . . I think Waffles is alive."

"What?" His uncle hurried over and crouched next to him. He laid the axe down and ran his hands over the goat, then looked up, surprised. "He is. He is!" He grinned, wide and triumphant.

Blake grinned back, the horrors of the night already slipping away, the details fading like a bad dream. And then he noticed movement behind his uncle, past the corpse and outside the edge of the goat pen. Something else long and insectlike scuttling quietly back into the night.

His grin cracked, peeling away like a bad sunburn.

"What is it?" his uncle asked.

"I saw . . ." Blake blinked, but it was gone. Only trees waving gently, their branches glowing softly in the starlight. "Nothing," he said, and he almost believed it.

1.
RAE

Rae looked at the barbed-wire fence and the security cameras and knew she had made a huge mistake. This was exactly the kind of place she needed to avoid. The kind of place her dad used to work at, all concrete walls and secrecy. A place that would be easy to enter but almost impossible to escape.

A large sign out front proclaimed, GREEN ON! BECAUSE IT'S NEVER TOO SOON TO THINK ABOUT THE FUTURE.

Rae eyed the steel-reinforced doors, and the guard standing just outside them. He looked back, his face as impassive as the wall next to him. He reminded her of the men who had stormed her old house and taken all of her dad's things. He had that same air of efficient indifference; he would do his job and do it well, and anyone who got in the way would be squashed without a second's thought.

Her dad was the reason she was here now, she reminded herself. All of this was for him. A year ago, he'd gone into work and never come out again. He'd been an engineer doing some kind of secret contract work on a project called Operation Gray Bird. And he'd discovered something unusual. Something he hadn't been supposed to see. Proof of extraterrestrial life.

Rae was sure that was the reason her dad was missing—he'd been abducted by the government and was being held somewhere now against his will. She had sworn that she would find him, but until recently, she hadn't had any leads. Especially since her mom had moved her and her older sister across the country from their home in northern California to this strange little Connecticut town.

But everything changed last week when Patrick, the senior consultant at Green On!, had told her who assigned her dad's contract. *He was working on a new energy source. Who do you think would be interested in something like that?* Patrick had claimed he didn't have all the details yet, but he promised that if she took part in his company's internship program, he'd find them out.

Rae didn't trust Patrick, with his too-handsome face and his too-fancy suits and his tendency to show up at exactly the most convenient time. But she believed him when he said he could get her information about her dad's involvement with Green On!. Which meant she needed to follow through on her end of the bargain, even if every instinct told her not to go into this place.

The six other kids from her school all trotted obediently through the doors. Only the last one hesitated, a short girl with dark hair and a humongous backpack—Rae's best friend, Vivienne. "Rae-Rae, you coming?" she called.

Rae glanced at the camera lurking just above the open doors. The light on top of it blinked like a single bloody eye, and she imagined Patrick watching her. It was too late to back out now.

She pasted on a shaky smile. "I'm just admiring the view."

Vivienne laughed. "This"—she waved her hand at the building—"looks like an ugly brick, I know. But it's nice inside."

Which obviously meant Vivienne had been here before, either to visit her mom, who was the head of the nuclear division at Green On!, or . . .

Or when she had started secretly working with Patrick.

Rae didn't like to remember that. Still, the truth stared out at her, as large and uncomfortable as Vivienne's ever-present backpack. Her friend had been the first person in Patrick's internship program, doing who-knew-what, and she hadn't said a word about it to Rae until after Rae almost got herself killed by a monster from an alternate dimension. And still she was keeping most of it secret.

But then, Rae was keeping secrets too.

The only person she'd been completely honest with was her neighbor, Caden Price. With his dark eyes, messy black hair, and heavy silver jewelry, he was the kind of boy who stood out, even in a weird place like Whispering Pines. And just like her, he'd understood how isolating it was to know a truth that no one else was willing to accept. She'd been able to tell him her secrets, like what really happened to her dad.

But Caden thought this internship was a terrible idea. He

wanted no part of it, or anyone in it. And after Rae decided to join anyway, he had stopped talking to her.

Rae angrily shoved thoughts of Caden away and followed Vivienne inside, the doors closing behind them with a heavy thump like a cage door slamming shut. She paused just inside the lobby. Vivienne was right; it *was* nice in here, all bright lights and fancy decorations.

To her left, the entire wall was floor-to-ceiling windows that looked out onto the Watchful Woods, while to her right sat a long, sleek desk made of black swirling marble. Hung on the wall over it were a series of awards, framed newspaper articles, and large photographs. The floor had white and gold tiles, with several small tables and chairs set up in little clusters across it. As Rae walked farther into the lobby, she realized the shape of each of the tables was meant to represent a different element: a sun, a water droplet, swirly lines that were probably supposed to be wind, and an atom.

A man wearing a bright green polo shirt with the Green On! logo on the front popped up from behind the desk like a clown out of a jack-in-the-box.

Rae leaped back, almost falling over Vivienne.

"Hello, children." The man gave all of them a condescending smile. "Welcome to Green On! We're all *so glad* you get to join us here. Not only are we a cutting-edge energy research facility, but now, also, a daycare. How *fun*." He emphasized certain words, drawing them out the same way a person might draw their nails down a chalkboard.

Rae gritted her teeth, and Vivienne shifted her weight like

she wanted to tackle the guy, while the other kids muttered behind them.

"Doctor Nguyen is in the middle of a major scientific breakthrough, but she'll still take time out of her very busy schedule to show you around. Because nothing is more important than our *little interns.*" Another broad, insincere smile. "She'll be here any minute. Until then, please, make yourselves at home." He waved a hand at the tables and chairs, and then disappeared again beneath his desk as abruptly as he'd appeared. Rae wondered if there was a door under there or if he was just sitting on the floor, waiting for them to leave.

"Wow," Vivienne said. "That was the most passive-aggressive welcome I've ever heard."

"It was actually kind of impressive." Rae rolled her shoulders back and forth, then glanced around at the others to see what they thought.

Besides her and Vivienne, there were two other seventh graders. One of them Rae knew pretty well: Alyssa Lockett, Vivienne's other best friend. She stood near the desk, idly reading the awards above it and playing with a lock of her blond hair. Rae hadn't liked Alyssa at first, but now . . . now she wasn't sure how she felt about her. It was hard to dislike someone so sad. Alyssa's on-again off-again boyfriend, Jeremy, had been found with his eyes missing and his mind zombified, and Alyssa had taken it really hard. Not that Rae could blame her for that. It was horrible and frightening.

Jeremy had been one of the victims of the Unseeing, a monster that had escaped from an alternate dimension. It had targeted kids, killing one and claiming the eyes of eight others before Rae and Caden sent it back to the place it belonged. Now those kids were being treated by the medical staff of Green On!. For all Rae knew, they might be somewhere in this very building.

Rae swallowed and turned away from Alyssa. The Unseeing had targeted Rae, too. It had chased her through an empty cabin and cornered her in the basement, and only luck and Caden's timely arrival had saved her. She dreamed about the Unseeing almost every night and woke up sweating and shaking, huddled in a nest of blankets, and waited until the first hint of dawn filtered through her window so she could relax again. Until the next night.

Before the Unseeing, she'd believed that supernatural things existed in this world. But it was one thing to believe that and quite another to experience it directly.

Rae studied the other seventh grader, a tall, lanky boy who stood by the window, staring out at the woods. Even from here she could see the deep half circles under his eyes, like he hadn't slept in days, and his red hair was almost as messy as Caden's. He looked . . . scared. Like he could see something out there beneath the trees, something no one else had noticed.

Vivienne caught her looking. "That's Blake Crowley," she whispered.

"Are you sure he's in our grade?" Rae asked. "I've never seen him before." Even though Rae had only started attending Dana S. Middle School earlier this month, she was positive she would have remembered a boy with hair that color and a face that haunted.

"I'm sure. He dropped out of school a couple of weeks ago to study mushrooms in the woods or something." Vivienne shrugged. "He must have decided he was done with that. Honestly, I'm a little surprised Patrick picked him for the internship, but I guess he has his reasons."

"He just dropped out of school to live in the woods? Is that even legal?"

"It's not encouraged. But we've learned it's best to just let people go when they feel the call of the Watchful Woods. They always come back eventually." Vivienne hesitated. "Well, usually," she amended. "There was a girl a few years ago who decided she wanted to be a bird. She built a giant nest and refused to touch the ground for months. Then one day she just vanished. Most people think she joined a flock and went south for the winter, then stayed out there."

Rae couldn't tell if Vivienne was joking and decided not to ask. She'd learned that Whispering Pines usually lost a student or two every year, and that the people of this town accepted that as perfectly normal. Even Vivienne didn't seem to think there was a problem with it.

Rae glanced outside at the Watchful Woods. There was a clear patch of grass a good ten feet thick around Green On! before the line of trees began, their branches extending hungrily into it as if they longed to cross that space. It was too easy to imagine a girl lost among those tangled limbs, swallowed forever.

Rae turned her back on the woods and studied the remaining three kids. They were all eighth graders. One of them sat alone at the small sun table, his elbows resting on two of the pointed rays as he scrolled through his phone, ignoring everyone else. He had curly brown hair and glasses, and wore a T-shirt that was just a little too big for him. Rae had seen him in the halls occasionally and knew his name was Nathaniel Cliff, that he'd skipped a grade, and that he'd won some sort of chemistry competition.

The other two eighth graders, a boy and a girl, sat together at the water droplet table talking quietly. Rae thought the boy's name was Matt. Or Mike? He was one of the largest kids in the school, with broad shoulders and very little neck. He looked kind of intimidating until he glanced up at Rae and smiled, a goofy, full-faced expression that made him look less like a linebacker and more like an overgrown eight-year-old. She couldn't help smiling back.

The girl looked up too. Her eyes were a deep brown several shades darker than her skin and framed by thick lashes, and she wore crimson lipstick that made her look older than eighth grade. She didn't smile at Rae. Instead she leaned closer to Matt, dropped her voice, and said something else. Rae thought she heard her name and felt her face going pink.

"What is it?" Vivienne asked, turning and following Rae's gaze.

"I think they're talking about me." As soon as the words were out of Rae's mouth, she regretted it. They made her sound insecure.

"Probably wondering if the rumors are true," Vivienne said.

"Rumors?" Rae tried to keep her face neutral, but she couldn't stop herself from thinking of her last school and the way rumors had plagued her like rats in a dumpster, constantly nipping at her heels, shredding all of her friendships.

"About you fighting that eye-snatching creature?" Vivienne said.

“Oh. That.”

“Yes, that.” Vivienne grinned. “No one is supposed to know about it, so naturally the whole school has heard.” She waved at the girl, who ignored her. “Rude.” Vivienne frowned. Raising her voice, she added, “That’s Becka Wilson. She thinks she’s a famous actress just because she starred in a hemorrhoid commercial six years ago.”

“It was *not* a hemorrhoid commercial!” Becka snapped.

Rae giggled.

“It’s not funny,” Becka said.

Vivienne adjusted her large backpack. “I don’t actually remember what she was advertising,” she admitted to Rae in a low voice. “So I just make up the most embarrassing things I can think of. It’s a pretty fun game.”

“How do you know her?”

“We were in chorus together last year.”

“Chorus?” Rae raised her eyebrows. “You?”

Vivienne grinned. “I was lead alto. Ahead of Becka, I might add.”

“Why aren’t you doing it this year?”

Vivienne’s grin fell away. “Not enough time. You know, with this internship, and, um, everything.”

And there it was, the shadow of a secret across her face. Rae hesitated, not sure if she should ask. But before she could decide, the glass doors at the far end of the room opened with a soft gasp, and a short woman in a long white lab coat stepped through. She waved a hand and gave them all a quick, harried smile. “So sorry I’m late. I’m Doctor Nguyen. If you’ll follow me?” And she turned and went right back through the doors without waiting for a response.

"Guess this is it, huh?" Alyssa said, joining Rae and Vivienne. She managed a weak smile. "Maybe they'll let us visit Jeremy and the others while we're here."

"I . . . don't think they will," Vivienne said carefully. "I'm sorry, Alyssa. I asked my mom about it the other day, and she told me they weren't allowing any visitors yet."

"Why not?" Rae asked.

"She didn't say."

"Are you coming?" Becka asked them from the doorway.

"It's not fair," Alyssa said. "Patrick promised—" She stopped abruptly, her lips pressing together.

"Promised what?" Rae asked, thinking of her own promise from him.

"Nothing. Let's just catch up." Alyssa strode away after Becka, leaving Rae and Vivienne to hurry after her.

They caught up with everyone else partway down a long, tiled hallway that led past a series of ordinary-looking offices. Patrick had made it sound like the whole company was behind this internship program—a chance for the kids of the future to help save that future. But so far no one here seemed enthusiastic about the idea. So why was he doing it? He'd said in his school presentation that the kids he picked would need to help save the world, but if that were really true, then Rae was pretty sure the world was in big trouble.

"Why isn't there anyone else here?" Nate asked.

Rae blinked, realizing he was right; all of the offices they had passed had been empty.

"Because it's Sunday?" Alyssa suggested. The seven of them had been dropped off at school, where they'd caught a bus out to the lab as a special "interns only" weekend field trip.

"Green On! is productive seven days a week," Doctor Nguyen said with a hint of pride. "Science doesn't stop for the weekends. This is where our admin team works, but they were given the afternoon off today."

"All of them?" Vivienne asked.

"It appears so."

"That's strange." Vivienne glanced at Rae. "They aren't very generous with their time off around here. Especially lately. My mom has been working twelve to sixteen hours a day for the past week."

"Wow, brutal," Rae said. "Doing what?"

Vivienne shrugged. "She doesn't like to talk about her work much. It's all very 'need to know' stuff, apparently."

"And you don't need to know," Rae said. "I get it." Her dad's work had been the same. Of course, that hadn't stopped him from telling her about some of it anyhow.

"It was your mom who actually gave the team here time off," Doctor Nguyen told Vivienne.

Vivienne's eyes widened. "That's even stranger."

They kept going, the hallway eventually turning right, then right again. The offices they passed grew less impressive, and soon they were just small rooms full of boxes, as if the kids were moving into the less-used storage area. There were still almost no other people around. Moments later and the hall dead-ended at an elevator.

"Where are we going?" Rae asked, her voice shaking.

"Yeah, this doesn't exactly look like a highly trafficked area," Blake said. He seemed extra twitchy, even more nervous than Rae.

"We had a new lab built recently that Patrick wants you to use." Doctor Nguyen pressed the elevator button. "It's a little deeper underground than most of our other labs, and this elevator is the only easily accessible entrance."

"That doesn't sound ominous at all," Rae muttered.

Ding!

The elevator door slid open. There was barely enough space for all of them inside, and Rae found herself crammed in the back. As the door closed, a strange panicky feeling gripped her stomach. She remembered the stench of mold, the feeling of bugs crawling through her hair and down her shirt, the splintery wood of the bed frame scraping against her back. And the feeling that she couldn't move an inch. That only a rotting mattress and a few lumpy pillows stood between her and a monster. *Rae, I know you're in here . . .*

Rae clenched her hands, resisting the sudden urge to flail her arms and leap over everyone's heads. She reminded herself for the hundredth time that the Unseeing was gone, banished forever. She wasn't trapped. She was safe.

But she didn't feel safe. She felt like she were seconds from something horrible.

"Breathe in through your nose," Vivienne whispered next to her, "and out through your mouth. Count four in, four out. It helps. Trust me."

The elevator lurched downward, and Rae slowly breathed in while a little screen in the corner tallied the floor level. She watched it for a few seconds and realized the numbers were negative. It was bizarre, but then, so many things in Whispering Pines were. So Rae tried not to notice and just concentrated on her breathing as they crept downward.

Each level they passed seemed hotter, like they were traveling to the center of the earth. Rae could feel the sweat sliding down her back and beading along her hairline. And was the elevator getting smaller? The light overhead flickered, plunging them into darkness for an eyeblink before coming back on. A soft, ominous grinding noise echoed down the chute, and Rae forgot about counting her breaths as the elevator wobbled and slowed. What if they were trapped here?

Vivienne took her hand and gently squeezed it. "We're almost there," she whispered.

Rae smiled at her gratefully.

The elevator finally creaked to a halt at floor minus-twelve. As soon as the doors opened, Rae almost knocked Blake over in her rush to get out. She sucked in a long, deep breath, enjoying the feeling of space all around her. It helped, until she realized they were deep underground, and suddenly she could feel the weight of all that earth pressing down on her.

"Your lockers are right here," Doctor Nguyen was saying, pointing at a small alcove just down the hall. Rae did her best to ignore her growing panic and joined the others, even as the pressure inside her built up like a shaken soda bottle. There were eight floor-to-ceiling lockers, each one wider than Rae was. Seven of them had labels with each of their names.

"Are we expecting anyone else?" Nate asked, standing in front of the blank locker.

"Only Patrick knows," Doctor Nguyen said. "Well, have a look inside. They're not locked yet."

Rae opened her locker. On one side hung a white lab coat, the other a bulky green hazmat suit. What would they be doing that would require a hazmat suit? Had her mom read the fine print before agreeing to send her here?

"What are you thinking about?" Vivienne asked.

Wordlessly, Rae pointed at the suit.

"Oh. Yeah. That." Vivienne grinned. "Patrick has some sort of secret mission for us. He hasn't told me any of the details yet, so don't ask. But I'm guessing that's what the suits are for."

"Strangely not reassuring." Rae closed her locker. But for the first time since she'd arrived at Green On!, she was starting to feel something other than that awful, crushing dread. The first whisper of excitement had caught hold of her. Hazmat suits and secret missions? Even if part of her was afraid of ending up the same way as her dad, the rest of her was eager to experience whatever Patrick had planned for them.

"Okay." Doctor Nguyen rubbed her hands together. "That's done. So next on the agenda is—"

Beep! Beep! Beep!

The bright overhead light faded to an angry pulsing red, turning the small locker room into a sea of bloody shadows.

"Report immediately to your designated safe room," a robotic voice said. *"We are experiencing a nuclear meltdown. This is not a drill."*

Rae's mouth fell open. She stared at Vivienne, and then at Doctor Nguyen. "A *what*?"

Doctor Nguyen didn't answer, her own eyes wide and terrified, while behind her Nate had his arms wrapped over his head like he was afraid of the ceiling falling down on him.

Vivienne made a soft little whimpering noise. "Mom," she choked.

"Is she working today?" Alyssa asked.

"She works every day." Vivienne clutched at Doctor Nguyen's sleeve. "What does this mean? Is everyone in the nuclear division safe?"

Doctor Nguyen shook her off. "Of course not. But it's not worth worrying about."

"How can you say that?" Becka demanded. "It's her mother!"

"Because we won't be able to reach the safe room in time, not from all the way down here," Doctor Nguyen said grimly. She looked around the room, the red lights gleaming in her dark eyes. "So none of *us* will be safe either."

The robot voice boomed again, "*We are experiencing a nuclear meltdown. I repeat, we are experiencing a nuclear meltdown. You must be in your designated safe room now. Green On! will be sealed in five . . . four . . . three . . .*"

2.
CADEN

Caden sat cross-legged on the floor in his mom's study, a blindfold over his eyes. "This feels very *Star Wars*," he muttered.

"Shh," his mom said. "Concentrate."

He sighed. This was ridiculous. But he went through the motions anyhow, imagining roots bursting from his body, digging deep into the soil below, grounding him firmly. Next he pictured a large bubble full of soft white light surrounding him in a protective embrace. And then, finally, he lowered his mental shields and let his awareness drift outward.

Caden had been an empath for as long as he could remember. When he was little, he'd been able to pick up the emotions of others as easily as a bird picking up seeds from a full feeder. But he'd learned—painfully—that other kids didn't appreciate that. Now he mostly kept that ability to himself. As far as he knew, it was his only strange skill. Well, that and the occasional prophetic dream. But his mom believed he might have other abilities, things he'd never discovered he could do. Things he'd kept buried.

"Can you sense it yet?" she asked.

Caden frowned, trying to feel the energies of the room around him. He could sense his mom sitting across from him. Sadness clung to her like a wet sweater, but beneath it he could feel another emotion, as solid and unbendable as an iron rod. Determination. A single-minded focus fueled by a desperation he didn't understand but that reminded him of someone . . .

Don't think about Rae.

He pulled back into himself so quickly it hurt and yanked the blindfold off. "I can't," he said.

"Can't?" his mom asked. "Or won't?" She sat cross-legged, mirroring him, none of the sadness he had felt in her visible on her face. In her hands she held a small rounded rose quartz. She'd been trying to get Caden to move that stone with his mind all morning, and he was tired of it.

"Aiden was the one with that ability, not me," he said. "I can't become him, no matter what you might wish."

She flinched and closed her hand around the stone.

Guilt enveloped Caden, thick and choking as car exhaust. Nine months ago, his older brother, Aiden, had torn open a hole into the Other Place, an alternate dimension full of monsters. He hadn't been able to control it, and as the evils of that place threatened to overwhelm him and escape, Caden had made the difficult choice to sacrifice his brother in order to close the rift and protect everyone else.

Then a few weeks ago, Caden had discovered that Aiden was still alive, trapped in the Other Place, and had tried to save him. But something happened after Caden reopened the rift. His brother abruptly disappeared, his energy vanishing so completely even their mom couldn't sense him at all. And she believed that this time Aiden was well and truly gone.

She had been in mourning ever since. And here Caden was, throwing his brother's loss back in her face.

He knew he should be grieving with her. But mostly all he felt was relief. He'd never noticed before how much his brother's presence weighed on him, like a too-full backpack he couldn't take off. Without Aiden around, Caden had been free to be himself. He'd even made friends. For a little while, anyhow.

He thought of Rae again, picturing her wide, gentle eyes, the contradictory set of her jaw. The way she threw herself into danger like a diver falling into a deep pool, headfirst, never questioning, never looking back, the echo of her own past failures snapping constantly at her heels.

He let that memory go and made himself look instead at his mom. She had her black hair wound in a low braid, a pair of amethyst chips glinting in her ears, matching the uncut purple stones in her thick necklace and on one of her large silver rings. Amethyst stones helped to ground and protect, to clear the mind, and to soothe the grief over the loss of a loved one.

"You're right, you are not your brother," she said quietly. "And regardless of what you think, I'm not trying to turn you into him. That would be impossible."

Just like that, the guilt surrounding Caden soured, curdling like milk left out for days and turning into bitter resentment. His older brother hadn't always been the nicest person. He'd used his abilities to hurt people, had terrified Caden and stolen magic from their mom, but still he'd been her favorite. His mom denied it, of course. She said she loved both her sons equally, that she'd spent more time with Aiden only because she knew he was experimenting with things beyond his control. She didn't have to worry about that with Caden. Careful, cautious Caden, who didn't need her protection.

His mom could say what she liked, but he'd seen the truth for himself. He was nothing but a poor substitute for his more powerful, talented brother.

"Then what are you trying to do?" Caden asked harshly.

"I'm trying to help you find the boundaries of your power while there's still time." She looked up, and there was something in her eyes, an emotion she'd managed to keep hidden from his inner senses.

Fear.

And abruptly he was afraid too. "What is it? What's going on?"

She studied the rose quartz in her hand, turning it over and over as if it held the secrets of the universe within its soft pink walls. "Do you know why the Other Place was created?"

Caden couldn't hide his surprise. "I didn't think you'd want to talk about that."

"I'm not going to ignore everything about that dimension just because it causes me grief. I can't afford to. Guarding the boundary between our world and that space is the most important job us Prices have." For a second her sorrow rose up, a deep-blue wave cresting around her and then smoothing out like the tides of the sea. She swallowed, composing herself. "I told you that the first Price came to Whispering Pines in the 1650s, right?"

"After fleeing the Hartford Witch Trials," Caden remembered. "She made a deal in order to escape, promised to oversee the line between our world and the Other Place."

"Good memory."

"It's not really the kind of thing a person forgets," Caden said wryly. "Cosmic family obligation and all that."

His mom laughed. "True. Well, that isn't the whole story."

"Oh?" Caden sat up straighter.

"I'm not going to bore you with the details."

"I don't mind."

She gave him a small, secretive smile. The kind that told him the story would be anything but boring . . . but that she wasn't about to share it anyhow. "Maybe someday," she hedged. She held the rose quartz out to him, and he took it in his hand, the stone warm against his skin. "For now, you just need to know that part of her deal was to help *create* the Other Place."

"How?"

Again the small smile.

"Fine," Caden grumbled. "Then why? It's an awful place."

"It's meant to be. It's a prison."

Caden frowned. "For who?"

She met his eyes, her own deadly serious.

"Or . . . for what?" Caden guessed.

She nodded. "That would be more accurate. She is many things. Evil, certainly. Destructive. Greedy. Ravenous. But human?" She sighed. "Maybe once, a long, long time ago." She ran her thumb over the amethyst in her ring. "And she is restless. Very restless. I could feel her this past week when I searched the Other Place for signs of what happened to your brother. She is testing the walls of her cell. And I know they have grown weaker."

"Then why keep her imprisoned? Why not destroy her?"

"True evil can never be destroyed. The best we can do is contain it and stop it from spreading."

Caden wasn't sure he believed that. He squeezed the rose quartz in his palm and felt the energy inside. Love, and protection. Maybe the problem was that destruction itself was an evil act. So trying to destroy something evil would be like trying to put out a fire with more flame. But there had to be another way.

"I—" he began, then froze. He'd sensed something. A disruption. It felt almost like a hole where a tooth should be. He poked at it with his awareness, trying to feel out the size of the gap.

"What is it?" His mom sat up very straight, and he didn't need any special powers to notice the alarm stamped all over her.

"I think . . . something has broken our warding circle." Caden poured salt in a ring around their house every week as part of a ritual of protection, a way to warn them if anything supernatural tried crossing over it. Ever since the Unseeing incident, he'd widened that circle to include their yard as well.

His mom pressed her lips together, transforming her face into a series of sharp, worried lines.

"Want me to check on it?" Caden asked.

"I'll go." She rose abruptly to her feet and walked out of the study, leaving Caden to scramble down the hall after her.

He caught her just as she reached the front door. "Wait, Mom—"

She yanked the door open like she was snatching something hot from a fire.

Caden flinched, but nothing flew at them, and all he could see through the open doorway was his empty front yard. He relaxed.

"There's someone out there," his mom whispered.

"What?" His relief evaporated immediately. "Where?"

"Over there. See?"

Like most of the houses in this part of Whispering Pines, their yard bordered the edges of the Watchful Woods. Sometimes Caden swore the trees that ringed their yard were stealthily creeping closer, and one day he would wake up and discover that the forest had reclaimed all of their land.

He followed his mom's gaze over to those trees. A person stood in front of them. A tall, slender person with a buzzed head, wearing a bright green uniform. He looked lost. Or maybe drunk? Caden frowned, feeling uneasy as the stranger stumbled closer. Casually he let his awareness drift outward.

At first he couldn't sense anything from the intruder at all. And then he felt a gentle tug, as if he had brushed against something sticky.

Caden tried probing that sticky spot. He concentrated, and pain lanced through his brain like he'd just eaten something very cold way too fast. He gasped, instinctively pulling inward again. His hand went to the pendant around his neck, the one he always wore for luck and protection.

"What's wrong?" his mom asked, gripping his shoulder.

The figure stepped out from beneath the trees, and now they could see him clearly: large, dark eyes, a sharp nose, full lips, hollowed-out cheeks. It was a handsome face. A *familiar* face. His eyes were a little too big, his lips chapped, and he moved strangely, as if he'd been out at sea for months and was just getting used to walking on land . . .

But still Caden recognized his older brother.

Caden felt the surprise from his mom, an explosion of bright yellow lanced through with worrying squiggles of black. But his own emotions were as flat and empty as a brand-new notebook.

This wasn't real.

Caden knew that. It was a dream. Any second now and his brother would vanish, melting away like ice cream left out in the sun.

As Aiden staggered toward them, Caden felt his mom's grip on his shoulder tightening, her fingers digging in painfully. He focused on that sharpness. It grounded him much more effectively than imagined roots.

His brother was gone. Exorcised. Destroyed completely. How could he possibly be standing here now?

“Please,” Aiden said, his voice a harsh rasp, his thin body swaying. “Help me?” He held his hands out toward them. “They’re looking . . . for me. I need . . . hide . . .” His eyes rolled up in his head, and he collapsed at the edge of their yard in a tangle of limbs.

3.

RAE

Rae was suffocating, her breath rasping through her helmet, filling her ears, competing with the sound of the alarm still blaring overhead. The flashing lights made her head pound, turning the whole scene into disjointed pieces like shards of a broken mirror.

"Hurry!" Doctor Nguyen shouted above the noise.

Rae tried to hurry, but her hazmat suit was heavier than it looked, and it felt like she were wading through sand.

"—not a drill. Green On! has been sealed for the protection of the citizens of Whispering Pines. This is not a drill. You cannot leave the premises. All employees must be in their designated safe rooms at this time. This is not a drill. Green On! has been . . ."

Rae tuned out the alarm, focusing on Vivienne in front of her. Or maybe it was Becka? Rae couldn't tell. They all looked pretty much the same in their matching Green On! hazmat suits. Only Doctor Nguyen stood out in her flimsy lab coat, looking small and vulnerable, her mouth a thin, determined line. She'd spent several tedious moments helping them all into their suits, which were specially made by Patrick. She'd shouted that they had upgrades only he knew about and might provide some protection. Meanwhile, she had nothing for herself. They'd checked the eighth locker, but it was empty.

Not that Rae believed any hazmat suit, regardless of how well made it was, would help them in the event of a nuclear meltdown. But getting suited up was better than sitting there, waiting to die.

Don't think about dying.

She wondered what her older sister, Ava, would do without her. Would Ava still attend college out here and then follow through on her plan to go looking for their dad? What about their mom? Rae pictured her, with her sad eyes and messy hair, how she would often drift in and out of conversations like part of her had been taken away too. Would Rae's death take the rest of her?

Would it hurt? To die in a nuclear accident . . .

Don't think about dying!

But it was hard to think of anything else. Rae gasped, her breath turning into a long, awful wheeze. She was having an asthma attack, and she didn't have her inhaler. She needed to calm down, try to slow her breathing on her own. Panic only made it worse.

". . . not a drill! I repeat . . ."

Rae was definitely panicking. She staggered, almost falling, her entire world narrowing to a thin tunnel of flashing light. Blood roared through her ears like an oncoming train, blocking everything else out. Dimly she watched Doctor Nguyen frantically trying each door they passed, using her key, tugging, pounding her fist. It didn't matter. Everything was sealed except this impossibly long hall.

Rae didn't want to die like this, hot and afraid, everything chaotic around her. She longed for cool darkness, for quiet, for fresh, clean air. She thought of Caden telling her *I've got your back*. Would he be sad too? Or would he feel like she'd brought this on herself by joining this internship? She couldn't picture him smug and vindicated.

He wasn't like that. She knew he wasn't.

Someone had Rae by the arm and was dragging her down the hall. Rae didn't know who it was and didn't care. Her lungs were sandbags in her chest, heavy and useless. She tried breathing through them anyhow, tiny sips of air.

They were at the end of the hall now, standing in front of the final doors, tall and intimidating and very firmly closed. Doctor Nguyen lifted her key card again in one trembling hand. Rae felt bad for the scientist. She had been saddled with babysitting duties, and now she was doing her best to save them all, and it wouldn't be enough.

Rae mentally got a grip on herself. She had survived a deadly game of hide-and-seek with a monster. She was not about to give up now. She forced herself to take a slow, careful breath, counting like she'd done in the elevator. She only managed to get to two, but it was something.

The doors popped open.

Doctor Nguyen leaped back, then froze, staring at the empty rectangle beyond before shaking herself. "Go, go, go!" She started shoving at the kids, nudging them through. Rae stumbled forward with the others, and the door slammed shut behind them.

Immediately the constant noise of the alarm went soft and manageable, as if someone had taken it off the wall and stuffed it under a pillow. Rae gasped, the high wheezing of her own lungs even louder in this relative quiet.

They were at the end of another hall, this one lined with cement: floor, ceiling, and walls. Overhead, several long electric lights flickered, casting a pale-blue glow that was a welcome relief after the angry red from before. Rae couldn't see any doors, just the corridor extending a good twenty feet in an unbroken line before turning a corner.

"That door should have been sealed." Doctor Nguyen frowned.

"Are we safe in here?" Blake asked.

"I don't know," Doctor Nguyen said. "This part of the lab was newly built to house our most sensitive experiments. So . . . maybe?"

"Well, that sure is reassuring," Alyssa muttered.

Rae wanted to agree with her, but she was too tired to respond, her eyelids heavy. Only the hand under her arm kept her standing.

"You okay?" Becka whispered, and Rae realized she'd been the one dragging her along.

"Asthma . . . trouble," Rae wheezed.

"I figured. You sound like my little brother when he's having one of his attacks. Do you have your inhaler?"

Rae shook her head.

Becka sighed. "Owen forgets his a lot too. Of course, he's ten. Not sure what your excuse is."

"Left it . . . in my other . . . hazmat suit," Rae managed.

Becka stared at her, eyes wide behind the glass front of her helmet. Then she grinned. "You might be okay after all, Rae Carter."

"Can we take off our helmets?" Matt asked.

"Absolutely not!" Doctor Nguyen said.

"What kind of experiments?" Alyssa asked abruptly.

"What?" Doctor Nguyen looked confused.

"You said this was a new lab for the most sensitive experiments. What are they?" By the tight, high-pitched tone of her voice, Rae knew Alyssa was thinking of Jeremy and the other Unseeing victims. But surely Green On! wouldn't keep a bunch of injured kids deep below the ground, hidden inside cement walls. They'd be somewhere with fresh air and sunlight and twenty-four-hour care. Wouldn't they?

"They are secret, is what they are," a woman at the other end of the hall said. She had black hair sprinkled with a few white streaks, several strands escaping from her otherwise tight bun, and her cheeks were pink as if she'd been running. She smoothed a hand down the front of her lab coat as she walked toward them.

"Mom!" One of the lime-green shapes hurtled forward, almost knocking the woman over, and now Rae recognized her as Mrs. Matsuoka, Vivienne's mom.

Mrs. Matsuoka hugged her daughter, pressing her face into the hardened outer shell of the hazmat suit. "I forgot the internship was meeting here today," she said, finally letting Vivienne go. "I'm so sorry."

"What's going on? Is everyone okay?" Vivienne asked.

"Yes, what's going on?" Doctor Nguyen asked. "Why are you down here and not in your designated safe room?"

Rae could have sworn Mrs. Matsuoka looked a little guilty, but then that expression was gone, hidden neatly away beneath a mask of professionalism.

"There was a malfunction in our alarm system," Mrs. Matsuoka said. "I came down here to check on the labs."

"A malfunction?" Alyssa asked. "So we're safe?"

"You're safe."

"But . . . how did it happen?" Doctor Nguyen asked.

"We were running a few tests and accidentally triggered this response. But it's nothing for you to be concerned about."

Doctor Nguyen's mouth fell open. "Nothing to be *concerned* about?" She waved her hands around like agitated birds. "The meltdown! The children! There is a *lot* to be concerned about!"

"These children signed their waivers." Mrs. Matsuoka crossed her arms. "They knew what they were getting into when they came here."

"Like heck we did," Becka whispered behind Rae.

She wheezed in agreement.

"Fine," Doctor Nguyen said, biting the word out. "I'll take this up with Patrick later."

"Oh, I'm sure you will."

"He'll probably want to know about this door, too."

Mrs. Matsuoka frowned. "The door?"

"They are all supposed to be sealed during an alarm, only this one wasn't." Doctor Nguyen glanced at the door behind them.

"I don't see any reason why we need to involve Patrick in a simple malfunction. He is so busy."

Doctor Nguyen crossed her own arms. "But you know how he feels about things not working properly. He'll definitely want to look into it. Personally."

Rae couldn't tell what was going on, just that there seemed to be a whole secret conversation silently creeping beneath their words. It was hard for her to focus, everything fading around her.

"Maybe you and I can discuss this later?" Mrs. Matsuoka managed a tight smile. "I think these children have been through enough for one day. Perhaps we should call the end of the tour and get them all home. That one"—she pointed right at Rae—"looks like she's about to collapse."

Rae realized she was leaning against the wall and pushed herself up straight. Immediately the world blackened around her in a rush.

". . . needs her inhaler," Vivienne's voice said. She sounded small and scared. Rae wanted to tell her it was all fine. She was okay. They weren't going to die, and it was only relief that had made her weak. But it felt like way too much energy to say anything, so she lay there silently.

Lay there?

Rae blinked, becoming aware of the hard ground under her. Maybe she was worse off than she'd thought. Caden had probably been right about this internship, Rae decided. Signing up had definitely been a bad idea.

4.
CADEN

Caden sprinted around the house, checking that all of the windows were closed and locked, the blinds pulled firmly over them.

"Unplug everything too," his mom called. "And turn out all the lights."

"What?" Caden paused in the kitchen. "Seriously?"

"Just in case. I'll light candles."

In case of what? Caden didn't trust Green On! either, but their family had opted out of the Green On! energy monitoring system. And anyhow, even if Green On! were somehow still tracking their energy usage, it wasn't like they could use that to spy on them inside the house.

Or . . . could they?

He stared at the coffeepot, his eyes following the wire as it looped along the counter before connecting to the wall. It wasn't possible. But then, he really didn't know *what* Green On! was capable of. He thought of Patrick, the new senior consultant and the one in charge of the student internship program. Patrick, who had appeared friendly and ordinary, with his magazine-ready smile and cool blue eyes. But underneath, Caden had sensed something . . . *other*.

When Caden was ten years old, his parents had taken him and Aiden on a family camping trip to Bear Mountain. They'd left in the evening and were driving the last stretch to the campground at night, their mom white-knuckled over the steering wheel as she guided them along a narrow, twisting mountain road.

And then the headlights of the car went out.

Caden could still remember the utter darkness of that moment. It had been an overcast night, so no stars shone, no moon glowed. There was nothing but the pitch black of the sky and the inky stretch of road, and the terror that they might be heading straight off into nothing.

When Caden had brushed against Patrick, back at their school's Green On! assembly, he had felt something like that: the vast darkness of a midnight mountain road, and the fear that if he kept going, he might tumble over the edge and be lost forever. He hadn't tried sensing Patrick again.

Caden shivered and unplugged the coffeepot. And the microwave. And everything else he could see. Then he turned off the lights. The afternoon was fading, but there was still enough sunlight trickling inside, even with all the blinds down, for him to make his way down the hall and into his mom's study.

She'd lit several large pillar candles—black, Caden noticed, for protection—and had them set up around the room, their flickering light bouncing off the cushions they had just been sitting on, illuminating the boy lying on the floor, his eyes closed, mouth shut tight. His arms were crossed over his chest, making him look disturbingly like a corpse laid to rest. On his left thumb, a thick silver ring with a strange circular design seemed to soak in the candlelight like a succulent soaks in rain.

Caden moved closer, watching his brother carefully. His chest rose and fell, so he was alive, but Caden still couldn't sense him at all. What had happened to Aiden, trapped all that time in the Other Place? His mom said it was a prison containing some ancient evil, and Caden had seen the things that lurked around the edges—things with tentacles and too many teeth and an insatiable hunger for human blood. Yet somehow Aiden had survived in there.

But maybe it had cost him.

Caden remembered the Unseeing, the eyeless monster that had escaped from the Other Place to terrorize their town, ripping the eyes from children. And not just their eyes. When Caden had gotten caught up in the memories of the Unseeing itself, he'd experienced the way the creature devoured the souls of its victims after removing their eyes, leaving them empty vessels made of flesh and blood and nothing else.

What if Aiden wasn't really himself anymore?

Caden looked down at his brother's gaunt face and tried not to let his worry trickle out. His mom wasn't as good at picking up emotions as he was. She and Aiden had never been empaths.

But she could sense them if they were strong enough.

Aiden's eyelids flickered, his face contorting as if he were in pain.

"Help me lift him onto the bed," their mom said.

Caden grabbed his brother by the arms while his mom grabbed Aiden's feet, and together they carefully lifted him onto the small twin bed his mom kept in her study. She took off his shoes, then walked over and knelt next to his head, gently stroking her fingers through his short hair.

"Do you think . . ." Caden stopped, swallowed. "Will he be okay?"

"I don't know." She took a deep, shuddering breath. "I don't know what all he's been through."

"Has anyone else ever spent time in the Other Place and survived?" Caden didn't want to hurt his mom, but he had to ask.

She hesitated, and Caden felt the cold, hard edge of a secret looming, waiting to be uncovered.

Aiden's eyes popped open, so abrupt Caden took a quick step back, and his mom gasped. Aiden stared up at the ceiling for a long moment. Then he slowly turned his head and looked at Caden and then their mom. "It's so good to see you again," he croaked.

"Aiden!" Their mom threw her arms around him and kissed him on the forehead. "We thought . . . I thought . . ." She broke down, sobbing, her words a mangled mess, and Caden felt the outpouring of all that guilt and sorrow and relief like a river breaking free, washing itself out.

"It's okay, Mom." Aiden put his own arms around her. "I'm back. Everything is going to be okay." He looked over her head, his eyes meeting Caden's. The candlelight flickered in them, washing them from brown to amber. It made him look strange, like something inhuman was staring out through the mask of his face.

The hairs on the back of Caden's neck prickled, a shiver running down his spine. And he thought again of that night on the mountain road when their lights went out, recalling the sharp burst of panic—that they would swerve off the edge of the cliff or crash into the trees on the side and die in a blaze of fire and pain.

Only now, as he stared at his brother, did he remember that Aiden hadn't wanted to go on that trip. His brother had been angry, so angry, when their parents packed them up anyhow. And when the headlights shuddered back on, Caden had caught a brief glimpse of their mom praying, their dad sobbing in relief, and Aiden sitting there beside him in the car, smiling.

Aiden's lips curved in that same triumphant smile now.

Caden wanted to run and keep running, but he couldn't move, pinned beneath his brother's unearthly gaze.

Bad things happened to people who crossed Aiden. And Caden had shoved his older brother into a dimension full of horrors. Horrors that had then fed on him for nine months.

Things were definitely *not* going to be okay.

5.
RAE

Rae trudged into homeroom like a zombie, her feet scraping across the tiled floor. She was exhausted. She had ended up taking too many puffs of her inhaler yesterday, so between the jitters from the medicine and the nervous energy from her brush with death at the lab, she'd been too full of adrenaline to sleep more than about five minutes last night.

Caden was already there, sitting in his old seat near the front of the room. His black hair was as messy as always, matching the wrinkled black T-shirt and black jeans. He glanced up as she passed, and for a second their eyes met. And despite her weariness, Rae felt a jolt of energy, like electricity flowing between them. A connection forged through blood and adventure.

Her heart lifted. She hadn't realized how much she'd missed being his friend this past week. Had he forgiven her for choosing

Patrick's internship over his help? Monday mornings were a perfect time for starting over.

"Cad—" she began.

But he had already looked away again, his eyes adopting a faraway glaze, like he was staring into the spirit world. For all Rae knew, that was exactly what he was doing.

"Fine, whatever." She stomped past him, the hurt inside her bubbling up like a fountain. She did her best to squash it back down again. She didn't need Caden or his friendship. He could spend all his time with his ghosts, for all she cared.

She flopped down in her seat next to Vivienne and Alyssa.

"Rae-Rae," Vivienne said. "Good to see you alive and well."

"If that's what 'well' looks like, I'd hate to see her sick," Alyssa said.

"Nice to see you, too, Alyssa."

"Did you want to borrow some concealer? You look like someone punched you in the face."

Rae reminded herself that Alyssa had been through a lot recently. "That's sweet," she said dryly, "but no thanks."

"Suit yourself." Alyssa shifted closer, lowering her voice. "Did you know that no one here heard about the false alarm yesterday?"

"Really?" Rae asked. That seemed pretty surprising. A nuclear meltdown at Green On! would have affected the whole town.

"Apparently the alarms were restricted to the company itself. All of these people?" Alyssa indicated the students around them. "They could have been turned to ash and not even noticed."

"I'm sure they'd have noticed that," Vivienne said, grinning.

"You know what I mean." Alyssa fiddled with the end of her blond ponytail, frowning. "Even my mom didn't know about it. And she usually knows everything."

Alyssa's mom, Ms. Lockett, was the school's vice principal. She ruled the hallways with her intimidatingly styled hair and ever-present clipboard. Rae had met her on her first day at school and had done her best to avoid her ever since.

"Did you tell her about it?" Vivienne asked, her grin gone.

"No," Alyssa said.

"Good. Because we signed those nondisclosures, and you could get in a lot of trouble—"

"I said I didn't tell her, Vivi. Jeez."

"Good morning, Dana S. Middle Schoolers!" the loudspeaker bellowed. "Happy Monday! Just a reminder that whistling is prohibited in the halls of the school. Humming is still allowed on a case-by-case basis. Apply to Ms. Lockett for a pass if needed."

"Whistling?" Rae scratched her head. This school had all sorts of weird rules, and it felt like they changed every week. Trying to keep track of them was like trying to run up a sand dune.

"It's extremely irritating," Vivienne whispered.

"But . . . humming isn't?"

"It depends on the person humming. That's why you'd need to apply for a pass." She said it like it was the most obvious thing ever. It made Rae wonder if the whole point of these ridiculous rules was to train students not to question the oddities in their town.

". . . will have Tater Tots today," the announcements continued.

"That's the good news. The bad news is that our town has received enough reports to instate a code peach fuzz."

"Oh no!" a girl in the back said.

"That's terrible!" someone else added.

"What is *that*?" Rae asked Vivienne.

"It means animals are going missing. Dogs, cats. Possibly livestock as well."

"Oh." Rae thought about it. "This, um, happens often enough to warrant its own code?"

"It usually only happens once every couple of years," Vivienne said. "But it's good to be prepared."

"Every couple of years?" Rae was suddenly very glad she hadn't convinced her mom to get her a dog yet.

"Yes, keep Fido inside, folks, especially after dark," the loudspeaker continued. "And finally, all of our Green On! interns, please make your way to room seven after the announcements conclude. Thank you!" The voice cut out with a long, eerie creak like the closing of a rusted door.

Rae shivered.

"I guess that's our cue." Vivienne hoisted her giant backpack up over her shoulders.

As Rae passed Caden's seat, he put his head down. Probably worried she'd try talking to him again or something.

"Wow, that is a dark look," Vivienne said as they left homeroom. "Why the fearsome scowl?"

"Do you think being in this internship is a bad idea?" Rae asked, the words bursting out of her. "I mean, yeah, it could lead to a scholarship, and—" And Patrick had promised to help her find her dad. But Vivienne didn't know about that. "And it'll be an interesting experience," Rae finished awkwardly.

Vivienne gave her a sidelong look, like she knew Rae was keeping something secret. "I guess it just depends on your reasons for doing it."

Rae bit her lip and followed Vivienne and Alyssa down a hallway she'd never explored before. The lighting almost seemed dimmer over here, the floor strangely dusty. "Did your mom figure out what went wrong last night?" Rae asked, deciding a topic change was in order.

"If she did, she's not telling me." Vivienne's eyebrows drew together. "Something is up with her, though. She's been super distracted lately. And my mom is *never* distracted."

"Do you think that's what happened?" Alyssa asked. "She made some kind of mistake?"

Vivienne shot her a look.

"What? Everyone makes mistakes sometimes. And she definitely didn't want Doctor Nguyen talking to Patrick about it."

"I don't know," Vivienne said shortly.

Rae glanced between the two of them. Alyssa had confided in her that Vivienne seemed to be drifting away, changing into someone else, someone she barely knew. Rae could practically feel the gulf between the two of them widening. She might be in competition with Alyssa for the top spot in Vivienne's friend list, but it still made her heart ache to see them growing distant. She knew what it felt like to lose a good friend.

"Is that Blake up ahead?" Alyssa said. "I'm going to go walk with him."

"You do that," Vivienne said.

Alyssa glanced over like she wanted to say something else, but then she tossed her hair over her shoulder and sped up.

Vivienne watched her go, her eyes narrowed. Then she sighed. "Sorry."

"You weren't mean to me."

Vivienne ran a hand down her face. "I know. It's just, my mom actually did have to talk to Patrick last night. And he was . . ."

"What? Angry?"

"He doesn't really get angry. But very disappointed. And I don't really like how Alyssa is throwing that in my face."

"I don't think she meant to," Rae said quietly.

"Maybe not." Vivienne stopped outside a plain wooden door. "And here we are." She stared at it like it might leap out and bite her.

"Should we, um, go in?" Rae asked.

"Probably." But Vivienne didn't move.

"Everything okay?"

Vivienne gripped the straps of her backpack. "Yeah. I just . . . I had a bad experience in this room. I didn't think I'd have to come back here ever."

"Bad . . . experience?"

"Are you talking about the Emmett incident?" a boy asked behind them. Rae turned to see Nathaniel Cliff, his hands shoved deep into the pockets of his baggy corduroy pants.

"What's that?" Rae asked.

Nate's eyes widened behind his glasses. "You don't know?"

"She hadn't moved here yet," Vivienne said.

"This used to be one of the science labs," Nate said. "Specifically, the fifth-grade science lab. They had a pet rabbit, Emmett, who stayed here throughout the day. Near the end of last year someone broke in at lunch and drained all the blood out of poor Emmett, then stuffed his corpse in a locker."

Rae felt sick. "Alyssa did mention something about that when I moved here," she whispered.

"It was pretty traumatic," Nate said. "There was blood all over this room. No one wanted to study in here anymore, so the whole class was moved. And it's been empty ever since." He raised his eyebrows and smiled in an obviously ironic fashion. "So if you're still wondering, yes. This internship is a tremendously bad idea."

"Were you spying on us?" Rae demanded.

"I was walking behind you, and you're loud."

"Hey, weren't you the one who found the rabbit?" Becka had come up to the door and stood with her arms crossed, watching Vivienne.

Vivienne's expression didn't change, but it was the kind of *unchanging* that stood out thanks to its lack of variation. Like Vivienne was afraid if she let something show on her face, it would be too powerful and would overwhelm her, so she was very carefully not showing anything. It reminded Rae of a person gripping a railing very tightly as the ground under them dipped and wobbled.

She knew that look well. She'd done the same thing at her old school whenever she heard anyone gossiping about her or her dad. And since everyone seemed to want to gossip about it constantly, she'd had a lot of practice.

It hadn't helped that another engineer vanished at the same time as her dad. A woman, young and beautiful. Of course everyone assumed he'd run off with her. Even though, if they knew her dad at all, they'd know that was way less likely than government abduction.

"Yeah, it was in my locker," Vivienne said finally.

"Did anyone ever figure out who did it?" Matt asked, joining them. Rae shifted over to give him more room. It was beginning to feel like that cramped elevator here in this hallway.

"No," Nate said.

"Emmett was probably just in the wrong place at the wrong time," Vivienne said breezily. "Let's go in, shall we?" She tugged the door open.

"Wrong place and time?" Nate said, following Vivienne in. "He was a pet rabbit in a cage. It wasn't like he had a lot of other options."

Rae tried not to imagine what it had been like for Vivienne, opening her locker to find that sad, dried-up thing. She was a little surprised Alyssa hadn't mentioned that it was Vivienne's locker when she'd told her about it.

The room where it happened looked just like a normal science room, with a chalkboard up front and two large rectangular blocks made of some hard black stone that were tall enough for a group of students to use as a standing desk. Each block had a deep sunken basin and faucet at one end, and a strip of power outlets lining the middle. Above those desks hovered a metal chute that led up to the ceiling. The whole place smelled strongly of disinfectant—lemon scented—and something else, sharp and metallic. Blood.

Rae shivered. It was just her imagination. There was no way that smell would have lingered here for a year. But she kept her arms wrapped around herself as she followed Vivienne, who glanced over at the desk that Alyssa and Blake were standing next to and then went to the other one. Nate joined them, leaving Becka and Matt to head to Alyssa's desk. They all stood around silently, until Patrick Smith waltzed into the room.

"Good morning, interns," he said, stopping in front of the chalkboard, hands on his hips as he surveyed them. He looked exactly the same way he always did: dark, carefully styled hair, pale eyes, wide smile, and fancy black suit. He was young for a senior company executive, probably in his midtwenties. Rae's older sister thought he was good-looking. Rae thought he was good-looking the same way a mountain lion was: powerful and dangerous, and best viewed at a distance. He glanced at her as if hearing her thoughts, and his smile dropped away like an unnecessary coat. "Ms. Carter."

Rae froze under that gaze.

"I heard you had some trouble at the lab?"

She felt her cheeks flush. "It was fine," she mumbled. She didn't like to think about how the other students had carried her out of there like a sack of dirty laundry. She especially didn't like to think of Patrick hearing about it. She didn't want him to believe she was weak.

"Glad to hear it." He let his gaze move off her, studying the rest of them. "All of you had an exciting initiation yesterday. Everyone still on board for this program?"

Nods and a few murmured "yeahs" filled the room.

"Good, good. I won't keep you here long, then. Just a few quick items and you can get on with your day." He paced slowly across the room, drawing their eyes like a magnet. "You may be wondering why, exactly, I've chosen you for this internship. Some of you are great students." He glanced at Nate. "Some of you are not." This time his gaze landed on Blake, who turned almost as red as his hair. "But all of you have a certain special . . . quality. A talent that will allow you to complete a very important task for me. For all of humanity, really."

"What task?" Rae asked.

Patrick stopped pacing. "My department is in the middle of a scientific breakthrough. It will permanently alter the way we view energy and will transform this planet forever. But . . . in order to make it work, I need a group of students to complete a crucial mission. A *secret* mission. So secret that most of the people at Green On! don't even know about it."

Rae found herself leaning forward, barely breathing.

"And . . . it's dangerous." Patrick looked at each of them, his gaze heavy. Rae felt it pressing against her skin and shivered.

"Why students, then?" Blake asked.

"All will be revealed in due time. But first I need to decide who deserves the right to go."

Rae blinked, confused. She glanced around the room. Everyone else looked just as bewildered as she was. Except for Vivienne, who didn't seem at all surprised.

"Oh, yes," Patrick said. "I only have space for four students on this mission. In order to be considered for one of those coveted spaces, you'll first need to master using your hazmat suits. I understand that Doctor Nguyen helped you into them at your lab tour. I have had them delivered here to this room today—spend the rest of this class period testing them out, if you would. They will be crucial for this mission."

A mission where hazmat suits were crucial? Rae felt a thrill of excitement that might have been terror uncurling inside her stomach.

"I've also asked that you all be excused from your normal science classes. You're to report back here instead, where I'll have various tasks written on the board for you to complete. I want you to become proficient at taking samples, studying slides, writing out detailed reports. All the boring tasks that make up a scientist's normal daily life."

"Fun," Nate whispered. He sounded serious.

"But the most crucial quality, the thing that will be of the utmost importance in my mission, will be your keen observation skills. And in order to determine who is best suited at that, I'm going to have a contest." Patrick grinned. "A little healthy competition always leads to better results. I see you're already divided into two groups, so let's go with that."

Vivienne glanced over sharply at Alyssa. "Wait, can't we choose—"

"Now, now, Ms. Matsuoka. No arguing." He gave her the kind of look a parent gives a small child, the kind that says, "don't make me count to three," and Vivienne went quiet. "The winning team gets to go on the mission. The losers settle for being my alternates." The way he said the word "alternates" made it clear he really meant "failures."

"What's the competition?" Rae asked.

"It's simple, really. I want my winning team to be capable of seeing what is right in front of them. A problem that no one else notices. And then to be proactive in fixing that problem, whatever it takes. So." Patrick spread his hands wide. "First step: find something hidden in plain sight."

"Something hidden?" Blake said. "Like a mystery?"

"Exactly, Mr. Crowley. A mystery. This town has plenty of them, so it shouldn't be hard. Find one, and solve it." He paused. "And in case the opportunity to be part of my groundbreaking research isn't enough motivation, all members of the winning team will earn a full-ride scholarship to the university of their choice."

Nate stood up straighter, his hands gripping the edge of the desk.

"There will be other rewards too," Patrick continued. "Work hard for me, and I'll work hard for you." He glanced at Rae. "I'll also grant the winners a favor. Anything within my power." He gave her a small nod, and she felt the hidden meaning in those words. If she won, then he'd help her find her dad. If she didn't . . . she wasn't sure what he'd do. Go back on his original promise? She frowned. That didn't seem fair at all.

"Good luck, everyone," Patrick said. "I'll see you all very soon."

After he left, Rae turned to Vivienne and Nate. "What do you guys think?"

"I think being the alternates works for me," Nate said.

Rae frowned at him.

"What? Did you not hear the man? Dangerous, top-secret mission?" He shook his head. "Like I want to volunteer to go first for that. But . . ." He sighed. "I do want that scholarship. So I guess we'd better go for it." He glanced at the other team already forming their own huddle. "It's not fair, though. We have one less person on our team."

"I think Patrick is hoping someone else will join us," Vivienne said.

Rae thought of Caden and his unique abilities. She knew exactly who Patrick wanted to join them. "He can hope all he wants. I'm pretty sure it's just going to be the three of us." She tapped her desk. "So, any ideas?"

6.

CADEN

Caden's sketchbook lay open on his lap in front of him, the blank page daring him to draw something, anything, but he just couldn't seem to focus on art lately. His last sketch had been eyes, which he used to love drawing, but now they just gave him nightmares. So he had torn out that page and hadn't been able to create anything new since then.

Today looked like it was going to be no different.

Rae wasn't on the bus, and neither was Vivienne. Which meant . . . what? That they were at Green On! again?

It didn't matter. It wasn't his business. Rae had made her choice. And now he'd made his—to not get involved. Whatever she was up to, it had nothing to do with him. He had enough problems of his own.

He pressed the tip of his pencil into the page, his thoughts drifting away from Rae and zooming in on his brother.

Last night Aiden had been too tired to talk about his experience. He hadn't explained how he'd escaped the Other Place, or why he was wearing a Green On! uniform, or who he was hiding from. He'd promised them all an explanation today when Caden got home from school and their dad got home from work.

Caden's pencil snapped, the tip rolling off the page and onto the floor of the bus. He blinked, finally noticing the swirling darkness he'd drawn, graphite covering every square inch of the once-white page like storm clouds bubbling across a summer sky. It felt about right. Sighing, he closed his sketchbook and put it and the broken pencil away, then stared blankly out the window until the bus rolled to a stop outside his house. He blinked. There were two people there, standing at the bottom of his driveway. His brother, and . . .

And Ava, Rae's older sister.

She was laughing at something Aiden was saying, her eyes half closed, mouth open. Caden almost forgot how charming his brother could be, how much everyone seemed to like him. Yet another way the two of them were so different.

"Hey, kid! You getting off my bus or what?" the driver barked.

Caden got off, his stomach a tangled knot, like he'd forgotten to study for a test and now found out it would be worth half his grade. Aiden glanced up. He was wearing one of their dad's nicer button-down shirts and had scrubbed all the dirt from his face, leaving a couple of small scratches visible on his left cheekbone. His face still looked too skinny, but the deep shadows were gone from under his eyes. He looked . . . healthy. Vibrant, even. Like the old Aiden. Not like the ghostly, sickly version Caden had been haunted by the past few weeks.

Aiden put on his biggest smile, like he was genuinely pleased to see Caden, but then he'd always been a good actor. No way was he going to let it go that Caden had pushed him into a hellish dimension.

Caden clutched the protective talisman he wore around his neck and made himself walk over.

"Welcome home," Aiden said cheerfully. "Have you met our delightful neighbor?"

Ava lifted a hand in greeting. Long, wavy brown hair tumbled around her shoulders, framing an oval face with wide brown eyes and full lips. She looked like Rae, only older, and—Caden had to admit—prettier. Rae's face was all sharp angles and determined chin, whereas her sister had softer features but the same big doe eyes.

He liked Rae's face better.

Stop it, he told himself firmly. "We've met," he said. "Hi, Ava," he added, trying to be polite despite the racing of his heart. He didn't know what his brother was playing at, but he was sure Aiden was up to something. Why was he out of the house? Last night he'd refused to even stand in front of a window.

"Oh, that's right," Ava said. "We did meet. Just before you helped my sister with her breaking-and-entering scheme."

"Caden did that?" Aiden widened his eyes, clearly shocked, even though he'd been there in spirit, spying on Caden and Rae as they trespassed through Doctor Anderson's house. "My little brother, a criminal?"

"Don't hold it against him. Rae can be very persuasive."

Aiden grinned. "I look forward to meeting her."

Caden could feel the tangled knot in his stomach freezing into a hard lump as Ava invited him and his brother over for dinner sometime. She might not know what Aiden meant, but Caden knew.

It was a threat.

Caden remained silent until Ava walked across the street to her own house, vanishing safely inside. Then he turned on his brother. "What are you doing?"

Aiden shrugged and started up the driveway.

Caden went after him, grabbing his arm. "Stay away from the Carters."

Aiden turned, yanking his arm free, his face hard and angry. "Or you'll do what?"

Caden opened his mouth, then shut it, unsure.

Aiden's smile did nothing to soften his face. "That's what I thought. You're too tenderhearted. Don't bother threatening me until you are willing to back it up." A car sounded down the road, and Aiden glanced over, his shoulders hunching instinctively. He stalked the rest of the way up the driveway, moving quickly, Caden following a step behind.

Aiden opened the front door and slipped inside, waiting until Caden closed the door behind them before his shoulders relaxed.

"Where does Ava think you've been?" Caden asked.

"She thinks I was volunteering with Doctors without Borders. I told her I couldn't sit here a moment longer, thinking of all those poor sick people in the world and doing nothing, so I ran away to help. But then eventually they found out I was only sixteen and sent me home." He chuckled. "I made that up on the fly, but I'm quite proud of it."

Caden shook his head. His brother had always been good at lying to make himself sound good. Caden was the only one who could usually see through those lies, as it was difficult to fool someone who could feel your emotions. Right now, though, he couldn't feel anything from his brother. It was as if there were no one standing next to him at all.

But he felt his mom's energy, all nervous excitement as she rushed into view.

"See, Mom?" Aiden said. "Back inside, safe and sound."

"I see that." She gave him a big hug, something she hadn't done since he was little. Then she turned to Caden and gave him a little pat on the back while Aiden smirked at him. "Come join me in the kitchen?"

Caden slipped off his shoes and dropped his backpack by the door, then followed his mom and brother.

His mom sat down at the small, round kitchen table, Aiden taking the seat across from her. "This is nice," she said, sipping from her steaming brick-red mug.

"This is wonderful," Aiden agreed, picking up his matching mug. He stared over the top of it at Caden. "Well? Are you going to sit with us?"

Caden hesitated. Already Aiden and his mom looked cozy and comfortable, like the past year's absence had never happened. It was amazing how quickly his brother slid into his old life. And how fast Caden could go from "only son" back to "unnecessary extra."

Caden's stomach twisted, but he kept his face neutral and pulled a chair back from the table, positioning it so he could leap out of Aiden's reach and sprint to the door if needed.

"You're eyeing me like I'm some kind of unpredictable monster." Aiden sighed. "Little brother, I promise, you don't have to be afraid of me. I'm not mad at you."

"Aiden understands it wasn't your fault," their mom said, her voice just a little too eager. She was obviously trying hard to smooth over any awkwardness. *We all know you didn't really mean to almost kill your brother, just like he didn't really mean to almost kill all of us by unleashing the monsters in an alternate dimension. Let's let bygones be bygones, shall we?* Caden almost laughed, it was so ridiculous. But in the end, he just sank into his chair, silent.

His mom relaxed slightly. "Want some tea?" she asked. "It's rooibos."

"That's okay." Caden wanted to keep his hands free. Was he being paranoid? He looked into Aiden's smiling face and didn't think so.

The front door opened, and their dad rushed in, his arms full of balloons and a large flat cardboard box. "Sorry I'm late! I made a few stops on my way home." He put the box down on the table and opened it with a flourish. A dozen jelly doughnuts lay nestled inside. Aiden's favorite. "Welcome home, son." His eyes glistened as he handed Aiden the balloons. They were brightly colored, a rainbow of red, orange, yellow, and green, with one in the middle in the shape of a star that said IT'S YOUR DAY TO SHINE in big bold letters.

"Uh, thanks, Dad." Aiden held the end of the balloons awkwardly, their strings all tied together in a large plastic clip.

"They didn't have any 'nice job escaping a hellish dimension' balloons, so I had to compromise."

Caden laughed, but Aiden didn't even crack a smile, and neither did their mom. "Tough crowd, Dad," Caden said.

His dad shrugged but looked happier than he had in months as he sank into a chair. Caden could feel the contentment radiating off him like the steam off his brother's mug. Strangely, this time it didn't make him feel resentful. He'd gotten so used to his dad's miasma of guilt and sorrow since Aiden vanished that he'd almost forgotten what his dad was like before that. It was nice to get a reminder.

Aiden set the balloon clip down on the table and looked at the doughnuts.

"Go ahead," their dad said.

"Maybe in a bit. I'm not hungry."

Caden gasped, his dad's mouth dropped, and even his mom sat up straighter in surprise. Aiden had *never* in his life turned down a jelly doughnut. Aiden broke into a wide grin. "Just kidding." He snagged a doughnut from the middle and ate the entire thing in three quick bites. "Mmm, better than I remembered."

Caden took a doughnut and ate it more slowly, trying not to

make a mess. Powdered sugar and black clothing were a terrible combination.

"So, Caden," Aiden said.

Caden almost choked on his doughnut. "Hmm?" he managed.

"I hear you've started training to take over the family business." Aiden licked the sugar from his fingers, watching him.

Caden felt the mood at the table shift, his dad's easy smile vanishing. He had blamed Aiden's disappearance on his involvement in Paranormal Price. And he had blamed their mom for allowing that involvement. He wanted Caden to stay far away from all of it. Honestly, that was what Caden wanted too. He didn't want to learn any more about his strange powers, or the family business, or the Other Place, or any of it. He just wanted to keep his head down, get through school, and eventually move away from Whispering Pines. But he'd never been able to tell his mom that.

"Um, just a bit," he said, very aware of his dad's weighted gaze and the simmering fury beneath it. Obviously his dad hadn't known that his mom had begun that training with him. "But I guess I won't have to do that anymore now that you're back." Caden felt a strange twinge of something. Regret, maybe? Or relief? He spent so much time analyzing the emotions of other people that he sometimes had trouble untangling his own.

"Actually, I won't be much help in that regard. Not anymore."

"What do you mean?" their mom asked.

"Something happened when I was torn from the Other Place. My Price abilities, all my magic, is gone."

Shock swirled around Caden. He'd been bracing himself for

Aiden to do something terrible to him to get revenge. And all this time his brother had been powerless. "Really?" Caden asked.

Aiden nodded. He looked annoyed and resigned. Not angry. Not desperate. Just mildly inconvenienced. It was so unlike the brother Caden knew—the one who craved power more than anything—that Caden didn't know what to think. Maybe Aiden had changed in his months sealed away, his priorities shifting.

"I'm . . . sorry," Caden said.

"I imagine you're also probably relieved."

Caden flinched but didn't argue. Unlike his brother, he didn't like to lie.

"I think it's time you told us the rest," their mom said, her voice gentle but firm.

7.

RAE

Rae took a huge bite of cheesy pizza.

"Best idea ever right here," Vivienne said, taking her own bite.

Rae chewed happily, gazing around the Eastbury Mall's tiny food court. In addition to Papa Joe's Pizza, there was a Chinese food restaurant literally just called "Chinese Food," never a good sign, a sandwich place called "Sub-a-Dub-Dub," and an ice cream parlor called "Eye Scream" that reminded Rae uncomfortably of the Unseeing. A dozen greasy plastic tables and chairs clustered in the middle of the floor. Rae was pretty sure the greasiness was mandatory for all mall tables, and she tried touching theirs as little as possible.

"Hey! You jerks!" Nate said, stomping over. "We're supposed to be working!"

Nate's mom had picked the three of them up from school and dropped them off here. Apparently the Cliffs lived in the townhouses just down the road from the mall, and Nate had suggested it as a place to try searching for something "hidden in plain sight," whatever that was supposed to mean. Rae doubted they'd actually find anything at this sad little shopping plaza, but since she didn't have any better ideas, here they were. After a few minutes of mindless wandering, Nate had decided they'd be more productive if they split up, and they'd all gone off on their own.

Rae had made her way to the end of the mall, where her former therapist, Doctor Anderson, had his office. A CLOSED FOR BUSINESS sign hung on his door, the office inside dark and empty.

Rae and Caden had found evidence that Doctor Anderson was the serial eye snatcher, and he'd been taken into Green On!'s custody. After the real eye snatcher was discovered, Rae had just assumed the doctor had been released. But staring at that sign made her wonder . . .

Vivienne had found her soon after, and they'd decided it was time for a pizza break.

Sitting in the food court, shoveling down melted cheese and tomato sauce, Rae was able to forget about Doctor Anderson. At least for now.

Rae took another bite of pizza and pushed the box on the table toward Nate. "Peace offering?" she mumbled around her food.

"Gross."

"You don't have to eat it," Vivienne said.

"I wasn't talking about the pizza. I was referring to the person eating it with her mouth open." He gave Rae a disgusted look, then carefully took a slice out of the box and put it on a paper plate. He went over to the counter, then came back with a fork and knife and sat down at their table.

"You have got to be kidding me," Vivienne said, watching him cut his pizza up into tiny squares.

"What?" Nate asked.

"Only serial killers eat their pizza like that."

"It makes it less messy." Nate took a tiny bite.

"Spoken like a true serial killer." Vivienne shook her head.

"Actually, a true serial killer would probably be less obvious about it," Rae said without thinking.

Vivienne and Nate stared at her.

"Know a lot about serial killers, do you?" Nate asked, his tone as dry as the crust on their pizza.

"Only a little." Rae managed a weak chuckle. She had actually read quite a lot on serial killers. It was a favorite subject for her, along with government conspiracies, alien abductions, and unexplained missing persons. But one thing she'd learned at her old school was never to let anyone know about her unique research.

She'd broken that rule already with Caden. And look where that got her.

"Now *that*"—Nate jabbed a fork at her—"was a serial killer response." He took another careful bite of pizza, chewed, and swallowed, then asked, "So did you find anything at all?"

"Of course we did," Vivienne said.

"Like what?"

"Well, for starters, I saw our good friend slash mortal enemy Matt here," Vivienne said.

"Mortal enemy?" Rae asked. "That's a little strong, isn't it?"

"He's in the other group. Ergo," Vivienne said, as if that settled the matter.

"What about Alyssa? She's in the other group, and isn't she your friend?" Nate asked.

Vivienne winced. "Yes, well . . . Alyssa isn't really talking to me right now."

"She isn't?" Rae asked.

"She's mad I didn't stand at her table in the science room, especially since that meant we got put on separate teams." Vivienne shrugged like it didn't bother her at all. But Rae could tell she was just pretending. She recognized that forced casualness. "She'll get over it. Probably just in time to be mad again when our team wins."

"I like your confidence," Nate said. "So, what about Matt?"

"Well, it turns out that he is a total nose picker. Also, our homeroom teacher's husband, Mr. Murphy, was hitting up the New Age store." She gestured toward Divine's Divinations and Crystals. Its glowing, swirly purple letters were just barely visible to the left of the food court. "I wonder if Caden's family shops there?"

Rae shrugged. The last thing she wanted to do right now was talk about Caden.

"Why are you staring at me?" Vivienne asked Nate.

"Please tell me that you didn't write down 'nose pickers' and 'crystal buyers' on our notes for the internship project."

"Of course I didn't write that." Vivienne beamed at him. "I

wrote down exact details." She pulled a heavily folded sheet of paper out of her back pocket and slowly peeled it open. "Ahem." She glanced down at it and read, "'At three twenty-eight, Matt went for the world record, digging at his interior nose canal for a solid forty-three sec—'"

"Okay! And you can stop there." Nate turned to Rae. "And what did you find?"

"I found it odd that everything here looks so new."

"That's because it *is* new. What's odd about that?" Nate finished his slice of pizza and gently placed the crust back in the box.

"How new?" Rae asked.

"Well, the Town Square behind us was cleared about twenty years ago," Vivienne said.

"More like nineteen years ago," Nate muttered.

Vivienne glared at him, then continued, "And they built a mall on the edge of it. But then they were forced to bulldoze that place and rebuild this one. I think it was finished about a year ago?"

"Closer to ten months," Nate said.

"Would you stop?"

"I thought you liked 'exact details.'" He made quotation marks next to his head as he spoke.

Rae could see Vivienne's annoyance gearing up and quickly asked, "Why did they have to bulldoze the first mall?"

"Oh, because it was totally haunted," Vivienne said.

Rae glanced from her to Nate and back, waiting for the punchline. Then she realized Vivienne was serious, and Nate wasn't correcting her, which meant he believed it too. "I see," Rae said slowly.

But it reminded her of an article she had read a few weeks ago about a woman walking her dog through the Town Square. Her dog had found a bone . . . a *human* bone. "Wasn't this place originally an old colonial graveyard, or something?"

"Was it?" Vivienne said.

"It was. The town moved the graves to another location," Nate said.

"I heard the town moved the gravestones but not the bodies." Rae shivered.

"That would explain the haunting." Vivienne smiled.

Rae wondered if she would ever get used to the matter-of-fact way people around here accepted hauntings and other supernatural strangeness. Maybe there was something in the water that just brainwashed everyone into thinking things like this were normal. "Would that be a secret hidden in plain sight?" she asked.

Vivienne frowned. "Maybe."

"Hold up," Nate said. "Are you suggesting we go out there and look for some human corpses?"

Rae shrugged. "It's either that or Matt's marvelous nose-picking feat . . ."

Nate shoved his chair back from the table. "Okay, let's go find us some dead people!"

8.

CADEN

Aiden settled back in his chair and took a sip of tea. Caden could tell he was enjoying the feeling of all eyes on him. He'd always liked being the focus of everyone's attention. Yet another way he and Caden were so different.

"My time in the Other Place is all kind of a blur," Aiden said at last. "Trying to remember it is like trying to remember a long-ago dream. All the details keep changing in my head. I just have a vague sense of the throbbing light, the constant pain, the endless terror. And the feeling of betrayal."

Caden flinched.

"It could have been hours, or days, or months. Or maybe years. Every moment impossibly long, and yet the whole thing ended in seconds. The rift tore wide open, and three people smashed their way through wearing very odd bright green suits with helmets and thick boots. They grabbed me, and the next thing I knew, I was out."

"So Green On! managed to open the rift," their mom said, looking sick. "I can't believe it."

"I don't think it worked out well for them, if it makes you feel better. Those suits didn't protect the people who went into the Other Place; all of them are dead. Or as good as."

"Strangely, that does *not* make me feel better."

"Oh, I didn't mean to sound cruel. But they were messing around with powers they shouldn't have been, and they paid the price for it. I know how that goes better than anyone." Aiden's lips twisted. "I've learned my lesson. And hopefully Green On! has learned theirs. Although I don't think so. I think they'll try again. I'm not sure how much luck they'll have, though."

"Why is that?" his mom asked.

"They haven't figured out how to create the right kind of energy needed to open the rift."

"What do you mean?" his dad asked.

"I mean magic. They can't create magic," Aiden said. "It's one thing their science and technology is unable to replicate. For now, at least."

"Then how did they pull you out?" his dad asked, frowning.

"That would be thanks to our dear little Caden here."

Caden could tell his brother wanted to see his reaction, so he did his best not to give him anything. He pictured himself as a wall, smooth and unfeeling. It was something Aiden had actually taught him back when Caden was little.

No special powers are needed to read your emotions, little brother.

They are plastered all over your face, Aiden had said after finding Caden grinning in the yard at a pair of squirrels.

What's wrong with that? Caden had asked, his grin faltering.

He remembered how Aiden had studied him for a long minute before smiling and ruffling his hair. *Nothing is wrong. But it leaves you open. If people know what you're feeling, then they can manipulate you. I can show you how to protect yourself, if you'd like?*

Back then, Aiden was always teaching him little tricks, things to make himself stronger, safer, better. Caden used to believe it was his brother's way of showing his love. Now he wasn't sure what to think. When Rae was trapped in the cabin in the woods with the Unseeing, Aiden had helped him once again, guiding him through the first steps needed to open the rift that would send the Unseeing back to the Other Place where it belonged. But even there, Aiden's assistance had been self-serving; he'd needed Caden to help him get out.

Not that it had worked. Aiden had vanished before the ritual was completed, leaving Caden to figure out the rest on his own. What if he'd messed it up somehow, given Green On! some kind of opening?

Caden managed to keep all these worries tucked away, his face as blank as he could possibly make it.

Aiden gave him a tiny nod now, almost as if in approval. "When Caden opened the rift, Green On! was able to somehow suction the power he generated into their lab. They used it to tear their own hole into the Other Place, and the rest . . ." He spread his hands wide.

"How do you know all this?" his mom asked.

Aiden fiddled with the ring on his thumb as if debating how much to say. Then he sighed. "After they pulled me out, they kept me locked in a secret underground lab."

"They did *what*?" their dad demanded, his face darkening.

"They kept me 'for observation.' But really it was because they wanted to know more about the Other Place. About how it works, the power contained in it. They thought I'd be able to help them get back into it. But since my powers are gone, I couldn't even if I'd wanted to." He frowned. "I wonder if that's why they haven't tried to find me again. Maybe I'm not useful enough to them."

"Didn't they let you go?" his dad asked.

"Let me go?" Aiden laughed. "No. I escaped."

"How?" Caden had seen pictures of the Green On! lab. It looked like a fortress, all concrete walls and chain-link fences.

"Apparently Mom did a favor for someone who works there." Aiden winked. "She arranged a distraction so I could get out, but first made me promise to keep her name a secret."

Caden glanced at his mom. She had her fingers steepled together, her lips pursed. He got the impression that she knew exactly who Aiden was referring to, secret name or no.

"This is unbelievable." Their dad leaned back in his chair, scowling. It was an unusual expression for his face, pulling it into awkward lines that made Caden feel like he were looking across the table at a stranger.

"Could they have released the evil thing imprisoned inside?" Caden asked.

"The what now?" his dad asked.

Caden's mom shook her head. "There are safeguards in place that will keep it trapped there, rift opening or no."

"What kind of safeguards?" Aiden asked.

"What kind of evil?" their dad demanded.

She pressed her lips together in a firm, unyielding line.

"Seriously, Eleanor? Another secret?" Their dad stood abruptly, his chair scraping across the floor with a shriek of wood.

"Wait, Vincent—"

"You tell our son—our thirteen-year-old boy—truths that you won't allow me to know. How can I possibly protect him if I'm kept in the dark? Unless that's your plan?"

"You know that's not it."

"I don't know anything." He glared down at her, then shifted his gaze to Aiden. "I'm sorry, Aiden. I'm very tired, but I hope you know how glad I am to see you home. I couldn't care less about your magic, I'm just happy you're safe." He put a hand on Aiden's shoulder and squeezed before letting him go. Then he patted Caden on the head once before leaving. They could hear his heavy footsteps creaking up the stairs and down the hall above.

Caden saw the crumpled, defeated look that crossed his mom's face before she quickly smoothed it out.

"Can you tell us more about this evil?" Aiden leaned forward eagerly, his elbows on the table.

"Not tonight." She ran a hand back through her long dark hair, looking suddenly exhausted.

"Tomorrow?"

"Maybe, Aiden."

"It's just, it sounds dangerous, and I'd like to help. I might not have my powers, but I can still read spell books. If you'll explain how the barrier was created and tell me more about these safeguards, then maybe I can—"

Caden's head snapped up. "Someone's here." He could sense them approaching the front door. Whoever it was felt like a swirling cloud, the murky yellow color of fear. He thought of the scribbles he'd made on the bus ride home. They felt like that.

His mom stood so quickly, her chair clattered backward. "Aiden, hide."

Knock. Knock. Knock.

"I'll get it." His mom straightened her shawl and waited for Aiden to vanish up the stairs and into his room. Then she opened the front door.

A man stood outside. He was probably in his early forties,.with thinning brown hair and a short, badly trimmed beard. A musty animal smell clung to him. "Eleanor Price?" he asked.

She nodded.

"I believe I have need of your services. Immediately, if possible." He swallowed, his Adam's apple bobbing. "It might already be too late."

9.

RAE

Eastbury Mall framed one side of the Town Square, sitting kitty-corner to another long row of buildings. Rae noticed a bank, a church, and an antiques shop in that row. The other two sides of the square were hemmed in by Whispering Pines's ever-present trees.

The Town Square itself was a literal perfect square that had to be several acres, all of it flat and covered in nice, squishy grass. In the exact center of the square stood a giant concrete fountain in the shape of a goat sitting on its own square slab.

"What's up with the goats around here anyhow?" Rae asked.

"They have something to do with our town's original founders, I think," Vivienne said as they followed the long, wavy sidewalk that cut through the square, leading to the center. "Also they're supposed to be lucky." Her cell phone rang, and she stopped. "Give me a sec, would you?" She dug around in the front zippered pocket of her bag and tugged out her phone. "Hi, Mom," she answered.

Rae and Nate waited while Vivienne gave short, one-word answers. Finally she hung up, frowning. "Apparently my mom took today off work to recover from the stress of yesterday's malfunction, and she's mad that I didn't come home from school right away."

"You didn't tell her you'd be out here with us?" Nate asked.

"Nope."

"Are you in trouble?" Rae asked.

"Yep." Vivienne shoved her phone back into her bag. "How was I supposed to know my mom would be home now? She's been working until late every day. But of course the one day I decide not to go straight home, she notices." Vivienne scowled. "I don't know what's up with her. Did you know the other day I caught her arguing with herself in the mirror?"

"My mom does that all the time," Nate said, shrugging.

"Yeah, well, my mom doesn't. It was very odd. Between that and her overprotectiveness lately . . ." Vivienne's scowl faded, her expression going thoughtful, then sad. "I guess I understand that, though."

"Why?" Rae asked.

Vivienne blinked. "Oh, you know. I'm still grounded from that whole breaking-curfew thing."

Rae frowned. It had seemed like there was more to the story.

"Aren't you still grounded too?" Vivienne asked her. Rae, Vivienne, and Caden had all been exploring together when they violated the town's code yellow alert. Only Caden hadn't gotten in trouble with his parents. Apparently when your family owned a ghost-hunting business, you were given a little extra slack.

"My mom's loosened up a tiny bit," Rae said. "Honestly, I think the way Patrick pitched the internship program to her helped a lot. Also, Ava talked to her." Rae sighed. "She actually listens to Ava."

"Why are you both grounded?" Nate asked.

Rae and Vivienne exchanged looks. "It's classified," Vivienne told him, grinning. "We could tell you . . ."

"But then we'd have to kill you," Rae finished, laughing.

"All three of us are supposed to be a team, you know," Nate huffed.

"Yeah, yeah." Vivienne waved a hand. "Speaking of being a team, my mom told me she'll be out front in half an hour to pick me up, so we'd better hurry."

"If I were a dead body, where would I be?" Rae studied the fountain. Water spouted from the goat's horns, and its eyes seemed to stare right through her.

"Obviously in the ground," Nate said.

"Someone still sounds a little sulky," Vivienne said.

"I am not being sulky."

"Are too."

Nate sighed loudly. "I'm going to stop this now, because one of us needs to have a little maturity."

Vivienne stuck her tongue out at him.

Rae laughed. "Anyhow, I know dead bodies would be in the ground. I meant where in the square should we look? It's not like we came prepared with shovels."

"I have a shovel." Vivienne patted her giant backpack.

Rae's eyebrows shot up. "I guess I shouldn't be surprised."

"We'll get in trouble if we start digging here," Nate said.

"What about over there? In the trees?" Rae pointed. "That's where I'd want to start looking anyhow."

"Why?" Nate asked.

"See how those trees are smaller than the others? They're young, freshly planted probably in the last decade or two. If I were trying to cover up the bodies I hadn't felt like digging up, I'd consider planting trees over them."

Nate stared at her.

"What?" Rae asked.

"Are you sure you're not a serial killer?"

"Like she'd admit it to you." Vivienne looped her arm through Rae's. "Let's go."

They strode across the grass, avoiding a couple of middle-aged runners and a woman out walking three pugs before reaching the trees. As soon as they were under those tangled branches, Rae started second-guessing her plan. Did she really think they could meander around and just stumble onto a skeleton? What was she thinking?

There were plenty of mysteries in Whispering Pines. Rae was sure they could find something else hidden in plain sight. But there was something about this one that tugged at her. As she stepped over roots and ducked beneath branches, she felt a growing sense of premonition. It was like the knowledge that your phone was about to ring a second before it did. And she knew she would find something here.

She separated from Vivienne and walked slowly over the ground. There were wide spaces in between trees, like bald patches on a person's head. One of those spots did look a little loose, almost as if someone had been digging there recently.

Rae moved closer, noticing lines in the dirt. Like something heavy had been dragged across it.

"Hey, Rae-Rae?" Vivienne called.

Rae turned.

"I think I found—"

The ground underneath Rae gave way, and she fell, screaming, through the damp earth.

10.

CADEN

Caden followed Gary the Goatman into the Watchful Woods, his thoughts drifting back to his most recent experiences in this forest. Like the time he, Rae, and Vivienne had been chased through the trees by the Unseeing. Or later, when he ran through the woods to save Rae, accompanied by the ghostly presence of his brother. It felt a little like those times now, and tension thrummed through his body like a plucked guitar string. At least today he had really strong backup: his mom was with him.

Caden glanced at her. She had changed into a pair of jeans and tall hiking boots; the ticks in Connecticut were no joke. She was wearing her most expressionless face, her mouth a sharp line, and she'd put all her inner shields up in an impenetrable wall. Which meant she absolutely did not want Caden to guess what she was feeling.

Definitely not a good sign.

Gary, on the other hand, had fear leaking from him like pus from a yellow, festering wound.

They reached a short stone wall covered in moss and stretching in either direction before disappearing beneath the pines. Caden knew this wall wove all around the forest. Its stones were dark with age, dating back to the colonial days. Most people in Whispering Pines believed it was meant to separate property, but his mom had told him that a coven of witches had built it as some sort of protection against the supernatural. Supposedly its pattern shifted daily. Caden believed that. There was something a little strange about this wall.

He put his hand on top of it, feeling the soft moss, and beneath it, a faint vibration. Like he was in a car speeding down a smooth road, only the barest hint of movement noticeable.

Gary scowled. "These walls. Supposed to help, did you know that? Fat lot of good they did."

"Help with what?" Caden asked.

"Keeping us safe from the things that don't belong here." Gary shook his head. "My nephew was messing around with this wall recently," he told Caden's mom. "He couldn't have . . . you know, ruined anything?"

"I doubt that. The spells set in this stone are very strong." She put both hands on top of it and closed her eyes, concentrating. "The wards are still up." She opened her eyes. "But this wall was only ever meant to be a fail-safe. Not a first line of defense."

Gary sighed. "I know. That's why I had the goats." He hoisted himself over the wall. "Coming?"

They walked through the woods for what had to be a good hour. Caden tried not to be anxious. "Are we close?" he finally asked.

Gary frowned at Caden's mom. "Told you we shouldn't have brought the boy. This here is a job for adults. Not scared little kids."

"I'm not nearly as scared as you are," Caden said, annoyed.

Gary glanced sidelong at him. "That's just 'cause you haven't seen it yet." He sighed and added, "And it's not too much farther. I like to keep my goats close to water, so we've just got the creek to cross, and I'm in the clearing on the other side."

Everyone in Whispering Pines knew that the size and shape of the Watchful Woods shifted constantly, much like the walls woven through it. Maybe the creek wasn't just a place for Gary's goats to drink. Maybe it also served as a landmark, so he could find his way back home.

And maybe Gary wasn't the only living thing in these woods using that creek as a landmark . . .

"What did you say it was that attacked you?" Caden asked.

"I didn't say. It's one of those things you need to see with your own eyes to really believe."

Caden glanced at his mom, but she didn't seem concerned. He supposed that in her line of work, most things were probably unexplainable until they were experienced firsthand. If this became his line of work, he'd have to get used to that, too.

Just thinking that made Caden feel like he were being stuffed in a box, his whole life contained within this tiny town full of people who didn't understand him.

Rae had understood him, though. She'd known what it was like to have rumors destroy your reputation and separate you from your friends. And she'd been one of the few people who also recognized the strangeness running underneath the surface of Whispering Pines—recognized it and didn't turn away.

When Patrick had asked Caden and Rae to sign up for his internship, and they had both been united in their refusal, Caden had realized how much it meant to him to have a real friend. A solid ally. Before Rae, he'd only had his brother, and Aiden would always be about his own interests first.

But then Rae had changed her mind. Even though Caden had promised to help her find her dad, she'd decided to turn to Patrick and Green On! instead for their assistance. So obviously she didn't feel as strongly about their friendship as he did.

Caden ducked under a low-hanging branch, the echo of that betrayal clinging to him like campfire smoke. But underneath it for the first time he recognized another emotion: fear.

He was afraid of Patrick.

Was that the real reason he'd decided to block out Rae? Was he really that big of a coward?

"Creek's just through here," Gary said.

Caden blinked, and now he heard the sound of flowing water and the faint rustling of animals nearby. It was a comforting noise; animals usually went quiet when they sensed danger. He pushed his way through some scratchy bushes, and there it was.

It was a small creek, the kind that ran dry in the summer and flooded after a large rain. Right now it was still pretty shallow, barely more than a trickle since the fall storms hadn't come yet.

Caden followed his mom and Gary across it and over to a large grassy clearing. In the center stood a tall canvas yurt, the sides the same deep, dark green as the forest, the roof a charcoal gray. Next to the yurt stood a long, sturdy wooden goat pen. Inside, a trip of goats milled noisily about, eating the grass and watching the intruders.

A white goat with a wide brown patch over one eye picked its way to the edge of the enclosure. "Baaa," it called.

"Did you miss me, Blueberry?" Gary scratched the goat behind her ear, and she tilted her head back, her eyes closing happily. The yellow cloud of fear that had been bubbling out of him vanished for a few minutes, replaced by a pink mist of affection, so bright and warm that Caden thought it might actually be visible to everyone.

But then Gary dropped his hand and the fear came back in a rush. "This way." He led them around the back of the goat pen and over to a small shed hunched innocently next to the tree line. He unlocked the shed and threw the doors wide, flooding the space with afternoon sunlight, then reached along the side of the wall and flipped a switch. An overhead light flickered on, chasing away any remaining shadows and illuminating something large and lumpy covered by a rug in the center.

"I had to drag it in here," Gary said. "It made my goats nervous."

"Let's see it," Caden's mom said.

Gary bent down and gripped the edge of the rug. He paused, and then in one quick motion, he yanked the rug off.

Caden stared. For a few seconds he wasn't sure what, exactly, he was looking at. Whatever it was had hundreds of jointed legs, all curled inward. "A . . . giant bug?"

"Near as I can tell," Gary said. "Although I've never in my life seen a bug like that before. And living out here, I've seen my fair share of insects."

"Where did it come from?" Caden craned his head for a closer look, keeping his feet firmly planted outside that shed. The creature was almost as wide as a person, its exoskeleton an oily black like wet pavement. It reminded him of one of the prehistoric centipedes he'd seen in a science book. The kind that used to get seven, eight, nine feet long.

"From the woods." Gary wiped his hand on his jeans, as if the rug covering the thing had been contaminated.

"Did you decapitate it?" Caden's mom asked.

Caden wondered what Gary should have done with it instead. Kept it as a pet? Sure, the goats wouldn't have been amused, but it would have made one heck of a guard dog . . .

"Had to," Gary said. "First it attacked my goats, then it went after my nephew. Luckily I keep my axe nice and sharp." He bared his teeth in a smile that almost masked his worry.

"Did it hurt your nephew?" Caden's mom crouched, not touching the insect, just looking at the edge where the axe had split it. Some kind of strange goop had hardened around the wound and glistened sickeningly in the light overhead. Something about it just looked . . . *wrong* to Caden, and he knew it didn't belong in this world. It had come from somewhere *else*. He could feel the truth of that knowledge just as sharply as the fear still leaking from Gary.

"My nephew was fine. Scared him away from the outdoor life,

though." Gary shrugged. "Probably for the best. I'd been trying to get him to go back home for weeks."

"He was living with you?" Caden glanced at the yurt. It didn't look that big.

"Yeah, it was a tight fit, but family is family, right? I couldn't exactly kick him out. He's doing well now, though. Last I heard he got placed in some fancy internship or something."

"Internship? At Green On!?" Caden's stomach sank.

"Where else?"

"Where else indeed," Caden's mom said. She stood up, frowning. "Sorry about your goat."

"My goats are just fine too. I gave Waffles away to my nephew. Poor thing was too shook up to stay out here, but I got another one—"

"One of them is missing." Her frown deepened. "Or did I miscount? I only saw eight."

Gary's eyebrows lifted, his forehead turning into a map of wrinkles. He turned and ran for the goat pen.

"How many is he supposed to have?" Caden asked, amazed that his mom knew one was missing.

"He needs nine if he wants to live safely in the Watchful Woods."

"Why? What happens if he only has eight?"

She pursed her lips. "Possibly nothing. But . . ." She looked up at the sky, where the sun had started slowly sinking. "Hopefully he can get himself a ninth goat before sundown so he doesn't have to find out."

Caden glanced at the bug, then away again quickly. There was something about all those legs and how they were curled inward that seriously freaked him out. "Do you think it"—he jerked his chin at the thing—"came from the Other Place?"

She shook her head, a strand of black hair sticking to her sweaty forehead. "It doesn't feel like it." She prodded the bug gently with one booted foot. "Honestly, I don't know where it came from." She turned her back on it. "I'm going to check on Gary." And she left Caden standing there in the doorway of the shed.

He made himself look at the giant centipede again, opening up his other senses to try to feel it out. He braced himself for the Other Place's energy to roll over him like a wave at the beach, but nothing happened. Maybe his mom was right. But . . . where else could it have come from? Green On! had opened a rift to pull Aiden out, and their lab wasn't far from this spot. The only thing that made sense was that this thing had skittered out with Aiden.

Caden walked closer to the bug. Something else about this corpse bothered him, some other fact that niggled against his brain like a half-remembered song lyric. He knelt down near the head. Against the dark carapace, he picked out the details of a face. Almost humanlike, only with multiple eyes stacked one beneath the other, and a mouth full of pinchers.

He could imagine that face scuttling toward him, pinchers wide . . .

He stumbled back from the shed, almost tripping over his own feet in his rush to rejoin his mom and Gary.

"—can't get Waffles back," Gary was saying. "That would break my nephew's heart. But there's a farm not far from here. They've been having some trouble with their own livestock vanishing, but I should still be able to get another goat from them." He ran a hand through his hair, his expression bewildered. "I just can't believe Priceless Art wandered off. I checked the fence this morning."

"Maybe she will turn up," Caden's mom said. "But the sun's almost down, so . . ."

"I know. I know. I'm going. Are you—"

"We'll be here for a little longer to search the area," she said. "But we can't stay long."

Gary looked up at the sky. "I understand. And . . . thank you."

"Don't thank me yet. I'm not sure what I can do about this except hope it's just a onetime occurrence."

Gary opened his mouth, then closed it again with an audible snap. Caden got a wave of emotion from the man, but it was a tangle as chaotic as a bag of yarn left in a room full of kittens. "If you find anything . . ." Gary swallowed.

"We'll let you know." She smiled and rested a hand on his shoulder. "You did good, Gary. I know it wasn't easy for you, coming to see me."

He nodded, then set off again through the woods without another word.

Caden watched him vanish into the trees. "What's with the goat names?"

"Oh, he names them after their favorite food."

Caden thought about "Priceless Art" but didn't ask. "What are we looking for?" he asked instead.

"Gary . . . doesn't like people. He rents out his goats, you know, to help trim weeds in yards, that sort of thing. So he'll talk to the folks in town then. But otherwise he keeps to himself. And yet he came to me."

Caden frowned. "That corpse wasn't fresh."

"Exactly. He killed it days ago. So why come to me now? And with such urgency?"

"You think he saw more of those things?"

"I think," she said slowly, "that his goat isn't lost in the woods."

Caden tried not to imagine more of those bugs skittering through the grasses. Suddenly he wanted to climb very high up a tree and stay there forever. "Did it eat the goat?" he asked, his voice small.

"I don't know," she said sharply. "I'm not an entomologist." She sighed. "Sorry, honey. I'm just . . . I'm not a fan of bugs." She wiped her hands on her pant legs, then gave him a quick, tight smile. "So let's do this search quickly and get out of here. I don't want to be in these woods after dark, either."

An hour of bushwhacking later, and Caden was ready to call it quits and go home. His stomach had started growling, his nerves were shot, and his legs felt ready to collapse. Plus, he was dirty and sweaty and scratched all over. They'd discovered a large hole dug under the fence of the goat pen, but other than that, nothing. Still, his mom insisted on combing through every inch of nearby forest. Part of him was impressed with her work ethic. But it was a very small part.

He went to kick a pile of sticks, then froze.

They weren't sticks. They had too many joints, and they were the wrong color—dark and shiny.

"Mom?" Caden's voice trembled, but he couldn't help it. "Mom!"

"Coming!" He heard the sounds of crunching and branches snapping, and then his mom was there, her hair hanging in sweaty clumps, her face as scratched and dirty as his. "What? What is it?"

Wordlessly he gestured at the sticks in front of him. She stared, confusion pulling her eyebrows together, before realization shot them up. "It must have shed its exoskeleton," she breathed. She found a stick—a real one—and nudged the exoskeleton, flipping it easily. It crinkled as it moved, a sound like someone digging inside a potato chip bag for the very last crumbs.

"It's huge," Caden said. "Bigger than the one Gary killed."

"They're growing." She dropped the stick. "And look. Do you see that mound there?"

Caden looked past the bushes and the bug skin and—and he saw it. A large hole, the opening wide enough for a person to climb into. "Did it come from there?" He couldn't look away from that darkness.

"I would imagine so."

"Should we . . . should we go look?"

"Nope."

Caden sagged in relief. This nightmare was almost over. Then he thought of another nightmare. "If they were going after goats before, and now they're getting bigger . . . what will they want to eat next?"

"I'm pretty sure we both know the answer to that," she said grimly. "I'll call Gary when we're home, give him a warning. We'd better hurry back."

Caden gave the exoskeleton one last look. He definitely wanted a different line of work.

But now that he knew these things existed, could he really pretend they didn't? Even if he left Whispering Pines behind, would he honestly be able to live a different kind of life?

As they rushed back through the woods, Caden found it impossible to imagine a version of himself that was any different from the version here. It wasn't this town, or his mom, or even the family business that had trapped him in a box.

It was himself.

By the time they stepped out of the woods and onto their street, Caden was ready to be done with this whole night. He could hear his mom's footsteps as she followed him up the driveway. He focused on his own feet and thought of the hot shower he would take. The image of that exoskeleton flickered through his mind. A hot shower and a whole bucket of soap, he amended. Maybe two hot showers, and—

And someone was standing in their doorway.

Caden froze. In an instant, he knew exactly who it was. Where his brother felt like nothing, this person felt like the deep, cold void of space. Caden's inner sense brushed against that presence and recoiled instinctively. "Patrick," he gasped.

Patrick Smith, senior consultant to Green On!, turned and smiled, his teeth perfect and gleaming in the setting light of the sun. "Ah, young Mr. Price." He looked past Caden. "And Mrs. Price. You look . . . well."

Caden knew they looked like they'd just spent the past few hours bushwhacking through the forest.

"What are you doing?" his mom demanded, moving to stand in front of Caden as if she might shield him with her body. "You are not welcome here."

"Oh, don't worry, I was just leaving. Mr. Price, I've kept a spot open for you in my internship. Should you decide to reconsider your position, it will be waiting for you. I'm sure your friends would welcome you back."

Caden didn't say a word, his lips pressed together so tightly his whole face ached.

"Leave," his mom said.

Patrick gave her a nod, then stepped around them and walked down the driveway, his dark suit blending into the growing shadows. As soon as he was gone, Caden's mom threw open the door and rushed inside. "Aiden? Aiden!"

"I'm right here, Mom." Aiden was leaning against the kitchen counter looking perfectly relaxed. "Everything is okay."

"But, Green On!, that man—"

"It's okay, Mom," Aiden repeated. "I talked to him." Where Patrick's smile had been large and gleaming, Aiden's now was small and secretive. "We came to an understanding." He glanced at Caden, then away again, his smile wavering.

And Caden was filled with a deep, heavy sense of dread. It reminded him of the prophetic dreams he sometimes had, his nights filled with glimpses of upcoming possibilities. He could feel the same sense of a future pressing against him now. A terrible future. One that his brother had just set in motion. And he knew, somehow, that it revolved around him.

And that he wouldn't be able to stop it.

11.

RAE

Rae hit the bottom of the hole hard enough to knock the air from her lungs. Wheezing, she put her arms up over her face and curled protectively onto her side as dirt and rocks cascaded over her in a wave.

It was done in seconds, everything going still as the ground settled. Rae felt the press of dirt above her, around her, the moist earthy scent filling her nostrils. She tried to sit up and found she couldn't.

Panic clawed at her chest like a living creature. Trapped. She was trapped! She flailed in the dark, scrabbling at the dirt, desperate, but it was like shoveling dry sand at the beach, more falling to replace any she managed to move away.

She was buried alive. She was going to die here, cocooned in the ground, slowly suffocating in darkness.

Rae needed to calm down. She knew it, but her mind had no control over her body anymore. She sobbed and thrashed, and one of her wildly swinging hands brushed against something that wasn't dirt. Rae dug toward it immediately, reaching for it.

Her fingers sank into it a little before stopping, like pushing through thick wet carpet to the hardwood floor beneath.

She froze. She didn't want to know what she was touching, didn't want to realize the truth of it, but she could smell it now, something worse than the dirt that surrounded her. The stench of garbage left outside on a hot summer's day, the sickly sweet scent of decay. And for one heart-stopping moment she was back in the basement of a creepy forest cabin, tangled up in a murdered boy's rib cage, wet pieces of him clinging to her skin, soaking into her clothes.

It was a sensation she would never forget, one that still woke her up sweating in the night, her blankets snarled around her.

Rae couldn't move, couldn't think, couldn't breathe. She was stuck in that purgatory of stink and dark and dirt, and—

Hands grabbed under her arms—strong, warm, *living* hands—and yanked her up.

Rae's head burst free from the mound of loose dirt, and she drew in a large, dusty breath, then hacked and coughed until her eyes ran.

"It's okay," Vivienne murmured, patting her on the back. "It's all okay."

Rae stayed like that for long minutes, coughing and panting until she could breathe normally again, only a slight hitch, a tiny wheeze. "I thought," she gasped, "that I would die, buried alive like, like. . ." She tried to think of something appropriate. "Like a vampire."

Vivienne's hand froze on her back, limp and heavy, before she withdrew it. "Technically vampires aren't alive."

"Okay, then, like . . ." Rae couldn't think of anything. "Like a worm?"

Vivienne laughed, the sound a little too loud. "Not sure that works either. But luckily for you, it looks like you'll live to see another day. No thanks to Nate, though."

"Hey, someone had to stay up here," Nate called down. "Otherwise how would you get out?"

"Good point," Vivienne said. "Um, Rae-Rae?" she asked, her voice abruptly changing, growing small and nervous. "What's that?"

Rae's panic had ebbed enough for her to look around. She was in some kind of air pocket about six feet below the ground, still buried up to her waist. The sun's rays filtered dimly through the trees overhead, outlining Nate's concerned face up top, Vivienne standing next to her, and . . .

And the half-covered body of a dead goat.

Rae lurched backward and kicked until her legs were free of the dirt, her back pressed against the soil wall behind her. She wiped her hand against her jeans, smearing the dirt in and not caring.

Most of the body was still buried, only the head, shoulders, and one leg exposed, the flesh sagging off it, the mouth hanging open. Rae could see the shriveled black tongue, and it made her want to throw up. Why would a dead goat be buried out here?

"What?" Nate asked, leaning over the edge, a trickle of dirt sliding around him. "Is that . . . is that a dead goat?"

"I guess that *was* what we came here for," Vivienne said, sounding strangely calm. "A corpse, right?"

"No," Nate said. "No way. We were looking for skeletons. For people who had decayed long ago. Not . . ." He turned away, and Rae could hear him retching above them. She didn't blame him.

She breathed as shallowly as she could. But she had never run from the truth before, even if it was ugly, and she wasn't about to start now. So she forced herself to look around. On three sides of her there was nothing but loose dirt—and the goat, of course. But behind her was a dark hole extending away into blackness, the walls glinting with yellowed shards of old bone and the splintered edges of rotting wooden coffins. A tunnel, half collapsed.

Vivienne noticed it too, and gasped. "So they did leave the bodies."

"Some of them, at any rate." Rae shivered, then noticed something else. Another large shape barely visible in the darkness. She inched closer.

"Careful, Rae-Rae. I don't think this tunnel is very stable."

"I'm not going in. But, look. Do you see it?" Rae pulled out her cell phone and used its glow to see.

It was the body of another goat, patches of bone glistening beneath the rotted skin. Behind it there were other lumps. Other dead animals. Rae thought she could see a dog and a couple of cats, although she tried hard not to look. It was too heartbreaking.

"Oh my . . ." Vivienne backed away.

"I think we've figured out where all those missing animals are."

"But why? How?"

"I don't know. And I don't think I want to stay down here and find out, either," Rae said grimly.

She caught movement out of the corner of her eye and whipped around. There was something shifting on the first goat—a long, wriggling, pale-pink something with way too many legs, climbing through the corpse's matted fur. And it wasn't alone.

More began popping up all around the body, a half dozen at least, each of them the size and shape of a hot dog. They climbed around the exposed skin, avoiding the beams of sunlight, scuttling back into the dark.

Rae realized they weren't actually pink, either. They were a milky yellowish-white. The pink color came from the blood staining their bodies. Because they were *eating* the goat, tearing off strips of rotting flesh and then scurrying back into the soil with them.

Rae's stomach roiled, and she clapped a hand over her mouth.

Vivienne gave herself a little shake, almost like a dog coming out of the river, and pulled off her ever-present backpack. She reached inside, tugging out a large plastic bottle, like the kind a person would bring on a hiking trip. She emptied the water, then used her own shirt to dry the inside of it. "It's not perfect, but . . ." She shrugged.

"But what?" Rae asked.

"For us to research." Vivienne darted forward, sliding her bottle over one of the bugs and then snapping the lid on, trapping the bug and several handfuls of soil inside.

"Research?" Rae said. "Like, for our internship project?"

"Exactly."

"What about the bodies?"

"I think this"—Vivienne shook her water bottle—"will be a bigger mystery. I've never seen a bug like this before. And we don't know what's killing these animals. So . . ."

"You think *bugs* did this?" Rae shook her head. "There's no way."

"Well, how did it die?"

"I . . . I don't know."

"Should we dig it out and look at it?"

"Ugh, no!" Rae wrinkled her nose. Then she remembered her earlier determination not to hide from the truth. "Maybe," she amended. "If you think it's important."

"I think we should go," Nate called from above them. "Your mom is going to be here in . . ." He paused, then said, "Seven minutes."

Rae made herself look at the goat again and sighed. The facts were always important. "Let's do it."

Vivienne rummaged around in her backpack again and produced a small folded shovel. She unfolded it with a flourish. "Ta-da!"

"Nice."

"Yeah. Never thought I'd be using it to unbury a goat." Vivienne began scooping dirt and rocks away, slowly uncovering more of the body. It didn't take long; the soil was all pretty loose from the tunnel's collapse. "Hmm."

"What?" Rae moved closer, peering around Vivienne. The smell hit her, blood and worse. The guts of the animal had been exposed, a giant hole gaping in its stomach, like something had ripped it out. "What do you think did that?"

Vivienne didn't answer, her eyes wide and dark as she stared at the wound.

"Vivi?"

"I think . . . I think I need to get out of here," Vivienne whispered, backing away from the goat. Her face had gone strangely white, her nostrils flaring.

"Me too." Rae stared up at the edges of the hole above them. "Should I give you a boost, or—"

"I have a rope."

"You seem to have everything in there."

"Good thing, right?" Vivienne flashed a weak grin, then shifted so her body blocked Rae's view as she dug around in her pack.

Rae had asked Vivienne about her backpack once, and Vivienne had promised to tell her what she kept in there—and why she insisted on keeping her bag close—but only if Rae exchanged her own secrets. Rae wasn't ready to do that yet. Vivienne was funny, and brave, and ready to leap into a hole in the ground to save a friend. But that didn't mean she wouldn't ditch Rae like a bad habit. Like Taylor had done at her old school. Like Caden had done here.

Rae didn't want to risk opening herself up to that again.

Vivienne pulled out a long, coiled rope. "Nate?" she yelled. "Stop your puking and help us, would you?" She tossed the rope up and waited for Nate to grab the other end. She gave it a tug, and Nate stumbled forward, almost falling.

"Wrap it around a tree," Vivienne said. "You're no good to us if you fall down here too." She rolled her eyes at Rae.

"You know what they say," Rae managed, her throat tight. "Good help is hard to find, right?"

Vivienne grinned. "Exactly so." Her grin slipped, and now Rae could see the fear hidden beneath it, and suddenly Rae felt a whole lot better.

She didn't want to be the only one afraid.

"We'll go talk to the police," Vivienne promised. "See what they can do for . . . for these poor animals, I guess." She tucked the bottle with the creepy bug inside her backpack and hoisted it over her shoulders.

Rae nodded. And when Nate told them the rope was secured, she told Vivienne to go first, even though every nerve in her body was screaming for her to hurry, to climb, to run into the sunlight and never leave it.

Alone in that dark pit, Rae looked into the goat's face. "I'm sorry," she told it. She blinked rapidly, her vision blurring, and didn't allow herself to think beyond that, to wonder about the other animals buried here, to picture the families who were looking for them.

Rae wasn't sure what had dragged them all down here, or why. But she would find out. And then, she would avenge them.

12.
CADEN

Caden didn't sleep well, his dreams full of giant, flesh-eating bugs and Aiden's cruel smile. He woke in a tangle of sweaty sheets well before his alarm went off.

When Caden was little, he'd been afraid of the dark because he didn't know what hid inside its shadows. Now that he was older, he was afraid of the dark because he *did* know. So he always slept with at least one lamp on. Not that it would save him. Not when the monsters could move in the light, too.

He blinked against the bright glare, waiting for his breathing to slow. He couldn't remember exactly what he'd dreamed, just tiny pieces. Aiden screaming for help before vanishing inside the Other Place. Aiden trapped behind a mirror, slamming fists against the wrong side of the glass. Aiden standing over him, grinning triumphantly . . . and bugs everywhere he looked, scurrying along walls and dripping off ceilings, long and skinny and stuffed full of legs.

Caden scrubbed a hand over his face, trying to wipe the dreams away, but the feeling of unease remained. No, not unease, he decided. It was that same sense of dread he'd felt last night.

Something was going to happen soon. Something awful.

He sat up, shoving his blankets to the foot of his bed, and did a quick glance around his room. He'd been shielding it for years, but ever since the Unseeing incident, he'd added additional protections. Besides the standard rose quartz in every corner, he now burned sage nightly and hung a talisman over his door, and another over his closed and shuttered window. It all looked and felt secure.

It was almost worse that way. If something had seemed out of place, then he'd know that was why he felt so . . . anxious. Like he was sitting in the front seat of a car a second before it crashed, fumbling with his seat belt and knowing he'd never get it clipped in time.

He got dressed quietly and slipped out of his room. Aiden's bedroom door was firmly closed at the other end of the hall, but Caden didn't want to chance his brother hearing him, so he crept down the stairs, easing his weight down one slow step at a time.

Aiden had been home for two days now and still hadn't done anything terrible. Not even a passive-aggressive comment. He'd been super nice instead, making dinner for the family, doing chores without being asked, volunteering to watch documentaries with their dad or run errands with their mom. Caden, he mostly left alone. It was weird. Caden had built up all of that foreboding and didn't know where to put it now. Maybe his brother really had forgiven him.

It would have been easier to know for sure if he could sense Aiden's energy. Caden hadn't realized how much he relied on that gift. *Too* much.

As Caden got to the bottom of the stairs, he realized he felt someone else's energy now. Angry, roiling, bitter energy. It was like stepping into a cloud of exhaust, all dark and acrid.

His parents were arguing.

Caden swallowed, the heavy feeling in his stomach growing thicker. He glanced back up the stairs, but now he could make out words drifting toward him from the kitchen.

"—literally held my son prisoner for days, and we can't even report them," his dad was saying, his voice rising. "Instead, they send someone here to our house to offer fake apologies?"

"Shh," Caden's mom said.

"Don't shush me, Eleanor. It's wrong, okay? That company owns this town. They can do anything they like with impunity. What if they change their minds about Aiden and demand we give him back?"

"What do you want to do?" Caden's mom asked fiercely. "You sure complain a lot, but do you have any solutions?"

Caden winced at the sharpness in his mom's tone. It was like being stabbed with a thousand tiny knives.

"We can't change how things are here. But we *can* leave."

For a second, Caden thought he'd misheard his dad. Leave? Whispering Pines? His heart leaped.

"You know we can't," his mom said.

"Maybe *you* can't."

Caden's heart came crashing back down.

He'd thought that it was Aiden's absence that had been destroying his parents' marriage. That once his brother was back, they'd return to being a loving couple. Instead, it felt like Aiden's sudden return had only driven a bigger wedge between them.

He could feel the yellowish-green of his mom's hurt, her rejection. He took a deep, cleansing breath and pulled his shields around himself tightly, blocking everyone else's emotions out. Then he walked up a few steps and noisily came down them again, practically stomping his way into the kitchen.

His mom had already retreated. Only his dad sat there at the table, drinking tea and reading the local paper as if nothing out of the ordinary had happened. "Hey, Caden." He looked up and grinned, his smile just a little too wide to be natural, the newspaper rattling in his shaking hand. Caden caught a glimpse of the front-page article:

Three Green On! Employees Still in Critical Condition After Experiment Gone Awry

Whispering Pines, CT. Alternative energy company Green On! isn't afraid to push the boundaries of science. "We can't afford to be complacent in our quest for clean, reusable energy," says senior consultant Patrick Smith. "There is too much at stake in this world. But unfortunately, sometimes there are unintended consequences." He was unwilling to provide specific details about his company's newest experiment, which left three workers in a catatonic state and—

His dad set the paper down before Caden could read more. "Sleep well?" he asked.

Maybe you *can't.*

Caden forced himself to smile back. He didn't want to think of the conversation he'd just overheard, didn't want to imagine his dad leaving. *He* was supposed to be the one who moved away. "I slept okay." He turned his back on his dad and rummaged in the pantry for a banana that he wasn't sure he could eat. "I think I'm going to head out early."

"Got a date with the neighbor girl, eh?"

Caden flinched. His dad thought he and Rae were still friends.

"You should have her over for dinner one of these nights."

It reminded Caden that yesterday Aiden had been chatting up Ava, extracting his own dinner invitation from her. That feeling of dread in his stomach returned full force, and he set the banana back on the counter. "Maybe I will," he told his dad. He scooped up his backpack. "I'll see you tonight. Have a good time at work."

His dad laughed. "The best time. Always." He waved and went back to his pretend newspaper reading as Caden left.

Outside the air had that heavy feeling that meant it would probably rain in a few hours. Already clouds billowed, dark and ugly, across the slowly lightening sky. Caden watched them as he walked down his long driveway to wait for the bus. He was early, but it felt good to stand outside, storm clouds or no. Before the sun rose, it seemed like maybe anything could happen.

Maybe something good, even.

Movement across the street caught his eye, and he saw Rae

and Ava in their driveway. He couldn't hear them, but it looked like they were arguing. Not like his parents had been, not a real fight. He opened his senses just a little, enough to feel the good-natured energy, the bickering annoyance. It was strangely comforting.

He and Aiden had never had that kind of relationship.

A pang of loss hit Caden deep in the pit of his stomach. He watched Ava get in the car and drive off without Rae, watched Rae stomp down the driveway, scowling, her brown hair pulled back in a high ponytail that bounced with every step.

She saw him and stopped, one foot lifted. And then she turned away, wrapping her arms around herself tightly.

He wasn't quick enough to pull back his senses, and so he was hit with the haze of greenish-yellow that swirled around her. It was so like his mom's own hurt and rejection that he couldn't look away.

Caden knew his mom could never leave Whispering Pines. She was in charge of keeping the rift between their world and the world of the Other Place closed. It was why he could never leave either, unless Aiden somehow got his powers back. A Price had to stay here to guard that barrier and the cosmic evil trapped behind it.

His dad knew it too. Even if he didn't fully understand it. He knew their mom would never swerve away from her duty, no matter what. So if he left Whispering Pines, he would be leaving her, too.

Caden was hit with the realization that he was angry with his dad. Not just angry. *Furious.* It wasn't his mom's fault that she was stuck here. His dad wasn't being fair, threatening to leave, demanding that she fix things that were broken beyond her abilities. Forcing her to choose between him and her biggest obligation . . .

As Caden stared at Rae's hunched shoulders and clenched jaw, the truth smacked him hard enough to drive the air out of his lungs, leaving him gasping.

He was just like his dad. He'd demanded that Rae choose between her friendship with him, and her obligation to find her dad. Sure, he had promised to help her in her search, but Patrick, with all the resources of Green On!, probably did have a better chance of assisting Rae. Obviously she couldn't turn that down.

All this time he'd been mad at her for rejecting him when it was really the other way around.

"Would you stop staring at me?" Rae demanded, whirling to face him.

"I'm sorry," Caden said.

"Don't be sorry. Just stop."

"No, I mean . . ." Caden paused, his mouth dry. He swallowed, tried again. "I'm sorry, Rae. For . . ." But the words escaped him again. For what? Ignoring her? Gaining her trust and then stomping it into pieces? He wasn't sure what he could say to make up for any of that.

Rae's eyes widened, then narrowed dangerously. "You're *sorry*?"

"I am. Really."

She shook her head. "Unbelievable."

Silence fell, thicker and harder than the road between them. Then Rae sighed, loud and dramatic. Still scowling, she stalked across the street and stood a few feet away from him. "You are *not* forgiven."

"I understand."

"Don't do that!"

"What?" Caden asked, bewildered.

"Don't act all contrite and reasonable! You haven't talked to me in more than a week! Not only that, you pretended I was a ghost."

"Not true," Caden said. "I talk to ghosts, remember?"

Rae's scowling mouth wobbled, her lips turning up in a brief, amused smile before it was gone again.

"I don't trust Green On!," Caden said.

"I don't either. But Patrick told me my dad might have been working on a Green On! contract when he disappeared. He didn't have any other information yet, but he promised to dig into it if I signed up for his internship." She adjusted her backpack. "That's the only reason I'm doing it."

"Did you still want my help too?" Caden hated how small his voice sounded. Of course Rae was going to turn him down. He'd messed up everything, and she'd moved on, and he never should have said anything now, should have left well enough alone. His thoughts ran in a circle of anguish, trapped like a rat in a wheel.

"That would be nice, yes," Rae said.

Caden blinked. "What?"

"Also, you owe me ice cream."

"Me?"

"Obviously you." She scrutinized him, her brown eyes serious and searching. Caden wondered what she was looking for. He stood up straighter, feeling strangely vulnerable under that gaze. Like for once someone was actually seeing him. Not seeing Aiden's brother, or one of the Price kids, or that weird boy. But *him*, Caden Price.

He hoped she wasn't disappointed.

"Don't ever do that again, okay?" she said.

Caden nodded.

She looked away, and the quiet crept up again around them. "Now this is awkward," she muttered.

Caden laughed. "I know, right? Where's that bus already?"

Rae smiled at him, a full smile this time. And for the first time since Aiden had reappeared, Caden could feel the knot in his stomach loosening.

13.

RAE

Rae spun her locker combination, her mind whirling just as fast as that small dial. She wasn't sure how she really felt about Caden's apology. It had hurt more than she wanted to admit when he'd started ignoring her. But then again, he *had* saved her life when she'd been attacked by the Unseeing. That probably earned him a second chance.

Her locker popped open, and she hung her backpack inside, moving slowly, her arms and back still aching from her fall yesterday.

She didn't want to think about yesterday. About that goat, and the tunnel, and those other dead animals. And the bugs, stained pink with blood . . .

Nate had gone for the police as soon as Rae had made it out of the pit. He lived close enough to walk home, so he promised to take care of all the reports while Rae hitched a ride home with Vivienne and her mom.

"Rae-Rae?" Vivienne said.

Rae turned. Vivienne was looking very odd, her hands twisting together, her mouth doing something similar. "Everything okay?" Rae asked.

"Well. Um, you remember that bug we found?"

"No, I've totally forgotten it." Rae rolled her eyes.

"Yeah, okay. Silly question. I'll just get to the point." Vivienne took a deep breath. "The bug is gone."

Rae stared at her. "Gone? What do you mean, gone?"

"I mean, it's no longer here."

"Like, dead?"

"No." Vivienne sighed and set down her backpack, rummaging inside and producing her water bottle. "Like, missing." She held the bottle out, and Rae took it.

There was a pile of dirt, and something in the dirt. Something gross and slimy-looking. And . . . there was a hole in the top. A small, chewed-up hole, right through the plastic lid. "It *ate* its way out?"

"Looks that way to me." Vivienne took the bottle back. They both eyed her backpack. "I already checked," she said. "It's not in there. Man, I really hope it's not in my house. My mom would flip out."

Rae shuddered.

"At least it left us this present." Vivienne shook the bottle, and that disgusting lump inside oozed a little.

"What is that?"

"I'm pretty sure it's, um . . ." Vivienne coughed. "It's, uh, you know."

"Poop?" Rae guessed.

Vivienne nodded.

"You don't want to say the word *poop*, do you?" Nate asked, popping up behind them.

Rae and Vivienne both spun.

"Would you stop lurking around us?" Vivienne snapped. "Jeez."

"We're teammates. I have a right to lurk." Nate adjusted his glasses importantly. "Now. My fellows. What is this I overheard about our specimen going astray?"

"Faster, Roadrunners!" Coach Briggs bellowed. Rae sped up, the finish line in sight. Rain fell against her in sheets until it felt like she was swimming more than running.

She crossed the line and stumbled to a halt, breathing hard.

"You okay?" Vivienne stopped next to her, barely winded.

Rae nodded. "Used . . . inhaler earlier . . . ," she gasped. "Just . . . tired."

The rest of the Dana S. Middle School cross-country team finished their final lap, all of them wet and shivering and exhausted.

Coach Briggs blew her whistle. "Circle up!"

Rae and Vivienne huddled with the others in front of her.

"You're looking good out there, but not good enough," Coach Briggs said. "It's almost like you're afraid of a little rain."

"A *little* rain?" a boy asked incredulously.

Coach Briggs fixed him with a stern eye. Her long brown hair swung in a braid down to her waist, and she wore her usual neon shirt and shorts. The only concession she'd made to the weather was that she'd pulled her socks halfway up her calves. "At least you have daylight," she said. "Do you know when I train?"

No one answered.

"I do my running at night. After the whole town has gone to sleep. You keep whining, and I'll make our next practice a midnight one." She stared around at everyone, then blew her whistle again. "Dismissed!"

"Can she really do that?" Rae asked Vivienne as they squelched across the wet grass and back to the school. "Make us run at midnight?"

"She's done it before," Vivienne said. "But it's still a code peach fuzz right now, so they probably wouldn't let her this time."

Rae thought of all the animals they'd found in the tunnel and then wished she hadn't asked.

"Hey," Alyssa said, catching up to them, her blond hair plastered down her neck.

Vivienne blinked, obviously startled. "Oh, so you're talking to me again?"

"I was never not talking to you."

Vivienne snorted.

"I just haven't seen you much, is all," Alyssa said defensively. "I mean, since we're on separate teams now."

"And we all know whose fault that is," Vivienne muttered.

Rae nudged her.

"Hi, Alyssa," she said, hoping to get past the awkwardness. "How's it going?"

Alyssa pushed her wet bangs back. "Right now? I feel like a fish."

"You look a little like one too," Vivienne said. "Your lips are blue."

There was a tense few seconds while Alyssa seemed to decide whether or not to be offended. But then she smiled. "Thanks. It's a new look I'm trying."

"Well, blue always has been your color," Vivienne said, smiling back. And just like that, some of the tension between them eased.

"How's your mystery going?" Alyssa asked. "I mean, unless you don't want to talk about it."

Rae and Vivienne exchanged a look. "Well," Vivienne said, "we found something strange. But we ran into a bit of a roadblock in solving it."

"It ran away," Rae added.

"It's bug related," Vivienne said. "That's all we can say, though."

"Yeah, pretty sure I don't want to know more." Alyssa ran her hands down her arms and shuddered dramatically. "I hate bugs." She pushed open the side door of the school and they walked inside, their shoes squeaking on the gym floor and leaving little dirt marks as they made their way to the locker rooms in back. "My mom is going to be a little annoyed about this mess."

"What about your mystery?" Rae asked. "Can you tell us anything about it?"

Alyssa glanced at her, and for a second Rae thought she wasn't going to answer. Then she shrugged. "Ours is . . . well. It's weird. Blake picked it. It has something to do with the Watchful Woods. That's all I can say, though." She flashed them a smile.

"Oh, come on," Vivienne said. "You told us practically nothing!"

"Hey, all you told me was that yours is bug related."

"Yeah, well, you said you didn't want to hear more. We can give you more details if you'd like."

"They're creepy-crawly little buggers," Rae said. "With lots of legs."

"So many legs," Vivienne added.

"Stop," Alyssa said. "Seriously. You're grossing me out." She opened her gym locker. Then she sighed. "Fine. You know that wall in the woods?"

"The stone one?" Rae said, remembering it. The last time she'd seen it was when she'd followed Ivan to his dilapidated home in the middle of the forest. She could still remember how he'd leaped over it, refusing to touch the stones. That should have been her first clue he wasn't human. But no, she'd gone ahead and followed him anyhow. Straight into a serial killer's shack.

"You okay?" Alyssa waved her hand in front of Rae's face.

"Sorry. Thinking." Rae twisted the combination on her gym locker.

"You're not much of a multitasker, are you?"

Rae frowned. "I can multitask."

"If you say so." Alyssa tossed her wet ponytail over her shoulder. "Anyhow. Blake's been studying it for a while, trying to figure out why its pattern changes. I guess that was the reason he moved into that yurt with his uncle. Or part of the reason, at least. So he suggested that for our mystery."

"Wait, hold up," Vivienne said. "Blake was already studying the wall before Patrick assigned this task? And now all of you are helping him with it?"

"That's what I said."

"But that's cheating! You can't jump into a half-solved mystery."

"Patrick said it was okay." Alyssa pulled her dry clothing out of her locker. "And besides, I really need to win this."

"Why?" Rae asked.

Alyssa chewed her lip. "I'm not supposed to say."

"Whatever." Vivienne yanked her locker open.

Alyssa sighed. "Fine. But don't tell anyone." She glanced around the locker room. There were a few other girls from their team in there, but none of them were paying any attention to their huddle. Alyssa still lowered her voice. "Patrick promised me that, if my team wins, I can help him fix Jeremy."

Rae's eyes widened. "Really? How?"

"I don't know the details, except that this top-secret mission we're competing for is somehow related to a cure for all the kids whose eyes were taken."

"Patrick told you all that?" Vivienne said, surprised.

Alyssa nodded. "It's why I agreed to join the internship." She closed her gym locker. "I'd better hurry. I'm supposed to meet Blake, Becka, and Matt now. Hopefully it'll stop raining soon, or it's going to be another long, wet evening." She got dressed, then waved at them as she rushed out the door.

"I wonder if Patrick promised everyone something different if their team won," Vivienne said as she finished dressing.

"Why? Did he promise you something?"

Vivienne shrugged and closed her locker. "Hey, I just realized we're already late. Will Ava leave without us?"

"She'd better not." But Rae got dressed quickly just in case and let her question drop. Obviously it wasn't something Vivienne wanted to talk about.

By the time she and Vivienne made it to the front of the school, Ava was already parked outside waiting for them. The rain slammed down so hard Rae could see it bouncing up again off the sidewalk. It looked very cold and very wet.

"Ready for this?" Vivienne said.

"Let's do it." They sprinted out the door and were immediately soaked, wind gusting around them, water sloshing down the pavement as they raced to the car. They pulled open the back doors and scrambled inside.

"I can't believe your coach had you running in this weather," Ava said as they settled themselves in the back seat. "Hard-core."

"Yeah, she's probably going on another run herself tonight," Vivienne said. "She's pretty intense." She buckled her seat belt. "Her rule for practice is that as long as we haven't lost our field to a sinkhole, we have to run. Rain or shine or sleet, or even tornado. Although there was that one time that practice was canceled because of the squirrels."

"Squirrels?" Rae buckled her own seat belt.

"Two years ago, Lizzie Jones forgot about the rule of not wearing red."

"What did the squirrels do to her?" Ava asked. "On second thought, I really don't want to know." She checked her mirrors, then pulled out of the school parking lot. "Mom's sleeping, by the way. She has a shift at the hospital tonight, so you'll want to be quiet in the house."

"Sure, sure." Rae could hear her phone vibrating angrily from her backpack and fished it out. "Hey, can squirrels even see red?"

"The squirrels around here can . . . and they hate it."

Rae and Ava exchanged glances in the rearview mirror. Ava raised her eyebrows as if daring Rae to ask more questions.

Rae decided not to. Instead, she opened her phone.

"Rae! Rae!" Nate howled at her.

"Nate! Nate!" she yelled right back. "Don't scream in my ear. I can hear you. In fact, everyone in the car can hear you."

"Hi, Nate!" Vivienne called back.

"Vivienne's with you? I've been trying to get ahold of both of you for exactly twenty-two minutes now!"

Rae took a deep breath. "You knew we were at cross-country practice." At the end of the school day, Nate had volunteered to take a look at their bug poop while Rae and Vivienne trained. They'd had a whole discussion about it where he'd called them both "social loafers" and insisted he was carrying their whole team. If he was calling to complain about that again . . .

"Yeah, sure," Nate grumbled. "But I didn't know that 'cross-country practice' was code for 'radio silence.'"

"Well, you've gotten ahold of us now. So, what's up?" Rae did her best to keep her voice even and patient, although she was starting to see why even super-friendly Vivienne got irritable with the guy.

"I prepared a few slides of the bug poop," Nate said, "and when I looked at it closely, I realized the pattern is all wrong."

"Wrong how?" Rae asked.

"I think you need to see it for yourselves."

"Well, that will be hard as we're on our way home now," Rae said.

Ava sighed loudly. "I can drive you back to school if you need." She put on her turn signal.

"Can't you just tell us?" Rae asked Nate.

"I could get into technical details, but I'm sure it would be way over your heads."

Rae gritted her teeth. "Yes, yes, you're very smart."

"Just spit it out already, Nathaniel," Vivienne called out, annoyed. "How is it wrong?"

"The poop was produced by something with a completely different organic makeup than it should have had." He waited a beat, but Rae and Vivienne just looked at each other in silent confusion. "Do I have to spell it out? It means the bug you caught does not originate from Earth!"

14.

CADEN

Caden drank his tea and listened to the rain outside, trying to ignore the truth.

The emptiness he sensed inside Aiden was getting worse.

He wanted to believe it was his imagination. But as his brother sat there across from him, idly flipping through pages in a copy of *Whispering Pines: Historic Downtowns*, Caden could feel that nothingness expanding outward, trickling past the outlines of Aiden's body to erase the energy of everything around him.

It was definitely different this afternoon than it had been the day Aiden returned. Then, Caden hadn't been able to sense his brother at all. It had felt like a hole. A rip in the energy fields. Now, it felt like a desolation. Like Aiden was slowly obliterating the entire world.

Caden shivered.

"What's wrong, dear brother?" Aiden glanced up. His expression was pleasant, his dark eyebrows drawn together in the picture of concern.

"Nothing." Caden took another sip of tea, feeling the warmth of it trailing down his throat and into his stomach. The heat did nothing to soothe him. What if his brother hadn't left anything behind in the Other Place? What if the real problem was that he'd brought something else back?

"I can tell you have questions." Aiden's long, elegant fingers plucked one of their mom's business cards off the table. The candle embossed on the front caught the light, the words PARANORMAL PRICE written at the top in dramatic swirling smoke. Aiden tucked the card into the book and closed it before looking up. "Ask."

"How did you survive?" Caden blurted. "You were in the Other Place for nine months. You told me that the things in there were feeding on you. I *saw* them drinking your blood." Caden pulled his mug closer, wrapping both hands around it. It had been an image impossible to forget, those questing, hungry tentacles tangling around his brother's arms, his torso, his neck. The sound of Aiden screaming . . .

Aiden tilted his head to the side. His hair was growing amazingly fast. Already it was long enough to frame his face in short, dark spikes. "I've often wondered the same thing, actually. I should be dead. I should have been dead long ago. And yet . . ." He spread his hands wide, the ring on his thumb gleaming. "Sorry to disappoint."

Caden watched the steam swirl across the surface of his tea. "I'm glad you're not dead," he whispered, and wondered if that were true.

Aiden sighed. "What happened to us?"

Caden blinked. "What?"

"You and me. We used to be close. It was us against the rest of the world; we shared secrets, power, dreams . . . when did that change? When did you start hating me?"

"I don't hate you." Caden wasn't sure where this was going. Since when did his brother care how anyone felt about him? "I told you, I didn't *want* to push you into the Other Place—"

"This isn't about that." Aiden frowned. "Something happened before then. You started avoiding me."

Caden looked away. "I didn't think you'd noticed."

"Just because I didn't say anything didn't mean it wasn't obvious. I may have taught you how to hide your emotions from other people, but *I* can always tell."

Caden doubted that was true.

"See, right there, you're feeling skeptical."

Caden glanced at him. His brother smiled and raised his eyebrows. "Okay, fine," Caden admitted. "You were right on that one."

"I'm generally right." Aiden tapped his fingers against the book cover, a slow, methodical beat like a heart.

"It was two years ago. The Zachary Mitchell incident."

Aiden stopped tapping. "Ah," was all he said. He was quiet for a long moment. Caden wondered if his brother was remembering the sight of Zach's face, red and raw and puffy, like a slab of uncooked hamburger, his eyes swollen with tears, blood leaking from his split lips. *Please,* he'd begged. *Please, let me stop.*

In fifth grade, Zach had spent months trying to bully Caden, until one day Aiden decided it was time to put a stop to that. He'd used his powers to somehow take control of Zach's body, making the younger boy slap himself in the face, over and over and over again.

Caden didn't like to think of it. It made him feel too many emotions at once. Fear of his brother, guilt that he'd helped cause this punishment, and, worst of all, triumph. Because Zach deserved to suffer, and part of Caden was glad to see it. That was why he'd started avoiding Aiden. He'd seen how easy it would be to become him.

"I understand how you might have found that upsetting," Aiden said into the silence now. "I was angry. I lost control of my better judgment." He ran a hand through his spiky hair, a familiar gesture, one that Caden had imitated often enough for it to become his own habit. "I'm sorry, Caden. It's something I'm working on." He dropped his hand. "It should be a lot easier now, since I no longer have those abilities at my disposal."

Caden wasn't sure what to say to that. His brother had chased power his whole life. It must be so frustrating to be stripped of it now.

"It's a relief, actually," Aiden said.

Caden's eyes widened.

"I told you you're easy to read." Aiden smiled. "I want to focus on my relationships. Just like our parents are doing now. All the magic stuff was getting in the way of that."

"What do you mean, like our parents are doing?"

"Oh, I just assumed they'd told you."

"Told me what?"

"They're attending a couples' workshop this evening."

"A what?"

"An intensive counseling session, little brother," Aiden sighed, as if that should have been obvious. "To work on their marriage."

"Oh." Caden frowned. It didn't seem like something his mom would ever agree to do. "When will they be back?"

"Tomorrow."

"Tomorrow?" Caden said, startled. They would be gone overnight? And without warning? "When did they decide to go to this . . . this thing?"

"After their fight this morning—you heard part of it, I believe?"

Caden nodded reluctantly.

"It made them realize they needed to focus on their marriage. So they left this afternoon."

"I can't believe they would be willing to go when you just got back."

"I may have also mentioned that you and I would benefit from a little quality brother time."

Caden swallowed.

"What's the matter?" Aiden asked. "Don't you want our parents to be happy?"

Of course he did. All those times his dad stayed late at work, all those nights his mom slept in her study. After Aiden disappeared, they became like the ripples of a lake, moving farther and farther away from each other. "I do want them to be happy—"

"But they're not." Aiden crossed his arms. "They are miserable. And whose fault do you think that is?"

Caden blinked. "Me? You're blaming this on me?"

"Well, little brother, *I* wasn't here."

Caden could feel a white-hot rage burning inside himself. He'd almost forgotten how Aiden could be—one moment acting like he cared about their relationship, and the next being this condescending, dismissive, entitled jerk. Caden used to ignore it. He was too afraid of his brother to call him out. But now? With Aiden's powers gone? He wasn't going to sit here and take it. "Stop calling me 'little brother.'"

"Why? Isn't that what you are?"

"I'm more than my relation to you."

Aiden lifted his eyebrows. "Someone has gotten a little uppity in my absence, haven't they? I'm not sure I like this new attitude of yours. *Little brother.*"

The rage inside Caden turned instantly to fear. He would be alone with Aiden the rest of today. And just because his brother didn't have his magic didn't mean he wasn't dangerous. He shouldn't have forgotten that. Caden could feel the tea in his stomach going cold and hard as ice.

Knock, knock, knock.

The hairs on the back of Caden's neck rose. He should have felt someone break through his wards long before they reached the door. Which meant the wards were down, the protections broken. And he had no idea when that had happened.

Knock, knock.

"Expecting someone?" Aiden looked nervously at the door.

"No." Caden stood slowly. They stared at each other, neither of them moving.

"Yo! Answer your door already!" Vivienne yelled from the other side.

Relief coursed through Caden, and he relaxed his awareness, let it drift outward until he was sure it was Vivienne out there. And Rae. And someone else. Someone radiating excitement and terror, those two emotions entwined too closely for Caden to sense which was stronger.

"Oh good, I've been wanting to meet your friends." Aiden stood and, before Caden could stop him, opened the door.

"Finally," Vivienne said. "We've been—oh! You're not Caden."

"No, I'm Caden's older brother, Aiden."

Caden hurried over, hovering behind his brother. Vivienne stood on the front porch, her hair and clothing soaked, next to an equally wet Rae and a curly headed boy in fogged-up glasses. Behind them the rain had slowed to a trickle, but it still looked pretty miserable.

Rae was staring at Aiden, her mouth hanging open, but she quickly snapped it shut and shot Caden an accusatory glare. He could practically hear her demanding to know why he hadn't told her that his brother was back.

Sorry, he mouthed, feeling guilty. Rae had been with him the night he'd believed Aiden had vanished for good. Of course seeing Aiden here now would be a shock to her.

"Everyone thought you were dead," Vivienne told Aiden.

"Well then, everyone was *gravely* mistaken." Aiden grinned, his full charismatic self on display.

Vivienne laughed. "That's a pretty good one."

"Thank you. Vivienne, right? I remember you from middle school. You were the first one up the rope in that weird challenge they made us do for Spirit Week."

"I can't believe you remember that!"

"Well, it's not every day that a tiny fifth grader beats out all the eighth graders. I thought I'd have that victory in the bag." Aiden chuckled. "You were so cute, with your hair in little pigtails. Wow, you've really grown up."

Vivienne's cheeks flushed, and she looked away, beaming.

Caden had almost forgotten how good his brother was at this sort of thing: charming people. Making them feel special. Making them like him. He'd also forgotten how uncomfortable it was to witness.

"And you . . ." Aiden looked at Rae, who met his eyes uncertainly. She'd seen Aiden trapped in a mirror and had heard the stories about him from Caden. Of everyone here, she was the only one who knew some of the truth about his brother. "You must be Rae."

"I am," she said. "Hi."

"Why are you here?" Caden asked quickly. He didn't know if Rae would fall for his brother's next act or not, and didn't want to find out.

"We needed to talk to you, Caden Price," the curly headed boy said.

"About what?"

"Poop."

"Say what?"

"What Nate means is that we found some bug coprolite that we need to discuss with you," Vivienne explained.

"Well, technically, it wasn't a coprolite," Nate said. "Since it wasn't fossilized."

Vivienne rolled her eyes.

"So, bug poop?" Caden asked.

"Basically, yeah," Rae said.

"Well, doesn't that sound like a fun conversation." Aiden wrinkled his nose. "I'll leave you all to it. And Rae? Could you please give my number to your lovely sister? She asked for it earlier, but I only recently got a cell phone." He handed Rae a card, a phone number written on the back in purple ink.

Rae took the card and tucked it in her back jeans pocket with obvious reluctance.

"Thank you. It was nice to meet you all. Have fun discussing . . . well. Whatever it is you need to discuss." He waved, and then disappeared upstairs.

"I forgot how cool your brother was," Vivienne said, craning her neck to watch Aiden leave.

"Puns are not cool," Nate said. "You made fun of me for telling one earlier today, remember?"

"They're not cool when *you* say them, true. But when someone as hot as Aiden does? Then they're just fine."

Caden felt very uncomfortable about the direction of this

conversation. "Why did you want to tell me about bug poop?" he asked, trying to steer them back.

Rae narrowed her eyes at him. The sudden reappearance of Aiden had obviously thrown her off-balance; her unease rippled around Caden like a cat with its fur brushed the wrong way. And he knew he owed her some explanations, but he didn't want to give them here, in front of the others, and with Aiden lurking somewhere nearby in the house.

"I mean," he added, "I'd love to stand around chatting about how hot my brother is—really, it's a favorite topic of mine—but it's just that I'm super interested in this bug poop."

Rae laughed, her agitation dissipating. "Fine. We'll move on. We think the bug that produced it isn't from Earth."

Immediately Caden thought of Gary and his giant bug carcass. And the sense he'd gotten that it didn't belong. That it was something wrong, something *other*.

"Since you're the only one I know who's dealt with creatures not of this world, you've become person of interest number one."

"Back to detective talk, huh?"

She grinned at him.

"I thought a person of interest was a suspect." Vivienne frowned.

"Not always," Nate said. "Sometimes they're just someone with valuable information that might help solve the crime."

"This guy"—Vivienne jerked a thumb at Nate—"always has to correct me."

"Not true. I correct everyone."

"But mostly me."

"It's not my fault you're wrong most often."

Vivienne scowled.

"Please, please help us, Caden," Rae cut in quickly. "You see what I'm dealing with here. I need you."

Warmth filled Caden's chest, chasing away the chill Aiden had left him with. "Actually, I think I might know what you're talking about already," he admitted. He stared at the three of them on his porch. It was something they had to see to really believe. "What are you doing tomorrow after school?"

"Nothing, as far as I know," Rae said slowly, exchanging glances with the others. "Why?"

"Want to take a hike?" Caden asked. "There's something I should probably show you."

15.
RAE

Rae hadn't stepped foot inside the Watchful Woods since the afternoon she'd followed Ivan through it almost two weeks ago. Now as she hiked, she kept thinking she could see him waiting for her behind every tree. In her imagination, he looked the way he had at the end, his face stretched out, mouth full of teeth, the skin smooth and unbroken where eyes should have been. Each branch that caught at her hair or snagged on her clothes reminded her of his arms reaching for her, his palms split down the center, those gaping holes ready to pull her eyeballs out so he could wear them himself.

She still couldn't believe she had walked so willingly into his trap. And here she was, marching through the Watchful Woods once more in search of monsters. She'd spent that entire day at school thinking of excuses to get out of it and had settled on a good one: it was pouring. Unfortunately the rain stopped just before school ended, and here she was. Even worse, the remaining rainwater kept trickling off leaves and sliding down the back of her neck like ice-cold fingers . . .

Ducking under another branch, she hurried to catch up with Caden, his black clothes turning him into a shadow as he led them through the trees. A few seconds later she heard Nate curse behind her.

"How much farther?" Nate asked. "I don't know how many more branches I can take to the face."

"Stop being such a baby," Vivienne told him. "We haven't gone that far yet. We barely passed the stone wall ten minutes ago."

They had wasted a few minutes at that wall wondering if Alyssa and her team were nearby and how close they were to solving its mysteries. Vivienne had claimed the pattern shifted due to some kind of magnetic field. Nate had told her that was frankly impossible, and it changed because of tiny constant shifts in the tectonic plates below them. Rae had no theories at all. And Caden . . . he'd gotten very quiet. Which made Rae wonder if he knew its secret already but wasn't allowed to share it.

"Actually, we passed the wall seventeen minutes ago," Nate said, glancing at the cheap plastic watch he wore on his wrist.

"Close enough," Vivienne said.

"No, it's not! It's a seven-minute difference."

"Then I guess we're seven minutes closer to our goal, right?" Vivienne grinned. She seemed more comfortable among the trees than any of them. Despite her heavy backpack, she loped along easily, dodging branches and roots like they were nothing.

Rae wished she could move so quickly and effortlessly. She felt like she were carrying several pounds of twigs in her hair alone.

"We don't even know what our goal is," Nate grumbled. "Or where, for that matter. We have been given zero specifics."

"Makes it harder for you to nitpick, doesn't it?" Vivienne said. "That's your real problem right there."

"Not true."

"Don't worry," Caden told Rae quietly. "We really are almost there."

"Should we tell them?" Rae jerked a thumb at Vivienne and Nate, still bickering behind them.

"Nah. Sounds like they're having fun."

Rae smiled. "So, what *are* we looking for?" She'd never admit it to Vivienne, but Nate was right: Caden hadn't told them anything. It made her feel like she was hiking in the dark with her eyes closed. She hated that feeling.

"We're looking for Gary," Caden said.

"Okay . . . that was almost informative. Is Gary some sort of supernatural expert?"

"No, he's the goat man."

Rae frowned. "Are you being intentionally vague?"

"No."

"Then what the heck is a goat man?"

"A man who owns goats." Caden glanced sidelong at her. "That one was intentional, by the way."

Rae laughed. It was either that or throttle him. "Fine. I can't say I get the whole goat thing in Whispering Pines, but moving on.

Why are we looking for a goat man?" But even as she said it, she was thinking of the goat they'd found, dead in a collapsed tunnel, its stomach torn out by . . . something.

Caden ran the back of one hand across his forehead, pushing his damp hair away from his face. "Because," he said slowly, "the other day, one of his goats was attacked by a giant centipede."

Rae rubbed at her arms, feeling sick as she pictured those large, bloodstained centipedes. Had they killed the goat they'd found? But how?

"I thought you should see its body," Caden said. "So you can tell me if it's the same kind of bug that you saw."

Rae was quiet as she crunched through damp leaves. "Your brother is back," she said abruptly, remembering the shock she'd felt at seeing him standing in Caden's doorway.

Caden paused, one foot up. "Yeah," he said, setting that foot down and glancing at her. "I meant to tell you about that. It's kind of a weird story, actually."

"Oh good. Those are my favorite kind."

Rae listened as Caden told her about how Green On! had pulled Aiden out and then held him for days until someone at the company helped him escape.

"The lab had a false alarm a few days ago," she said when Caden had finished his story. "I wonder if that was related?"

"Could be."

"Your brother seemed . . ." Rae hesitated. She wasn't sure how she actually felt about Aiden. He'd been a lot nicer than she'd expected after Caden's stories, but it was the kind of nice that felt like it had strings attached. Like he was trying to sell something.

"I know what you mean." Caden smiled wryly before shoving his way through a thick layer of brush. Rae followed him through and then across a small creek. The trees opened up ahead of them to reveal a large, grassy clearing. In its center hunched a strange circular structure with a cloth roof, which Rae assumed had to be a yurt. A blocky wooden pen stood next to it, the gate hanging open.

"The goats," Caden said.

"What goats?" Rae asked.

He looked at her. "Exactly. They're gone." Frowning, he glanced at the yurt. "We'd better check inside."

Rae looked at Caden's tight, closed face, and realized he was scared. Caden, who had dealt with a literal eyeless monster. Suddenly the woods seemed extra creepy, the moisture in the air slowly building into an eerie fog that rose around the trees. Anything could be hiding in it.

Rae looked around. "Where are Vivi and Nate?"

"We're coming!" Vivienne yelled. A moment later she and Nate caught up. "Sorry about that. Nate got his shoe stuck in a hole back there. Why are we staring at the outside of a yurt?"

"Because," Rae said, "we're afraid of what might be *inside* it."

They all looked at one another, the silence thickening like the fog around them.

"I vote Nate goes first," Vivienne said.

16.
CADEN

Caden carefully shut the door of the yurt behind him. It had been empty, but the bed wasn't made, and there were dishes in the tiny sink. He wasn't sure if that meant Gary had been planning on coming right back or if he was just messy. But it felt wrong.

Caden looked around the clearing. Everything was quiet, the trees wreathed in mist, drops of rain softly falling from their branches.

"What now?" Rae asked him, her eyes wide.

"I want to check the shed." Caden led the way over to it. Inside, a carpet lay over a lump in the center of the floor. He pulled the carpet back, revealing a giant charred husk.

"Was this the bug?" Rae asked.

"Yeah," Caden said. Even burnt to a cinder, it was clearly

recognizable, the blackened legs all curled inward. So many legs. "Is this like the bugs you found?"

"Similar," Rae said. "Only this is much bigger."

"Maybe the ones we saw weren't fully grown yet," Vivienne said quietly. They all looked at one another.

"Why do you think Gary burned this one?" Rae asked, breaking the uneasy silence. "I mean, it was already dead, right?"

"It's what people do. They destroy the things that scare them." Caden shrugged, trying to be casual, but he could feel the muscles in his jaw tightening. It was a reminder to him to be careful. He had started to feel a little too relaxed, like he belonged with this group of kids. But he was different from them. He could never forget that.

If Rae knew about his abilities, would she freak out like the kids in his elementary class? She knew some of it already. She'd seen him open the rift into the Other Place and hadn't been scared away. Maybe she'd be okay with the rest. But he couldn't chance it. He didn't want to admit it, but he liked having friends. He didn't want to be alone anymore, like he used to be before, when it was just him and Aiden.

"I don't think we can take this back," Nate said. "It would probably fall apart if we tried to move it." With a disgusted look, he prodded the bug with his sneaker, and the whole thing collapsed in a puff of ash and dust.

"Nice one." Vivienne coughed. "Well, this turned out to be a bust. Great job picking this little mystery, Nathaniel."

"Wait, you're blaming this on me? We could have chosen something else! I was not attached to the bugs!"

"I'm glad we picked them," Rae said firmly. "If there's some kind of weird infestation going on in our town, then I want to know about it."

"Hear, hear, Rae-Rae," Vivienne said. "Can you imagine a whole swarm of those things creeping and crawling under our houses?" She pointed at the pile of ash, and even though Caden wasn't trying to feel the energy of the group, their alarm hit him in little prickly spikes.

His mom didn't think these bugs were from the Other Place, but Nate said they weren't from Earth. So where else could they have come from? Caden knew the rift had been opened recently, both by him and by Green On! when they pulled out his brother. If these bugs had escaped during one of those times, then it was his job as a Price to look into it.

And if they'd somehow managed to drag Gary away . . .

He swallowed, hard. But according to Aiden, his mom and dad wouldn't be back until tomorrow, and Aiden didn't have any of his powers anymore. There was no one else. This was Caden's responsibility. "Hey, guys?" He waited until they were all looking at him and then made himself say it. "I might know where more of these are."

"Oh yeah?" Rae said.

Caden nodded. "Anyone up for a bit of spelunking?"

17.

RAE

Panic bubbled up inside Rae's chest. Vivienne had gotten way too excited when she heard the word "spelunking," and now here they were, standing over a deep, dark hole in the ground, contemplating going in. Apparently Caden and his mom had found an abandoned giant bug exoskeleton in front of this very cave and were pretty sure the thing was living somewhere inside it.

This was madness. Sheer madness. Rae breathed in and out slowly through her nose. She tried not to stare at that hole but couldn't help sneaking glances at it. It seemed to drink in the remaining light of the day, giving back nothing, and when she finally looked, *really* looked at it, it reminded her of an open mouth screaming.

She shuddered.

"It looks like it widens a few feet down, and then levels out just below that," Vivienne said, straightening. "Shouldn't be too bad of a drop." She rummaged in her backpack and pulled out her trusty rope.

Rae took another deep breath. "Are we really serious about this?" she asked as Vivienne secured the rope around the trunk of the nearest tree, tying it off with some kind of fancy knot.

"Yep." Vivienne dropped the other end of the rope down the hole. "Why not?"

"Because it's a terrible idea!"

"I gotta say, I'm with Rae on this one," Nate said. "I have never seen a horror movie where a pack of kids goes into a cave and all of them make it out okay."

"Wow, Nate, I'm surprised," Vivienne said. "I never would have pegged you for a horror movie guy."

Nate looked away. "Fine, so I don't actually watch horror movies—"

"Of course you don't."

"They give me nightmares, okay? But so will going into a creepy hole in the ground! I vote we leave here, find Doctor Nguyen, and tell her about this cave. Then she can send some Green On! people to check it out. *Grown* people, with proper equipment and training."

"I think that's a great idea," Vivienne said.

Relief enveloped Rae like a warm bath.

"*After* we do a bit of reconnaissance."

All of Rae's relief drained away immediately as Vivienne tossed her an ugly headband with an attached light and put a similar one around her own head. She glanced at Nate, standing white-faced away from the hole, and Caden, silent and brooding right next to it. "Sorry, I only have two headlights."

"You know, if even Rae thinks this plan is reckless, then maybe we'd better rethink it," Caden said slowly.

"Hey!" Rae said, even though she secretly appreciated the backup.

"What if Gary the Goatman is hurt down there and needs our help?" Vivienne asked. "We should at least look around a little. Especially since it's not night yet, and there are four of us. It'll be safe."

"You didn't see this bug," Caden said.

"Safe-ish," Vivienne amended. "And you boys don't have to come. You know, if you're too scared." She looked at Rae.

Rae swore there was a gleam in Vivienne's brown eyes. Like she was daring Rae to try to stop her. But now Rae was thinking about Gary, potentially stuck down a deep, dark hole, even though realistically she knew there was a much better chance that he'd just hightailed it out of the woods. Still, maybe they *should* look around a little, just in case. Reluctantly, she nodded, and Vivienne grinned wildly. "Catch you on the flip side, my friend." Then with a whoop of excitement, she swung down into the hole and was gone.

Rae slid the other headlamp around her head, carefully tugging her ponytail free, her hands trembling. She did not want to go in there.

Vivienne was counting on her to follow.

Rae grabbed the rope and squeezed her eyes shut. For a second she thought of Ava, remembering the last time they'd gone to an amusement park together.

It had been a year before their dad disappeared.

Neither of their parents liked heights, so when Ava had asked who was up for the Sky Flier, only Rae had been willing to go with her. Back then, Rae was willing to go anywhere with her older sister, even though she secretly didn't like heights either. The two of them had been clipped inside a harness side by side. Rae could feel her sister vibrating with excitement. And then they'd been hauled up into the air, so high they could see the entire park, with nothing but that flimsy harness and a long bungee cord keeping them from an untimely death.

"Ready?" Ava had asked, sounding so confident.

"No," Rae had said, but then Ava pulled the cord and they were falling.

Rae felt that same rush of terror now, but this time she didn't have Ava here to pull the cord for her. She would have to do the fall herself.

She opened her eyes. The hole stared back at her. Hungry. Waiting. "Are you guys staying?" she asked.

"No, I'll come," Caden said.

"Thank you," she whispered.

"I told you, I've got your back." He smiled. She could tell he was scared too, and somehow that made her feel a little better.

"Nate?" she asked.

"Let's see, option A, go into a hole to search for large carnivorous bugs, or option B, wait in the creepy woods alone, where large carnivorous bugs hunt for food . . . tough choices, but I think I'll take my chances with you."

"There's always option C: trace your steps back through the woods and go home," Rae said.

Nate sighed. "Yeah, I did think about that. That would definitely be the smart option. But you know how I feel about social loafers."

"Social loafers?" Caden asked.

"You know when you get assigned a group project how there's always that one kid who doesn't do any of the work and still gets the same grade as the others?" Nate said. "That's the social loafer."

Rae laughed. "The worst."

"They really are." Nate inched closer, peering into the darkness. "I'm totally going to regret this, aren't I?"

"I'm pretty sure we all are," Rae said grimly. And then she lowered herself down.

18.
CADEN

Caden could just make out Rae's light about ten feet below as he swung his legs down and grabbed the rope.

He held his breath as he eased himself down, moving his hands carefully, clamping his ankles around the rope below him to take some of the pressure off his arms, which were already burning with the effort. This was really not his thing. He tried not thinking about how he would have to somehow climb back out again, but suddenly that was *all* he could think about.

Several agonizing moments later and his feet touched bottom, sinking a little into the soil. Everything smelled like dirt, the scent so strong he could almost taste it. Only a thin trickle of light filtered in from the hole above, dimly illuminating Rae's silhouette next to him.

"Vivienne's checking ahead." Rae turned, her headlamp getting him full in the face. He flinched, throwing up his arm to shield his eyes. "Oh, sorry." Rae quickly flipped her light up. "Watch out!"

Caden had the barest glimpse of a muddy sneaker before a weight dropped right on his head. He staggered, Nate flopping with him, both of them slamming into the dirt wall before ending in a tangle on the tunnel floor.

Dirt and rocks rained down in a small shower. Caden caught his breath, not daring to move until it was over. After a few seconds the dirt stopped trickling down.

"Well, that was fun," Nate said, an edge of hysteria in his voice. "Why are we doing this again?"

"For the good of humanity and all that." Vivienne hurried over and hauled Nate up. "Or at least for the good of Gary. If he's even down here. The tunnel bottlenecks up ahead, by the way, but we should be able to get through it." She glanced down at Caden, careful to keep her headlamp pointed up. "You okay?"

"Never better," Caden croaked.

"Scared you, didn't it?" Vivienne's teeth flashed white in the tunnel.

"Um, yeah," Caden said. "I'm pretty sure it scared all of us." But even as the words left his mouth, he realized they weren't true. Vivienne wasn't scared at all. Instead, she radiated a strange, excited energy that reminded him of Aiden whenever he was about to try a new and dangerous spell.

"Don't worry, these tunnels don't collapse easily. They're surprisingly solid." Vivienne knocked one fist against the dirt wall next to her.

"You come here often, then?" Nate asked.

"Once or twice," Vivienne said. "My mom and I used to go exploring underground." Abruptly the eagerness Caden had sensed in her vanished. "We'd better hurry." She turned her back on them. "We can't be down here when night falls."

He frowned, a trickle of unease sliding along his spine, as gentle and disturbing as if a spider were walking on his bare skin. He knew a thing or two about secrets, and Vivienne was definitely hiding something from them. Something big.

He'd noticed it before but assumed it was that she was working with Patrick. Now, as Caden watched Vivienne and Nate take the lead down the tunnel, he couldn't help but wonder what other secrets she had buried beneath her cheerful, friendly facade.

Perhaps the reason *why* she had started working with Patrick in the first place.

"I guess we should follow them, huh?" Rae whispered.

Caden blinked, noticing Rae hovering there by the thin stream of light from above. Her fear fell off her in waves of a sickly yellow that made him feel slightly ill too. "Are you okay?" he asked her.

"I hope so."

"Not a fan of tunnels?"

Rae shook her head, her light bouncing off the wall.

"Me neither. Want to go first, so I can make sure nothing sneaks up behind you?"

"Oh good, something else to worry about," Rae muttered, but she started walking. Her steps were small and slow, like she was inching through the dark, and before long Vivienne and Nate were so far ahead that Caden could barely see their headlamp.

Caden watched Rae's light bouncing off the dirt, the trailing roots, the occasional rock. Her fear grew bigger and stickier, until finally he was forced to put up his personal shields, keeping his awareness locked firmly inside. He might not be able to sense any of the Other Place's energies like this, but in this small space it was too hard to think with someone else's emotions wrapping around him like a hungry octopus.

Rae stopped abruptly, and Caden almost smacked into her. "Um, I think this is the bottleneck Vivi saw," she said, her voice way too high-pitched.

The tunnel narrowed dramatically. Vivienne hadn't been kidding about that. "Want me to lead through this?" Caden asked.

"Only if you w-want to."

"I would love to." He stretched his mouth into a smile. "Then you can just follow right behind me, okay?"

"Want my light?"

He did. He really did, but he shook his head anyhow. He didn't think Rae would be able to get through that tight space without her headlamp.

Dropping to his hands and knees, he began crawling, the tunnel pressing down on his head as he moved forward. Eventually he had to drop all the way to his stomach and squirm, using his elbows to drag himself along, the rocks digging into his skin.

His breath felt trapped like the rest of him, echoing too loud in that small space.

Vivienne made it through this, he told himself. So he could too.

But then Vivienne was small and athletic. He remembered how she had sprinted through the woods in the dark without breaking a sweat. She was basically a superhero. There were probably a million things she could do that he couldn't.

Nate made it through this, he reminded himself, and that did give him a little more confidence.

Finally the pressure above him eased, and he was able to get back up to his hands and knees, and then to his feet, the tunnel widening again. Vivienne and Nate stood nearby, waiting.

"How did you manage to bring your backpack?" Caden asked, staring at that humongous thing.

"Easily. I pushed it through ahead of me."

"Why do you carry that around with you everywhere, anyway?" Nate asked.

"You have a backpack with you," Vivienne pointed out. It was true; Nate had a small pack slung on his back, hardly larger than a loaf of bread.

"Mine is tiny. Yours could eat mine and still have room for seconds. What are you even carrying in there? I mean, aside from rope."

"Stuff," Vivienne said.

"Stuff?" Caden asked.

"A girl can never be too prepared." Vivienne reached over her shoulder and patted the top of her bag like it was a favorite pet. Then she crouched closer to the bottleneck and called, "Rae-Rae? You doing okay?"

"Just . . . peachy," Rae grunted. A minute later and she climbed out of the bottleneck, her face white in the light of her headlamp, her lips pressed hard together. She hovered next to Vivienne, whose headlamp bathed her own face in light, making weird shadows under her eyes and nose, turning her features strange and unfamiliar. Where Rae was like a wild horse confronted by a wolf pack, two seconds from bolting, Vivienne seemed almost like a creature of the tunnels. Like she belonged here in the dark.

Vivienne's eyes locked on Caden's. And for one second he felt the presence of a hunger as vast and dark as the entire underground. Then she blinked and it was gone. Just Vivienne standing there. Friendly, cheerful, easygoing Vivienne. The same girl he'd known since elementary school.

They hadn't been friends then. But he'd always liked her. Or at least, he'd disliked her less than the others. She was popular, but in a casual, "of course people like me" way, her self-confidence refreshing amid the backdrop of all the other middle school insecurities. And while she was blunt and not always nice, she'd never seemed mean-spirited. He'd sensed in her a love of nature, and adventure, and fun. Nothing like . . . whatever it was he'd just brushed against.

She pulled the straps of her backpack tighter and turned away from him. "Let's move, people. We've got some bugs to find."

Caden shivered. Had he imagined all of that? He knew how fear could make you see things that weren't there, feel things that weren't real. And he *was* afraid. His heart beat too fast, his breathing was harsh and quick. Being underground in the dark was enough to scare anyone.

But he knew that wasn't it. As he walked behind Vivienne, he was sure that some other entity had been looking out through the mask of her face. And whatever it was, it had noticed Caden noticing *it*.

And *that* was what really scared Caden.

19.

RAE

Rae wasn't sure how long they'd been underground. It felt like hours. It might have been minutes, or days.

She wasn't going to be the first one to complain.

She told herself that over and over as she walked, her world reduced to a thin washed-out beam of light ahead, darkness crowding above, below, and to either side. The rocky ground was uneven enough that she had to concentrate to avoid stumbling, the walls and ceiling sometimes squeezing inward like a tube of toothpaste, brushing against her head, her shoulders, causing hysteria to rise up in her chest until it felt like her heart might beat itself to death against the bones of her rib cage.

She wouldn't ask to turn around.

She counted her breaths, drawing musty air in, thick with the smell of moist dirt, and letting it slowly out. The air grew colder, the tunnel sloping downward, and still Vivienne led them on.

Rae walked in the back of the group. She was very aware of that, of the feeling that something could easily creep up behind them, and then she'd be the first one to go . . .

She was *not* going to chicken out before the others. She would not be the first one to break.

Fear pressed against her lungs, making it hard to breathe. It reminded her of being in that hazmat suit, trapped underneath Green On!, thinking she was about to die. That same sense of suffocating panic.

Rae gasped for breath, trying to stay calm, but her nose and mouth filled with the rich, earthy scent of dirt, and suddenly she was remembering that cabin in the woods, and of running for her life through the dark and knowing something was following her. Something unnatural, with too-long arms and legs, and no eyes, and so many teeth.

Ready or not, here I come . . .

She was losing it. Spots flared up in her vision, and she stumbled, putting a hand against the tunnel wall next to her. She couldn't breathe. The darkness pressed in on all sides, and she could feel the weight of dirt above her, could imagine the ceiling crumbling, all of it crashing down on her head in an avalanche.

She needed to think of something else, quick. Something comforting.

Rae squeezed her eyes shut and thought of her dad. She tried to picture him walking next to her and couldn't. It was like grasping for someone's hand in the dark, the details of his face slipping past.

Her heart pounded. It felt like someone had gone into her brain with a scalpel and removed her dad. How could she forget what he looked like? Wildly she searched ahead, past Caden, focusing on Nate. On the edge of his glasses.

Glasses.

She seized on the image of her dad's favorite pair: ugly, boxy things with thick black frames. He complained contacts made his eyes feel too dry, and he didn't trust laser surgery.

Sure, it can fix my eyesight, he'd say whenever someone brought it up. *But can it make me look as good as these babies?* And he'd tap his glasses and wink, and ignore anyone arguing that as a highly specialized engineer, he should have more faith in technological advances.

Rae kept those glasses fixed in her mind and built the rest of her dad's face from memory around them. His energetic eyebrows, quick to knit together, to raise up or lower down, pulling his forehead into a series of lines and creases. Beneath the glasses, a wide nose that her dad claimed made him look like Harrison Ford, and thin lips. When he smiled, he did it with his whole face, teeth glinting, eyes gleaming, nose wrinkling. Rae's heart ached imagining that smile now, and what she'd give to be able to see it again, to have him ask her, *What's wrong, sugar cube?*

She blinked, her vision blurry. There were so many things wrong right now. Starting with the fact that her dad had disappeared over a year ago and everyone was pretending that it was totally normal. And now here she was, in a tunnel, looking for a giant bug and possibly another dead goat. And it was dark here, and scary, and she wished she were home.

She knew what her dad would tell her, though, if he were really here with her. *If you're going to do something, do it with all you've got. Study every detail. Commit it to memory. Break it down into parts.* He usually launched into a tree metaphor, too, talking about roots digging deep into the soil the way an inquisitive mind needed to dig into the facts.

Focusing on facts was a good way to detach from her fear, so Rae adjusted her headlamp and did what her dad would do. She studied the tunnel walls and floor and ceiling, everything she could see around Caden's spiky-haired silhouette in front of her. And as she mentally checked off the details of her surroundings, the tight grip of panic loosened, her lungs relaxing.

It seemed like a normal enough tunnel, as far as she could tell. Not that she'd been in many before. The ground under her feet had leveled out, only the occasional rock to trip her up. The walls, too, had gone pretty level. And the ceiling.

Rae stopped and stared. They were all symmetrical. Frowning, she moved closer to one of the walls, studying it in the light of her headlamp. She ran a hand over the dirt. It had been well packed, but as she scraped some of it away, she noticed that there was something solid beneath the dirt.

She glanced down the tunnel, where Vivienne's headlamp was getting farther away. "Guys?" she called. "You might want to see this."

"What?" Nate's voice sounded small and panicky. "Is something wrong? Is the tunnel collapsing?" He stumbled closer, almost falling into Caden.

Rae carefully pointed her headlamp up so she wouldn't catch either of them in the face, but she could see the gleam of Nate's too-wide eyes in the dark. "I don't think it *can* collapse. Look." She pointed at the spot on the wall she had scraped clean.

"Is that concrete?" Caden leaned in close. He touched the wall, then pulled his hand back as if it had been burned. "These tunnels were artificially created."

"Or at least this part was," Rae said. "The section back there seemed more natural."

Nate slid his backpack over his shoulder and pulled a small glass vial out, then carefully scraped a soil sample into it.

"Isn't there supposedly an abandoned military base somewhere beneath Whispering Pines?" Rae asked, remembering an article she'd discovered during one of her earlier research phases.

"Rumors," Nate said immediately. "I don't believe it."

"But you do believe that squirrels here attack anyone who wears red?"

"Well, yeah. Because they do."

"And your town has a goat man for good luck? And giant bugs? And your school rabbit was attacked by some kind of blood-draining vampire?" Rae put her hands on her hips, annoyed at the way the others were looking at her. It reminded her uncomfortably of the way the kids at her old school had stared and whispered "conspiracy nut" behind her back.

"What's your point, Rae-Rae?" Vivienne asked.

"My point is we know there are weird things that go on in this town. How can you immediately discount the idea of a secret abandoned military base? It's no stranger than anything else I've seen here." Rae rapped her knuckles against the concrete wall. "And if not a base, then what is this?"

Silence fell around her, thick and awkward. And then Caden said, "She's right. It *is* possible. I've often wondered why Green On! really set up shop here. Maybe they're working with the military? Creating secret weapons, hidden beneath the mask of 'alternative energy'?"

"Oh, stop," Vivienne snapped. "Your family just hates Green On!. My mom works there, and if she were involved in any conspiracy stuff, I would know about it."

"Would you?" Caden asked. "Does your mom tell you everything?"

"Everything important," Vivienne said. But then she frowned and looked away. "Or she used to," she admitted. "I think she's working on something big right now that she can't talk about." She adjusted her pack, shuffled her feet, and now the uncomfortable silence was focused around her. "But that doesn't mean it's anything nefarious or whatever."

"Speaking of nefarious," Nate called, "I'm pretty sure I found a door." He had his cell phone out, the blue-tinted glow illuminating a stretch of tunnel wall in front of him.

Rae squinted, noticing the deeper line of an indented rectangle set inside the smooth expanse of tunnel.

Nate's expression was bleak. "I retract my earlier skepticism."

Vivienne pressed both hands against the rectangle. Nothing happened. She ran her hands along the dirt next to it, stopping on a protruding rock.

"What are you looking for?" Rae asked.

Vivienne pushed at the rock. "Some sort of opening mechanis—ah!"

With a *whoosh* and a sprinkle of soil, the rectangle opened, revealing a small, windowless room, light glowing softly from the top.

They all looked at one another.

"I know what you're thinking," Nate said. "And the answer is no. No freaking way. Absolutely not."

"You sure are protesting a lot," Vivienne said. "Especially since no one has suggested anything."

"You want to go in there," Nate accused.

"Hey, there's an idea!" Vivienne beamed. "What do you think, Rae-Rae? Should we go inside, like Nate obviously wants?"

"I do not!"

Rae stared at that tiny box of a room and wanted to turn and sprint back down the tunnel. But it had been thinking of her dad that led her to this discovery, and he wouldn't have run away from something like this. He would have needed to know where it led.

Even if it led to his abduction.

"Rae . . ." Caden put his hand on her arm, his fingers cold and clammy. She glanced at his face and saw that he was terrified. "I know you care about that internship. But it's not worth it."

Rae pulled her arm free. "This isn't about the internship. This is about following the facts. Wherever they lead." She had to follow in her dad's footsteps or she would never find him. She stepped forward into the room.

Ready or not.

20.

CADEN

Caden knew he could turn around and go home. And then go back to the way things had been when he didn't have any friends and didn't have to care about anyone outside his family.

Things had been simpler then.

He looked at Rae standing in that small room, and at Vivienne joining her, and at Nate waiting to see what he would do.

"If you go in there, I'm gonna have to go in too," Nate told him.

"I'm sorry," Caden said.

Nate sighed. "Yeah. I figured this would happen." He straightened his glasses, brushed dirt off his pants, and tightened his backpack straps. "Let's get it over with, then."

Caden smiled. "You know, you're all right, Nate."

Nate smiled back. "Don't let Vivienne hear you say that. She'll totally argue."

"I will not," Vivienne said.

"See?" Nate stepped into the room.

Caden glanced once more at the inky blackness of the tunnel and then followed him in.

Rae pressed a button on the side and the door whooshed shut again. They all stood there, quiet, waiting.

Nothing happened.

"That was awfully anticlimactic," Rae said.

Vivienne peered at the button Rae had pushed. It glowed the same soft light as the ceiling. "What happens if we push this again?" She tried it.

The room plummeted so fast Caden's stomach shot up to his brain, and he staggered back against the wall. He caught a glimpse of Rae's openmouthed silent scream, of Nate curled in a tiny whimpering ball on the floor, and of Vivienne still standing upright, one hand delicately placed against the corner for support, her whole face straining in concentration.

Finally the downward hurtle slowed, giving Caden's internal organs time to adjust to their new position.

He still felt like he was going to throw up as they eased to a stop. He had no idea how far down they'd gone, but it felt like they'd been shot into the center of the earth. Whatever was hidden this deep beneath Whispering Pines had to be important if someone had put in a fancy high-speed elevator in order to more easily reach it.

Someone like Green On!.

Caden swallowed, his stomach gurgling.

Ding!

The door whooshed open.

21.

RAE

Rae stared out that doorway at the unknown, and for a second she was back in her old house, watching the blank-faced men in their identical suits moving through the rooms, bagging her dad's stuff, cornering her mom in the kitchen.

Mrs. Carter? We just have a few questions. About your husband.

She remembered how her mom had kept repeating in a tight, high-pitched voice, so unlike her normal tone: *I don't know anything. I swear, I don't know* . . . How her eyes had found Rae, frozen in the doorway, and pleaded with her to go. Hide, she seemed to say. Run. Don't let them catch you. Don't let them take you!

Rae blinked the memory away. Anything could be outside this box of a room. Anything at all. And that *was* scary. But it was also exciting. A high-speed elevator hidden deep in a tunnel? It had to lead to something interesting.

From somewhere nearby, she could hear noises: some sort of soft, rumbling vibration, people talking, the staticky burst of a walkie-talkie. She thought of the rumors about the abandoned military base, remembered all the articles she'd found in her research about people finding things they weren't supposed to see . . . and then vanishing forever.

People just like her father.

The safest thing to do would be to go back up to the surface and forget about this. But Rae knew the question of what was down here would haunt her forever, and she already had enough ghosts. So she stepped out of the elevator and poked her head around the corner.

A long stretch of tunnel extended outward, all of it hard cement. There was no disguising it down here with a covering of dirt. Light filtered from the end, filling the space with a predawn gloom. Rae clicked her headlamp off and looked back at the elevator.

Vivienne, Nate, and Caden all stared back at her, eyes wide.

"Let's go," Rae whispered. She crept down the tunnel, the sound of all of their breathing and footsteps loud in the muted quiet. The tunnel continued on straight for a good twenty feet before veering sharply to the left. Rae stopped and glanced at the others. *Wait,* she mouthed at them. Then she cautiously peeked around the corner.

The tunnel opened into a huge cavern, so massive Rae couldn't see the top, the whole thing lit up by floodlights wired around the walls. She had an impression of people in bright green hazmat suits standing in front of a large gleaming metal wall before she ducked back around the corner.

"What?" Caden whispered.

"There are people."

"Doing what?" Nate asked.

"I need to look again." Rae took a deep breath, getting her heart rate under control before sidling back.

"I want to see too," Vivienne whispered behind her.

"This isn't a good idea," Nate moaned.

"Shh," Caden hissed. Rae heard a gasp and a muttered curse as the three of them inched behind her, but she ignored them, trying to take in all the details as quickly as possible. It was hard, though; she couldn't figure out what, exactly, she was looking at.

The metal wall reached up as high as Rae could see. It was made of some weird silver-blue material, the whole thing smooth and rounded, almost like it had been melted and then frozen solid again, all the edges softened away. Like a giant spoon.

There was a small plastic barrier around that wall keeping people two feet away from it. Spaced around it were a handful of guards, none of them in hazmat suits. Instead, they wore face masks and rested large, scary-looking weapons against their shoulders. They stood facing the metal wall, their backs to Rae and the others, but she imagined they'd be able to turn and point their weapons very quickly.

Despite the guards and their obvious danger, Rae couldn't stop looking at that curve of metal behind them. It drew her eyes to it, and now she saw that the floodlights didn't reflect off its surface. Instead, the wall seemed to drink in their light and disperse it in beads, like little water droplets. It was the oddest thing.

The closest guard shifted.

Rae ducked back, tripping over Vivienne and crashing into Nate before Caden caught her. The inside of her head felt weird, like she'd been concentrating on a brightly lit screen inside a dark room.

"You okay?" Caden whispered.

"I . . . don't know." There was something about that wall . . . some detail she wasn't quite grasping. She pressed the palms of her hands against the cool rock of the tunnel. What if . . . what if it wasn't a wall at all? It had curved at the top, almost like . . . "Like a disk," she whispered.

"A what?" Caden asked.

"We should go," Nate said.

Rae thought of the project her dad had been working on before he disappeared: Operation Gray Bird. It had been top secret, but he'd mentioned that he was in charge of reverse engineering a fuel source from some kind of craft. Rae had asked him if it was a spaceship, and he'd laughed and stopped answering questions about it.

But later, after he vanished, she'd found that photograph he'd hidden of an alien . . .

Rae swallowed. Patrick had promised to look into her dad's disappearance, to see if it was actually connected to Green On!. But Caden didn't trust Patrick, and honestly, neither did she. What if his company had an alien craft in its possession? Maybe even the same one her dad had been working on?

It was madness. There was no way.

She needed to look at it again.

"I'm sure they have guards making rounds in this area," Caden whispered. "It's a miracle we haven't been caught already."

Rae ignored him, sticking her head back around the corner and staring again at that impossible thing. Now that she'd thought the word—*spaceship*—she couldn't see it as anything else.

Dimly she heard a burst of walkie-talkie noise, and a voice saying something about movement in the tunnel.

Caden grabbed her by the arm and yanked her back. "Rae," he hissed. "We need to go. It would be very bad if they found us here."

This time Rae let him tug her back down the hall and around the corner.

They crowded into the elevator and Vivienne hit the button, the door whooshing closed. "Ready?" she asked.

Rae widened her stance and put her back against the wall, then nodded. Vivienne pressed the button again, and they shot up. The skin on Rae's face sagged with the force of their velocity, and she closed her eyes and gritted her teeth, waiting for it to be over.

The elevator slowed and then stopped. The door whooshed open and Rae stumbled out first, the darkness of the tunnel almost a relief.

"I wonder where else this tunnel connects?" Nate said.

"What?" Rae blinked. The glow of the elevator outlined Nate's face, his eyes worried behind the sheen of his glasses.

"This tunnel extends farther that way." He pointed in the direction away from them. "I'm assuming it leads to Green On!'s headquarters. Otherwise why would they need an elevator right here?"

Rae squinted down the tunnel as if she could see what lay at the other end. Did tunnels crisscross beneath all of Whispering Pines? It was a disturbing thought. "You all saw that thing they were guarding, right?" she said.

"Yeah, we saw it," Vivienne said. "It was super weird."

"Do you . . . know what it was?" Rae asked.

"Besides super weird?" Vivienne frowned. "No idea."

Rae took a deep breath. "I think it's a spaceship."

Nate nodded.

"You agree?" Rae almost fell over.

"Those bugs we found had to come from somewhere. And it wasn't here."

"You think those are alien bugs?" Caden sounded strangely eager. "As in, from outer space?"

"I'm not about to make any conclusive statements yet," Nate said. "But I think it's a strong possibility. As bizarre as it sounds."

"How would the bugs have gotten out?" Vivienne demanded. "They have that ship sealed up. Or did you not notice?"

"Of course we noticed," Caden said. "But do you really think they're just guarding it? Obviously they'll have opened it at some point. How could they not?"

"You don't know that," Vivienne said.

"I know they have a habit of messing with things that they should leave well enough alone."

"Like what?"

"Like everything!" Caden said. "All of this 'alternative energy' they talk about. What do you think it is?"

"They are trying to save the planet. Or don't you care about that?"

"Yes, I care, but is that really what they're doing?" Caden asked.

"You just want some proof that Green On! is the bad guy your family always thought they were!" Vivienne had her hands balled into fists.

"And you just want to go on pretending that they are the good guys that you always thought they were," Caden fired back.

"Hey now, Green On! is a large company," Rae said. "I'm sure that there's both good and bad in it. Most groups are not just one thing."

"Yeah, what she said," Nate said. "Now can we stop arguing and go home?"

"We're not arguing," Vivienne snapped. "I mean, *he's* arguing." She jabbed a finger at Caden. "I am merely defending the company my mom works for, that she's devoted her whole life to, because it's a good company full of good people who are trying to do good things. They're not unleashing killer alien insects on the population of Whispering Pines, okay?"

"It might have been accidental," Caden said quietly. He would know about things like that; the Unseeing had slipped from the Other Place and into their town before Caden managed to seal the rift behind his brother.

Rae was suddenly exhausted. "Let's go home. We can talk this over when we're not buried deep in the heart of the earth."

"We haven't found any weird bugs yet," Vivienne said sulkily. "I thought that was our goal here?"

"I took a couple of soil samples." Nate patted his backpack.

"Oh, yeah, 'cause that'll be super helpfu—" Vivienne stopped.

She turned and cocked her head to the side. It was such a sudden, strange movement that it reminded Rae of the Unseeing. The way it had stared at her, all traces of humanity leaking from its face like water from a cracked pot.

Rae shivered. "Vivi?"

"I heard something." Vivienne peered intently down the tunnel.

"What?" Caden asked.

Vivienne clicked on her headlamp, its light washing over her face. "I'm pretty sure it was the soft, desperate bleating of a goat."

22.

CADEN

It didn't take them long to find the small crevice in the side of the tunnel. It was just a slit in the rock, barely wide enough for them to get through, and then only if they turned sideways. But now that they were close to it, Caden could hear the bleating of the goat too.

It sounded like a person screaming. And even though he did not want to slide into that hole in the rock, he knew he couldn't leave the goat there. He wondered if it was the goat Gary had been missing the other day. And then he wondered if Gary was in there too . . .

Caden thought of that unmade bed and felt sick. But Gary had seemed very capable. He kept his axes sharp, and he'd lived in the Watchful Woods for as long as Caden could remember. They hadn't found any sign of him down here yet either. He had probably just decided to move his remaining goats somewhere safer.

"What should we do?" Vivienne asked, her face white in the flickering light of her headlamp.

"Um, Vivienne?" Nate said. "Your light."

"What?" Vivienne tapped her light. It went brighter for a second and then winked out, the tunnel abruptly filling with more darkness like a bucket filling with ink. Only Rae's headlamp shone in the gloom.

"Uh-oh," Vivienne said. "It might need to be recharged. Sorry about that." She pulled the headlamp off and shook it, but nothing happened. Sighing, she stuffed it into her backpack. "At least we still have your light," she told Rae.

"Do you want it?" Rae asked. "Since it's technically yours."

"No, you keep it."

"Thanks," Rae said, obviously relieved.

The goat screamed again, long and pitiful. Caden flinched. Aiden had always accused him of being too tenderhearted—having the ability to feel the emotions of others did that to a person—but Caden knew he couldn't leave behind something that was in that much pain.

"I'll lead," he said.

"Don't be silly," Rae said. "Since I have the light, I should go first." And she slid into the crevice without looking back, leaving the rest of them in sudden darkness.

"Hey, since you have the light, you should go last!" Nate yelled after her, but she was already gone.

Caden shuffled sideways into the crevice after her. The ceiling was barely taller than his head, and he had to stay turned, moving his left foot and then sliding his right to meet it. The rock scraped against his back, damp and cold. A little farther in and it pressed against his stomach as well.

Rae's breathing turned into rough gasps ahead of him, terror rolling off her in waves, threatening to drown him. Behind him, he heard Nate stumbling closer. The feeling of being trapped—rock in front and back, people on either side—pulled Caden into one of his worst memories.

He was in a therapist's basement, staring at a rip in reality. A torn space bleeding a garish greenish-yellow light. And his brother stood in front of that rip screaming as hungry tentacles wrapped around him.

Caden had two choices: he could try to pull his brother free and risk all the horrors of the Other Place coming with him, or he could push Aiden farther in and seal that rift.

Caden had hesitated. But not for long.

And once his brother had vanished and he'd yanked the rift shut as tightly as a zipper closes a jacket, Caden had stood there, stunned and blank, staring through the doorway into Doctor Anderson's storage room at a bunch of boxes and stacked books. He'd been hot and cold at the same time, his hands shaking, mouth dry and bitter, stomach full of roiling acid.

That wasn't the worst part, though.

His parents had rushed down the stairs moments later, and Caden had turned to see their concerned faces. And he'd known he'd have to tell them what he'd done, known they would never forgive him. *That* was the worst part.

Because Aiden was the favorite son.

Hard on the heels of that thought came the same bitter, roiling resentment. Maybe if he were as powerful as Aiden, he'd be the favorite.

Caden shook away the memory and the dark feelings attached to it. His brother was back, his parents were getting help, and right now, Rae needed him. "I'm here, Rae," he whispered. "I'm right behind you. You're okay." He reached for the feeling of calm purpose, picturing it as a fluffy cloud the cheerful blue of a summer sky, and imagined it wrapping around Rae. He had no idea if that would help, but after a few seconds her breathing evened out.

Moments later he burst from the narrow space and into a wider cavern, almost running into Rae. She stood frozen, her face tilted up, the headlamp spilling across her features—wide, terrified eyes, open mouth, one hand clutched at her chest.

Caden slowly, slowly followed her gaze up. To the thing bathed in her beam of light.

A giant milky-white sac hung dripping from the low ceiling. And wrapped inside it, only the head and one leg sticking out, was the goat.

23.

RAE

Rae couldn't believe the goat was still alive. She watched its eyes roll, the whites gleaming in the darkness as it bleated softly. Hopelessly. It hung right at face level, the sac tangled around it and then smeared all across the ceiling. Almost more of a dripping web than a sac, really.

Rae turned, her headlamp pointed up so she wouldn't blind the others as they piled through. Incredibly Vivienne had managed to shove her backpack in front of her. She held one of its straps loosely as she stared up at the goat. "I guess we found our bug's hidden nest," she said.

"Looks that way." Rae heard her own voice, even and detached. She felt oddly calm right now. She should be screaming, but she wasn't.

"Where's the bug?" Nate asked nervously.

"That is a very good question," Caden said.

"Also a good question: Is there more than one?" Vivienne asked.

"Ugh, *that* is a terrible question." Nate shuddered. "Let's hurry up, okay?"

"Vivi," Rae said, "do you have a knife, or something sharp?"

Vivienne unzipped the front pocket of her backpack and fished around for a few moments, then tossed something small and shiny to Rae.

Rae caught it. "A nail file?"

"Give me a break. I have to take this bag with me to school."

Rae supposed it was better than nothing. "Nate, Caden, grab a sharp rock and help me get that goat down."

"I have a pair of scissors, too," Vivienne said, still rummaging in her pack. "I'll help you cut."

"Baa," the goat bleated.

"We won't let you fall," Rae promised it. She thought of the dead goat they had found earlier in the collapsed tunnel behind the Town Square. Did these tunnels connect? Were they littered with other dead goats, other dead animals? Even if they were, she couldn't do anything for them now. But she could save this goat here. She got a firm grip on the small nail file and dug its sharp tip into the egg sac where it met the ceiling.

There was a hardened membrane on the outside, almost like taffy candy, and she had to work to get her tiny blade through it. But as soon as she'd made it past that layer, her hand slipped forward like she were stabbing into a raw egg yolk. The liquid inside oozed out, thick and warm like snot, sliding down her hand, dripping onto her face, puddling around her legs. And with it, an awful smell, sharp and acrid. It reminded her of a skunk, with the same chemical burning effect.

Rae wrinkled her nose and tried not to breathe as she sawed away at more of the stuff.

Nate squeaked and dropped his rock, batting at his hand, his shirt, running fingers over his head.

And now Rae noticed the bugs.

They were *everywhere*, pouring out of that sac. Small and wriggly and bone-pale, with hundreds of little legs. They wriggled down Rae's arms, crawled along her shirt, slid through her hair. She could feel their tiny pinchers biting into her flesh.

"I think I'm going to be sick." Nate made a retching noise as he staggered away.

Rae gritted her teeth. She knew if she stopped now, she would never be able to make herself do this again. She kept sawing at the edges of the egg sac while Vivienne cut across from the other side and Caden scraped at it with his rock.

They got a little over half of it sliced, and then the weight of the goat tore the rest as it fell. Caden and Vivienne caught the animal together, staggering under the weight. They set it gently down to the ground, where it stood, trembling, its fur matted and damp with egg fluid. Caden brushed tiny hungry bugs off it. "It's okay, girl," he cooed. "We're going to get you home now."

Rae hurriedly slapped all the bugs out of her hair and flicked them out of her clothes, stomping on them. Then she helped Caden brush the bugs off the goat. She could still feel phantom bug feet all over her. It was awful, the worst sensation.

"It's okay, Priceless Art," Caden cooed.

"What?" Vivienne said, confused.

"The goat. I think that's her name."

"Weird name for a goat."

"Gary the Goatman names them after their favorite foods. I'm guessing there's a pretty good story behind this one's best meal."

"How do you know she's Priceless Art, and not some other goat?" Rae asked.

"I don't. But we need to call her something, so . . ." Caden shrugged.

Rae hoped this really was Priceless Art, and they could eventually reunite her with her owner. And she appreciated the way Caden sounded so calm and matter-of-fact. Like it was totally normal to be covered in the remnants of weird bugs and disgusting egg sac fluid while rescuing a goat inside a deep, dark tunnel.

Click. Click. Click.

Vivienne jerked back and stared across the cavern. "Not to alarm anyone, but there's something back there."

Click-click.

"Something big."

Rae turned. It looked like another tunnel extended out that way, and she caught a glimpse of more milky-white webbing dripping from the ceiling farther down before her light flickered like a candle flame in the wind.

Rae froze, not even breathing until it evened out again.

"Maybe I should have charged that headlamp too," Vivienne said.

"This is the stuff of nightmares," Nate moaned.

"Let's move," Rae said. "Nate, you go first. Then you, Vivi. Lead the goat, would you? Caden, help push it along from behind. And I'll go last." She could hear the clicking from behind her growing louder. It sounded like someone flicking a nail against their teeth.

Or like hundreds of large insect legs connecting with rock.

"Can we go any faster?" Rae asked.

"I'm . . . trying," Vivienne grunted. "Come on, goat. Move your Priceless butt already!"

They moved, and Rae crammed herself in after them, taking tiny, impossibly slow steps, trying not to imagine a giant centipede crawling after her, dragging her away, and stuffing her inside an egg sac.

"I'm out!" Nate yelled.

A second later, and Vivienne called, "I'm out too. And so is the goat."

Then Rae felt Caden move out of the way, and her headlamp illuminated the wide-open tunnel beyond him. She burst out into it, breathing hard.

Vivienne stared past her, her dark eyes narrowed as she gazed into the crevice. "I think it's noticed," she whispered.

"Noticed what?" Rae asked.

"That we destroyed its nest." Vivienne swallowed. "I think . . . I think it's angry." She looked at Rae.

Just as Rae's headlamp went out.

24.

CADEN

There was a moment of complete, suffocating darkness filled with a heavy silence, as if they were buried beneath an avalanche of snow instead of mounds of dirt. And then Vivienne screamed "Run!" and Caden was sprinting, his body reacting before his mind had a chance to register, stumbling off tunnel walls he couldn't see, tripping over rocks lying unseen beneath his feet.

"This way!" Vivienne yelled. "Nate, you idiot, follow my voice!"

Caden had a sudden terrible fear: the goat. They'd left the goat! A picture flashed through his mind of the poor creature standing alone in the dark, shivering and vulnerable. Ready to be cocooned once more. He stopped, turned back.

"Caden, what are you doing?" Vivienne shrieked.

He wondered how she could see him in the pitch black of the

tunnel. "Priceless Art?" he called, thrusting his hands out, searching.

"I have the goat," Vivienne said. "She's with me. Now run!"

Caden heard rocks breaking behind him, as if something very large were trying to squeeze its way through a crack in the tunnel wall.

He ran, feeling a strange wrongness behind him, like a cold spot in an otherwise heated pool of water. Rae and her little group were correct: this bug, whatever it was, did not belong on their world. But he could tell it wasn't from the Other Place, either.

Rae must be right. There was a spaceship buried below them. An actual alien spaceship.

Caden didn't have time to ponder what that meant. He could feel the thing behind him getting closer and picked up his speed.

There was something terrible about running in pure darkness. It felt like a nightmare, and he wondered if he was covering any distance at all. He could hear heavy breathing just ahead of him, the sound of footsteps, and from far back, the rapid *click-click* of insect feet scuttling along the stone.

Someone swore loudly from a few feet ahead. It sounded like Rae. "Bottleneck," she said. "Duck your heads."

Caden put his free hand out and slowed his steps a little, feeling for that overhang of rock. When his fingers connected, he stopped and reached both arms forward to trace the opening.

Click-click-click-click!

It sounded like it was right behind him! Caden threw himself into the small space, scurrying forward on hands and knees faster than he would have thought possible. He kept picturing that egg sac, the bugs pouring out of it, the giant centipede carcass at Gary's yurt. And the way it would feel to have those legs scuttling over him, to be pinned beneath its segmented insect body, the serrated mandibles opening wide . . .

The air in the tunnel shifted and Caden lurched to his feet, out of the bottleneck and into the last stretch of tunnel. He raced down it, the darkness slowly lightening until he could make out the silhouettes of the others ahead. Beyond them late-afternoon sunlight trickled sluggishly through the hole, illuminating the rope.

Rae reached the rope first. "Nate, up," she ordered, cupping her hands and bracing her feet as Nate staggered to a stop next to her. She was wearing Vivienne's giant backpack, and a second later Caden saw why: Vivienne had Priceless Art slung across the top of her own shoulders. The goat looked bigger than she was, but she stood there easily, waiting as Nate grabbed the rope and put his foot in Rae's hands, then hauled himself up.

Caden jogged the last few steps until he was standing with them. "Your turn," he told Rae, holding out his hands.

She hesitated, but just for a second. Then she grabbed the rope and let Caden boost her up.

Then it was just Caden, Vivienne, and Priceless Art.

"You next," Vivienne told him.

"What about the goat?"

"I'm going to tie the rope around her, and then you guys are going to haul her up," Vivienne said.

"Then what about you? How will you get up without ropes?"

She gave him a smile, small and knowing. It was the kind of

smile that clearly said she had a secret, and she knew he knew she had a secret. But all she said was, "Don't worry about me."

"Vivi . . ."

"Later, Caden." She glanced back over her shoulder. "It's almost through the bottleneck."

Caden turned and leaped at the rope.

25.

RAE

Rae hunched her shoulders, trying to make herself seem smaller. She was wedged in between Caden and Vivienne in the back seat of Ava's car, Priceless Art crammed in the back behind them, her head pressed up right behind Rae's. Nate had called shotgun, and the rest of them were too scared of Ava's furious glare to want to sit that close to her. Even dealing with goat breath was better than being up front.

"I just can't believe you," Ava said again. "We had a deal, Rae."

Rae had promised Ava she would keep her in the loop when she was investigating anything dangerous, and in exchange, Ava had promised to share her own research with her. "I did call you," Rae mumbled.

"Yeah, you did. After you spent all afternoon tromping around some random tunnel!"

"Cell phones don't work in the Watchful Woods, so I couldn't call you sooner." Rae glanced around, but none of the others backed her up. Nate looked like he'd gone to sleep, his head against the window. Caden was staring off into space, and Vivienne was purposefully not looking at her, as if afraid that any accidental eye contact would drag her into this fight.

"Yes, well, you could have called me *before* you went into the woods." Ava smacked the steering wheel with one hand. Never a good sign. She only did that when she was really trying to make a point. "Why did you need to go into that tunnel again?"

Rae swallowed. She hadn't told Ava the whole truth. Or even most of it. Her sister was mad enough without knowing about giant alien bugs and mysterious spaceships. Once she calmed down, Rae promised herself, she would tell her. For now, she decided to keep it simple. "Um, a goat had gotten lost down there."

"So you put your life and the lives of your friends in danger for a *goat*?"

Priceless Art bleated pitifully.

Ava sighed. "Yes, yes, I'm glad they saved you. Still."

"It wasn't all my idea, you know." Rae elbowed Vivienne in the side. "Right, Vivi?"

"Hmm, well, look at that," Vivienne said. "We're at the lab."

Just ahead loomed the chain-link fence that surrounded the perimeter of Green On!'s lab. Ava slowed as she approached the gate. A guard glanced at her from the small guardhouse next to it.

"Here to see Patrick Smith," Ava said. "He's expecting us."

Vivienne had texted Patrick as soon as they got in the car, and he promised to have the lab open and waiting for them.

The guard nodded and pressed a button, and the gate swung open for them to drive in.

"We'll talk more about this later," Ava said.

"I can't wait," Rae muttered. She glanced at Caden. He'd been super quiet this whole drive. Not that he was ever that loud, but he seemed even more drawn inward than usual. "You okay?" she asked him.

Caden blinked as if he'd been staring at something invisible and was just now noticing the world around him. She remembered the way he had looked when he'd opened the rift between their world and the Other Place that night the Unseeing had almost killed her. Maybe he really *was* watching something she couldn't see. It was a little freaky.

"Sorry," Caden said. "Just tired."

"Tired?" Vivienne asked. "Or sulking?"

Caden scowled. "I don't sulk."

"Oh yeah?" Vivienne said. "We all know how you feel about Green On!. But we need to talk to Patrick ASAP."

"I know, okay? I didn't argue with that, did I?"

"Why do you need to talk to Patrick so badly anyhow?" Ava pulled into the closest available parking spot. "Shouldn't we be going to, I don't know, a vet?"

Her sister had a point. A vet made more sense for a potentially injured goat. Unless that goat had been attacked by giant alien bugs. In that case, a science lab was probably the best place to be. "Patrick needs to examine Priceless Art first," Rae said.

"Why?"

Rae could feel Ava's gaze lasering on her through the rearview mirror, and she squirmed. Rae had never been good at lying. Especially to her sister. "The goat is, um, part of our internship."

"Really." Ava drew the word out, making it as skeptical as possible.

"Oh yes," Rae said, and it wasn't *technically* a lie. "We'd better hurry. Don't want to keep him waiting." She nudged Vivienne, who opened her door and got out. Rae scrambled out after. She closed the door, then noticed that Ava had gotten out too.

"I'm coming with you," Ava said.

Rae and Vivienne exchanged glances. "You'll probably be bored."

Ava shrugged. "I can survive boredom." She bared her teeth in a smile that had as much warmth as the deepest tunnels below.

Rae's shoulders slumped. Her sister was one of the most stubborn people she knew. There would be no talking her out of this.

"Mind carrying my bag?" Vivienne held out her humongous backpack. "I'm going to carry Priceless Art."

"Um, sure." Rae reluctantly took it and slung it onto her back. There was something about Vivienne's bag that made Rae very uncomfortable.

When Rae was little and didn't want to go to bed, she used to throw herself on the floor so her dad would have to scoop her up and carry her to her room. She'd learned that if she went completely limp, her dad would really struggle to lift her, so sometimes instead of going through all that, he'd give her five more minutes of playtime as long as she promised to go to her room on her own afterward.

Vivienne's backpack felt like that. Like it was purposefully making itself heavier because it didn't want Rae carrying it anywhere.

Rae shivered. She was being silly. A backpack couldn't have intent. She tried to ignore its presence—not that a backpack could have a presence, either—as she walked slowly up to the front doors of Green On!

Vivienne paused. "Do you hear something?"

"What?" Caden looked sharply at her.

"Someone yelling?"

And now Rae heard it too. She turned.

Nate was sprinting after them, his face red. "You jerks!" he yelled. "You didn't wake me up!"

"Oh, sorry," Rae said.

"Sorry? *Sorry?* As I keep reminding you, we're supposed to be a team!"

"Really sorry," Rae said.

"Really, *really* sorry," Vivienne added.

"We didn't realize you were still asleep," Rae said.

"Honestly, we kind of forgot you were even in the car."

"Vivi," Rae hissed.

"What?" Vivienne said. "It's the truth. No malice, just oversight."

Nate glared at both of them. "I see how it is." He marched past them and into the lobby, letting the door swing shut in Rae's face.

"I'm guessing he's still a little mad," Vivienne said.

Rae rubbed her nose. "You think?"

"Baa," said Priceless Art.

"I agree." Vivienne ran a hand down the goat's nose. "I never really saw the appeal of goats before this, but I'm kind of getting attached to this one."

"Maybe Gary will let you keep her." Caden pushed the door open for them. "He gave his nephew a goat, apparently."

"You mean Blake?" Vivienne said.

"Blake's uncle is the goat man?" Rae barely looked at the Green On! lobby this time as they walked across it to join Nate outside the smoky-glass doors that led to the labs. "Oh, the yurt!" she realized. "Alyssa said he'd gone to live there so he could study the stone wall. I was wondering how many yurts are in those woods."

"More than you'd think, actually," Vivienne said. "I know of at least three. Also a geodome. Oh, and a converted bus."

"Who's Blake?" Ava asked, following behind.

"One of our mortal enemies," Vivienne said.

"What?" Ava blinked.

"We're in a competition with him," Rae explained. "Ergo."

"Ergo," Vivienne agreed. She nudged Nate. "Come on, Nate. We're supposed to be a team, remember?"

Nate sighed loudly. "Ergo," he muttered grudgingly.

Ava shook her head. "You people are weird."

The inner glass doors opened, and Patrick stepped out, wearing his normal dark suit and confident smile. "Welcome back." He glanced at Caden, and his smile widened. "Mr. Price. I see you have reconsidered your position on our internship program?"

"No," Caden said shortly. "I'm just here to support, not to stay."

"We'll see." Patrick focused on Ava next. "And Ms. Ava Carter! How good to see you again."

Ava's cheeks went pink, and she didn't quite meet his eyes. Rae could hardly believe it. She'd never seen this side of her sister before.

"I hope it's okay for me to be here," Ava mumbled.

"But of course. Welcome to Green On!. Perhaps you'll even decide you'd like to work here one day."

"Maybe," Ava said uncertainly.

"My department is in the midst of some very exciting work," Patrick continued. "I have a feeling that a lot of people—smart, capable young people like yourself—will be interested in being a part—" He stopped abruptly. "Is that a *goat*?" He was looking at Vivienne now, his smile faltering. It was the first time Rae had ever seen him look uncertain.

"This is Priceless Art." Vivienne shrugged her shoulders, and Priceless Art lifted her goat head. "We think," Vivienne added.

"Baa."

"I . . . see." Patrick moved closer, reaching a hand toward the goat. "Not exactly what I was expecting when you said you found something interesting, but—"

The moment his fingers touched Priceless Art, the goat jerked back, legs flailing wildly. Vivienne cried out, and only Caden's quick lunge forward saved her from toppling backward with a heavy goat on her head.

"Shh, shh," Caden whispered, stroking the goat's nose. Her eyes rolled, the whites showing all around them, and then abruptly she went still. "I think she fainted."

"Goats do that," Patrick said. Only he wasn't looking at the goat anymore. He was looking at his fingers, the ones that had brushed against Priceless Art's flank. He rubbed them together thoughtfully, then brought them to his nose and sniffed. His eyes widened. "Where did you find this goat?"

"In a tunnel," Vivienne said.

"Where in a tunnel?" Patrick asked, a strange urgency to his words.

"In a cavern in the tunnel, stuck inside a giant egg sac," Nate spoke up.

Patrick frowned.

"Is something wrong, Mr. Smith?" Ava asked.

"Perhaps, Ms. Carter. Perhaps." Patrick pasted a smile on his face. His usual smiles were wide, pleasant, attractive things. They reminded Rae of toothpaste commercials and luxury car advertisements. But this smile wasn't selling anything that anyone would want. And when Rae looked at it, dread curled in her stomach, filling her mouth with the bitter taste of fear.

Rae inched closer to Caden, his shoulder brushing against hers. She could feel Ava at her back and was glad her older sister had insisted on coming after all. Even if she was upset with her.

"Let's get this poor creature to our lab," Patrick said. "Quickly now. You can fill me in on the details on the way." He tapped a panel and the doors opened again. "Oh, and please do call me Patrick," he told Ava. He strode past the smoky glass, leaving the rest of them to scramble after him.

Rae thought of the hole Caden had found, the way it loomed

there in the middle of the forest, deep and dark and mysterious. She remembered how she'd felt just before she went inside. The terror that came with the knowledge that they were about to follow a monster through a tunnel full of unknown dangers. And as she trailed behind Patrick through the long, empty hallway of Green On!, she couldn't shake the feeling that she was doing the same thing again.

26.

CADEN

". . . found Priceless Art wound up in a giant, disgusting egg sac, and of course we couldn't leave her there," Vivienne finished, rubbing the goat's nose. The goat lay across the hard marble slab of a table in the middle of their underground lab. Caden couldn't stop watching her side, how it moved up and down rapidly with her too-fast breathing, the only indication that she wasn't already dead.

"Of course," Patrick agreed. He leaned against the counter that ran along the side of the room. The electric lights of the underground lab washed his face in a harsh bluish glow, erasing every shadow, illuminating every line. He wore an expression of casual interest, as if he were watching the first episode of a new show and hadn't decided if it was worth seeing the rest of the season yet.

Caden frowned. He'd seen that exact same expression on his

brother's face before and knew what it meant: Patrick was hiding something. But then Caden was sure that Patrick had been part of the team that opened the rift to the Other Place and pulled out Aiden. And then kept him locked in a secret underground lab. So this was the kind of man willing to kidnap a teenager. He was probably hiding all sorts of things behind that bland exterior.

We came to an understanding.

Aiden still hadn't explained what that meant, just said Green On! wouldn't be bothering him anymore. Caden's stomach filled with that terrible sense of dread again and he pushed those thoughts away; he'd been through enough today and didn't need to add worry about future horrors.

Next to Patrick, Doctor Nguyen stood straight and stiff. She'd met them in the hall on their way into the lab and had listened to Vivienne's story with growing apprehension, her eyes widening behind her wire-rimmed glasses, her mouth pressed tight as if holding back a whole tide of words she knew she wasn't allowed to say.

Ava stood on Patrick's other side, her mouth also clenched. But if Doctor Nguyen's distress was a tide, Ava's was the building pressure of an ocean pulling inward before a tsunami. She wasn't just agitated. She was *furious*, the red of her anger combining with the black of her fear. It looked almost like a gaping, bleeding wound.

Caden looked away from her, uncomfortable. He knew Ava was upset because Rae put herself in danger again. Just as he knew his own older brother would never have cared so deeply about him.

But that wasn't entirely true.

Caden thought of the Zachary Mitchell incident again. Aiden

had said he'd lost his temper. That it was something he was working on now. But Caden remembered what Aiden had told him after he'd finally let Zach stumble away.

If someone hurts you, you don't just take an eye for an eye. You take the whole head.

When he said those words, Aiden's face had been filled with unapologetic fury. Where Ava's outrage shimmered with love, his brother's had been shot through with the entitled anger of a toddler who has just discovered someone else playing with his toys. He wasn't being a protective older sibling but a possessive one.

"I can't *believe* you," Ava finally burst out, rounding on Rae. "You told me you went in the tunnel to find a goat, not to track down some kind of mutant bug!"

"Six of one, half dozen of another," Rae said, attempting a sickly smile.

"What does that mean?" Nate asked.

"It's something our dad used to say," Ava said, still glaring at Rae. "It means the truth is a little of both things." Her eyes narrowed. "Which also means both things are a little bit of a *lie*."

Rae winced. "I was going to tell you the rest."

"When?"

"Eventually."

"Maybe now would be a good time to also mention the spaceship we found," Nate said.

Everything went still and quiet, the silence that perfect crystal moment right before something precious crashes to the ground. Caden could feel the inevitable shattering.

"Nate," Rae hissed.

"What?"

"We agreed not to talk about that." Vivienne scowled. "Remember? In the woods?" After they'd left the tunnels, they'd decided that it would be better—*safer*—not to let Patrick know they were nosing around secret Green On! stuff. Even Vivienne had thought it best. "But obviously some people have the memory of a goldfish."

"Actually, the whole goldfish memory thing is a myth," Nate said. "Current studies suggest that they remember things for months."

"So not the point, Nathaniel," Vivienne said. "The point is you have a terrible memory."

"Says the person who forgot I was in the car on the drive over here."

"So this is some kind of revenge?" Vivienne crossed her arms.

"No. I just think that since Doctor Nguyen joined us here, she deserves to hear all the facts."

"Suck-up," Vivienne fake-coughed.

"Totally," Rae muttered.

"Um, thank you, Nathaniel," Doctor Nguyen said weakly. "I appreciate your trust in me."

"See?" Nate told the others. "*Some* people appreciate me. Anyhow, it doesn't make sense neglecting to mention the ship if we think the bugs came from it. Besides, we were supposed to find a mystery. It was literally the assignment. We can't get in trouble for doing the assignment."

Patrick shifted, and all eyes turned to him. "This conversation has taken a rather fascinating turn. You children honestly believe that you discovered a spaceship hidden in a tunnel?" His tone didn't change, and neither did his expression, but he still managed to convey a whole bucket of skepticism.

Rae stiffened, and Caden could feel her indignation flaring. "That's exactly what we found," she said. "An alien craft, surrounded by Green On! employees."

"Hmm." Patrick steepled his fingers together in front of him.

"Don't lie to us," Caden said, his own anger building. "We saw it with our own eyes."

"I have said nothing against this . . . theory of yours." Patrick gave a tight smile that made Caden want to hit him, it was so condescending.

Caden shoved his hands deep into the pockets of his jeans. "We're pretty sure that when your employees opened that craft, they let something out. An alien bug or two."

"Accidentally," Vivienne added.

Doctor Nguyen fidgeted and looked from Patrick to the others and back again. She cleared her throat. "Patrick," she began tentatively. "Is it possib—"

"Doctor Nguyen." Patrick cut her off, his tone full of warning. And Caden noticed suddenly how odd it was that Patrick always used last names and titles for other people, while insisting that everyone call him by his first name only. It was some weird sort of power game, a method of keeping people off-balance.

"Did you really find a spaceship?" Ava asked, and she was so earnest about it that Patrick's expression cracked.

He sighed. "We found *something*, Ms. Carter. I am not at liberty to say more than that."

"You mean you can neither confirm nor deny?" Ava raised her eyebrows.

Patrick chuckled. "We no longer use that expression. Too many movies and television shows have ruined it for us."

"That's right. You used to work for the CIA, didn't you?" Ava said.

"I see someone did her research."

"Us Carters always do." Ava shared a smile with Rae. "Do you still work for them?" she asked Patrick.

He shifted uncomfortably. "I am now fully committed to my new career here as—"

A long, uncanny scream filled the lab, the noise echoing off the concrete walls. Caden's hands flew over his ears as he spun around.

Priceless Art's eyes had rolled back in her head, the whites glowing an eerie blue in the glare of the lights above her. Her legs twitched like she wanted to run but couldn't, her chest rising and falling even faster than before, her lips pulled back and that horrible noise pouring out of her, high-pitched and terrified.

And then she stopped and went silent.

Patrick inched back. "You might want to—"

The goat *exploded* as something dark and shiny erupted from her stomach and headed straight for Rae.

27.

RAE

Time slowed down for Rae, every millisecond sliced into a series of still frames like an old movie, every detail imprinted in stark relief. The feeling of blood, warm and sticky, dripping off her cheek. The horrible smell of torn guts stinking like a summer festival outhouse. The sight of that giant centipede, as thick and long as her arm, its legs splayed out on either side as it sailed toward her. And the knowledge that she would not be able to get out of its way.

Rae tried getting her hands up, but her movements were as slow as the rest of the world, and she'd barely lifted them before the insect slammed into her chest, knocking her back against the concrete floor.

Legs, hard and sharp, scuttled up her body, dug into her neck, pinched against her throat. Rae thrashed, trying to get a grip on the thing, but it was slippery with gore, and *fast*. Impossibly fast. It pinned her down, its bottom half pressing against her windpipe.

Rae gasped for breath, and the thing reared back like a cobra about to strike. She caught a glimpse of a face on its underside—large, gleaming black eyes and a mouth stretched wide around a pair of cruelly serrated mandibles—before it darted forward, those mandibles extending toward her own mouth.

Instantly she thought of the exploding goat and terror gave her new strength. She thrust her fingers up between the insect's body and her face, covering most of her mouth with the back of her hand and trying to shove the thing's head away from her. Its legs clung to her skin, the tips of its mandibles pressing into the corners of her mouth.

She brought her other hand around and jabbed the insect in the eye with her thumb. Hard. It felt like pressing against a warm M&M, her thumb cracking through a bit of resistance before sinking into soft eyeball goo.

The insect shrieked and pulled back, and Rae shoved it off her chest. It stumbled, and then righted itself and lifted its top half again, yellowish ooze sliding out of the crushed eye, its mandibles clacking together violently. Even though it was an insect, and it didn't—*couldn't*—have emotions, fury seemed to vibrate in every shiny, segmented line of its body.

It dropped down and charged at her.

Rae scrambled backward, trying to get to her feet, but it was moving so, so fast. It leaped.

Ava slammed something large and heavy against it, crushing it into the ground. Half of it was mangled, more of that yellow liquid leaking out of snapped legs and cracked body segments, but it still managed to drag itself forward, hissing, its single good eye fixed on Rae.

Ava swung her weapon again, and again, until the instrument broke apart in her hand. By then the bug was nothing more than a large yellowish smear on the floor.

Patrick grabbed her by the shoulders and gently tugged her back. "It's dead now, Ms. Carter. Extremely dead, in fact." He sighed. "Much like that microscope you're holding."

"Sorry." Ava set the remaining pieces of it down on the lab table. "Was it expensive?"

"Quite. But it can be replaced. Unlike your sister."

"Are you okay?" Caden crouched next to Rae.

She couldn't stop looking at the bug remains on the floor in front of her. "I don't know." She ran a hand over her face, feeling the sticky slime trail the insect had left behind, and shuddered. "But I'll probably feel a lot better after a shower."

"You and me both." Caden helped her to her feet. She noticed the blood smeared across his forehead and felt more of it squishing on his hands.

"Showers all around, I think," Ava said. She gave Rae a shaky smile, then wrapped an arm around her waist in a half hug. "I'm glad you weren't bug food."

"Me too." Rae hugged her sister back and felt her trembling. She realized suddenly that they were almost the same height. Rae wasn't sure when that had happened; she'd always viewed her older sister as much bigger.

Doctor Nguyen screamed, glass shattering around her.

Rae whipped around.

"The door!" the scientist shrieked. "Get the door!"

Rae saw something hurtling across the floor toward the open door. Nate jumped on a chair, and Vivienne—

Rae glimpsed her friend all the way in the far corner, her back to the room. It was very odd and brought Rae up short.

Patrick reacted quickly, however, leaping over a chair, sprinting at the door, and kicking it shut a second before the insect reached it.

The thing hissed and drew back, raising its upper half and clicking its mandibles together furiously.

Doctor Nguyen slammed a large glass jar over it.

The insect threw itself at the side of the glass, then fell back. Immediately it got back up, its segmented body moving smoothly, almost snakelike as it scuttled in a tight circle, testing the sides for weaknesses while Doctor Nguyen clamped the jar down with both hands, her face white.

"Smart thinking," Patrick said. "Very commendable."

"Th-thank you."

"Notice how Doctor Nguyen trapped us a complete, live specimen?" he told Ava.

Ava shrugged. "The other one deserved to die. Messily."

"Did it really?" Patrick asked. "It was only obeying its biological imperative. There was no malice to it."

Rae thought again of those black marble eyes and wasn't sure she agreed.

"I'm still not going to apologize." Ava crossed her arms.

Patrick chuckled.

The insect in Doctor Nguyen's jar had stopped pacing and now stood motionless in that way that only insects seemed capable of. It was slightly smaller than the one that had attacked Rae, but still impossibly large for a centipede, its body covered in streaks of goat innards. It must have followed the other one out of poor Priceless Art's stomach, and they'd been too distracted to notice. Rae wondered if that was an intentional evolutionary strategy: the first bug out went on the immediate offensive so the second could sneak on by. Or was she giving these things too much credit?

The centipede dropped low and sidled up to the side of the jar, thrusting its legs against the crack between the bottom edge of the glass and the floor. Doctor Nguyen grunted and shifted her grip to pin the jar down more firmly. No, Rae decided. Definitely not too much credit.

"It looks a little like the bugs we found in the town square," Nate said.

"Yeah, the same way a striped house cat looks a little like a tiger," Rae muttered.

"I think . . . maybe this one is a queen?" Nate was still on a chair, but he'd crouched down so he could peer in at the bug. "Maybe both of them were. They spent their gestation period inside a living creature where they would be most protected. The rest of their, um, swarm? Hive? What do you call a group of centipedes?"

"An infestation," Caden said darkly.

Rae shivered, and tried not imagining the soil below Whispering Pines filling with those wriggling creatures.

"The rest of them were wrapped around the outside of the creature," Nate continued. "Those must be the workers, or the males, or . . . I don't know. We'll have to study them."

Rae frowned. "Are you actually excited about this?"

"I didn't love crawling through tunnels or dealing with exploding goats. But the research?" Nate grinned. "I think I'll like that part. I mean, an alien insect, Rae! We can learn all kinds of things!"

"I think we should revisit the shower idea," Ava said. "Research can wait."

Right now, with goat blood drying on her skin and the memory of an insect trying to cram itself down her throat still fresh in her mind, Rae was more than willing to let a shower take precedence over research. "I call dibs first," she told Ava.

Her sister smirked. "I was going to insist you go first. You smell awful."

"Thanks, sis. Love you too." Rae paused by the lab table and finally made herself look at Priceless Art.

She had to look away again immediately, her stomach roiling. *That could have been me.* She didn't want to think like that, but the image of the goat's empty eyes and burst stomach was going to haunt her forever, she just knew it.

"It's unfortunate, I know," Patrick said. "But sometimes, regrettably, there are casualties in the name of scientific exploration. Priceless Art served her purpose."

"Oh yeah? And what purpose is that?" Rae demanded. "She didn't deserve to die like that."

"Of course not. But like Mr. Cliff here has said, the specimen we caught, thanks to this brave goat's sacrifice, will teach us so much."

Rae scowled. It wasn't fair. The goat didn't want to be sacrificed. She'd been trapped, and scared, and alone. And then she was safe. And now?

Rae looked again at that bloody shape stretched across the table. Vivienne had moved out of the back corner and was hunched over it, her shoulders shaking, almost like she was trying to pet the animal's flank.

"Vivi." Rae reached out a hand to comfort her friend. Then froze.

Vivienne wasn't petting the goat. She was sliding her fingers into the blood and then licking it off, her brown eyes flat and dark.

Rae gasped.

Vivienne looked up, her gaze snapping to Rae's, blood smeared all around her mouth and down her chin. She bared her teeth, and something deep in the back of her eyes flickered red like a banked fire.

Rae instinctively took a step back. Fear slammed into her harder and faster than any insect. Dimly she was aware of Nate saying he would stick around a little longer and get started on the research, but she couldn't look away from Vivienne. No, *not* Vivienne. From whatever was staring at her out of Vivienne's eyes.

"Rae?" Ava called from the door. "Vivienne? You coming?"

Vivienne blinked, and she was herself again. She wrinkled her nose and wiped her bloody fingers on her shirt. But she didn't seem to notice the smears of blood across her chin.

"Hello?" Ava said.

"I'm going to wait here for my mom to get off work." Vivienne turned away, not looking at anyone.

Rae hesitated, but she'd never ignored the truth just because it was a little terrifying. Okay, a *lot* terrifying. "Vivienne," she said. "Are you—"

"She's fine, Ms. Carter." Patrick put a hand on Rae's back and nudged her toward the door.

Vivienne didn't turn around, and so Rae let herself be guided out of the lab. She followed Ava and Caden down the hall toward the elevator, feeling like she'd just swallowed a whole tray of ice cubes. There was something terribly, terribly wrong with her friend. Something *supernaturally* wrong. And no one else seemed to notice.

Caden nudged her shoulder.

Rae glanced at him.

"I saw it too," he murmured.

"You did?" she said, relieved.

Caden nodded. "I'll talk to her about it tomorrow."

"I can do it."

"I know you can. But I think this might fall under my own area of expertise."

Rae chewed her lip. She didn't feel right leaving this to someone else. Vivienne was her friend, and—

Caden took her arm, pulling her to a stop. "Rae, let me help." His eyes were such a deep, dark brown, intense and serious, framed by long, thick lashes that curled upward. "You don't have to do everything on your own," he said quietly.

And Rae remembered that moment in the cave again when

she'd been stuck in the crevice, gripped by claustrophobia, and he had said *I'm here, Rae*. "Thank you," she whispered.

Caden nodded.

"Hey, I thought you wanted to get home and shower," Ava called from down the hall. "Stop flirting and start walking!"

Rae sighed. Trust her sister to ruin a nice moment. But as she took the elevator back up into the light, she left behind thoughts of dead goats, alien insects, and blood-drinking friends and instead focused on the one thought that gave her comfort: she was not alone in this.

28.

CADEN

When Caden woke up the next morning he could tell immediately that his parents still weren't back yet, the emptiness of their absence radiating through the silent house. The fact that they'd left town at all was honestly weird enough, what with the unusual insects in their woods and Aiden's sudden reappearance. That they were staying away so long was beyond strange.

Caden picked up his phone and dialed his mom. He hoped he wasn't interrupting some kind of last-minute additional couples counseling session, but he needed to talk to her.

Straight to voicemail. Caden listened to his mom's cheery voice, her "Name your Price!" and the beep at the end, and clicked off without leaving a message.

Scowling, Caden got ready and left his room, quietly closing the door behind him. He passed Aiden's closed door and wondered if he should check on him. But when he lifted his hand to knock, unease roiled in his stomach like an undercooked hamburger and he let his hand drop and backed silently away. He'd wait and let his mom check on Aiden whenever she bothered coming home. He had enough confrontation ahead of him today as it was.

At school he kept a close eye on Vivienne, watching her laughing with Alyssa, chatting with an obviously anxious Rae, mocking Nate. She seemed like her normal self. And when he met Rae for a few minutes at his locker, she admitted that there had been nothing out of the ordinary with her today. "I'm sure I didn't imagine it," she said. "But . . . I don't know. Maybe it was stress?"

"You think she was stress-eating *blood*?"

"Well, it sounds ridiculous when you put it that way, but . . ." Rae sighed. "I guess I just don't know what to think."

"Me neither," Caden admitted. "But I felt something from her in the tunnels, too." He gripped his pendant, the weight comforting in his hand. "Give me a little more time, and I'll talk to her."

The bell shrieked, announcing the start of the next class, and Caden waved at Rae and hurried off down the hall.

He had two more classes with Vivienne that day. In each of them, he relaxed his inner shields and reached out his awareness, but her energy felt like it always had. There was no indication that she was hiding anything.

As he walked toward the buses, he tried remembering Vivienne's expression in the cave, that sense of wrongness that emanated from her, but in the daylight it just seemed so unreal.

"Caden!" Vivienne yelled.

Caden jumped, almost feeling like he'd conjured her up with the power of his thoughts. He turned slowly to face her.

She stood against the side of the school, wearing her giant backpack and a grouchy expression, her black hair in braided pigtails that hung in front of her shoulders. "Did you want to say something to me?"

"Wh-what?"

"Don't stutter and act all innocent. You've been staring at me all day." She crossed her arms. "And not just staring, but doing that creepy thing where you look at me like you're digging into my brain."

Caden winced. "Sorry. I don't mean to be creepy."

Vivienne sighed. "I know you don't." She chewed her lip, and Caden realized her annoyance was just a cover, disguising the worry beneath it.

"Is there something *you* want to say to *me*?" he asked.

Vivienne was quiet for several long, pounding heartbeats. Caden could hear the rest of the students clearing out of the school, the buses turning on, the space around them emptying. Finally she nodded. "Not here, though." She turned and led him along the outside of the school to the maple trees in back. From there they had a view of the track field in the distance and the second field beyond it. Or at least, what remained of the second field after a giant sinkhole had swallowed most of it over the summer.

Vivienne slid her backpack to the ground beneath a tree and sat down next to it, waiting until Caden did the same across from her.

He felt a little like he always did when his mom made him practice with her. Just like those times, he found himself mirroring Vivienne's pose: cross-legged, hands on knees, back straight. He waited for her to talk first.

That was also something his mom had taught him.

Think of a new client like a nervous dog. You want to let them come to you. Don't rush at them or you risk driving them away.

"You're good at this whole silence thing," Vivienne finally said. "I almost forgot that you never used to talk before Rae moved here."

"I talked," Caden said.

Vivienne snorted.

"Okay, maybe not a lot," he admitted. He studied Vivienne's face. She looked different without her usual easy smile. Her lips seemed thinner, her forehead lined with worry, as if she were a middle-aged woman and not thirteen. "What's going on with you?"

She looked past him, out at the fields. "I told you my mom and I went caving last year, right? We were exploring the tunnels below Whispering Pines. And no, before you ask, I was never in the tunnels we found yesterday, okay?"

"I wasn't going to ask that," Caden lied.

"Yes, you were. I can read it all over your face."

"You can read my face?" Caden asked, surprised.

Vivienne smirked. "No, but you totally just gave yourself away."

"Okay, fine, I *was* wondering . . . I mean, you seemed so familiar in them. Even in the dark." He waited, letting that statement sit there between them like the last cookie on a tray, both of them eyeing it.

Vivienne bit first. "It wasn't familiarity. I can see a little in the dark."

"Oh. That's, um, useful?"

"Really? I tell you I have superpowers and that's your response?"

Caden shrugged. "It's not wrong, is it?"

She laughed. "No, it's not wrong." Her laughter died out. "It's not just my eyesight. I'm stronger now, too. And faster. Those are the perks. But," she said, sighing, "there are some real downsides."

"Like?"

"Like . . . the whole blood thing." Vivienne drew her knees up to her chest and wrapped her arms around them. "When I smell it, it's like I become a monster."

Caden thought of Vivienne's face in the lab, the goat blood smeared under her chin. "How did it happen?"

"My mom and I were exploring a tunnel when part of it crumbled, and I fell into this weird, huge cavern. The floor was solid rock, and there were all these stone columns in it. And in the center was this really creepy carved pillar . . ." She closed her eyes. "I remember my mom kept calling to me. She was still in the tunnel above, and she was screaming my name, and I heard her, but it was like I couldn't do anything. Like in a dream, you know? I knew something terrible was going to happen, and I kept telling myself to turn and grab the rope my mom tossed down, but I couldn't look away from that pillar. It drew me to it, and I reached out both hands and touched it." She opened her eyes. "And after that, I started changing."

"What did this pillar look like?"

"I couldn't actually see it that well." Vivienne laid her cheek against her knee. "Or maybe I've forgotten? I know that sounds weird. How could I forget what something looks like after it ruined my whole life?"

"It's not weird. It can be hard for the mind to hold on to the details of a traumatic event. It's your brain's way of protecting you."

"Nice of it," Vivienne muttered. "I remember the carvings a little. There were faces with lots of teeth, long and gleaming. And eyes. So many eyes. And when I touched it, I remember thinking that it felt gross. Sort of like when you go camping for a couple of weeks and you can't wash your hair? And then you try running your fingers through it? It was like that."

"That is pretty gross," Caden said.

"I know." She managed a small, weak smile, but Caden could feel the fear shimmering around her like a cloak.

"What happened next?" He kept his voice soft and gentle. He remembered how he'd projected calm at Rae in the caves and tried doing the same thing here. Blue light, warm and comforting as a late-summer sky, enveloping Vivienne, wrapping her in a soothing embrace.

"I started becoming . . . I guess *hungry* is the best word for it?" She let go of her knees, dropping hands to the grass. "But I thought it wasn't that big a deal. My mom figured it was a growth spurt. Until Emmett."

"Emmett." Caden thought about that a second. He'd actually had a prophetic dream about Emmett a few weeks before his untimely demise, but he'd been dreaming from the perspective of the rabbit, and so all he'd seen was the dark shape of some large predator looming over him before he woke up. Now, staring at Vivienne, he realized who that predator must have been. "That was *you*?"

"Not so loud, please," Vivienne said.

"Sorry." Caden tried picturing that calming blue again, but it was hard when his mind kept conjuring that little white furry body, drained of blood. Because *Vivienne* had drained it . . .

"I felt terrible about it. I still do. But it was like something *inside* me attacked that bunny. I couldn't stop it. I couldn't do anything but go along for the ride." She shuddered. "It was the most awful thing."

"I can imagine."

"Yeah, you probably can, ghoul boy." Vivienne grinned, but it wilted quickly. "We actually visited your mom over the summer to try to get help."

"You did?"

She nodded. "I wasn't supposed to tell you. Or anyone, actually. My mom doesn't like people to know we visited the ghost hunters."

Caden wasn't surprised by that. A lot of people in town called on his family for this exorcism or that house cleansing, but almost none of them admitted it. Especially not someone as highly regarded as Mrs. Matsuoka. He was honestly shocked she'd been willing to go in for a consultation with Paranormal Price, secretly or not. But then he thought of the way Vivienne had looked in the cave, and again last night, blood smeared all across her chin, and he could understand why her mom had gone. "Was my mom able to help you? Did she figure out what was going on?"

"She said I had a transference curse. Rare, and incurable, as far as she knew."

Caden's stomach dropped. "Oh."

"But," Vivienne said, "she did give me something to help." She pulled her bag closer to her and opened it.

Caden's breath caught. He was super curious about her backpack. A backpack that she'd only started carrying around with her at the start of this school year, he realized.

Vivienne reached deep inside, pushing away a layer of ropes, an extra jacket, a library book, and other items Caden couldn't quite see.

"Wow, you sure have a lot of stuff in there."

"A girl's gotta be prepared. Especially around here." She wriggled her arm around, then yanked out a rectangular blue velvet box about the size of a large old-fashioned encyclopedia. She glanced around. Caden did the same. They were alone, the school behind them, the fields ahead, and the trees above. Nothing else but their shadows dappling the grass. Still Vivienne hesitated for a long, tense moment before she undid a latch on the side.

The lid of the box pulled back like a book cover. Nestled inside was a large round pendant about the size of one of Caden's clenched fists. It looked like it was made of simple gray stone, a circular pattern carved into the front of it and filled in with green gems the color of deep forest moss.

Caden leaned forward, frowning. There was something about that pattern . . . when he blinked, it seemed to change shape. Just a little. Enough to make him question what he was seeing. It made him want to draw it, to commit the shape to pencil and paper and pin it in place.

"Don't touch," Vivienne warned, pulling the box closer to her.

"What is it?"

"Your mom called it a sealing stone. She said my curse would never go away, but it wouldn't get worse as long as I kept this thing as close as possible as much as possible." She shut the lid again, hiding the pendant away. Immediately Caden felt better, like he'd just unbuttoned a pair of too-tight jeans.

"Your mom was wrong, though," Vivienne said sadly. "It *is* getting worse. So my mom went somewhere else for help." She closed the latch on the box. "She went to Patrick."

"Ah."

"I know you hate him, but he really did help me for a while."

"How?" Caden tried to keep his voice neutral.

"He was making this elixir. I took some every day. But then on Sunday, I think my mom did something at work. Some kind of mistake? Anyhow, she accidentally set off an alarm, and Patrick stopped giving her the elixir for me."

"That's terrible!"

"Well, it was starting to lose its effect anyhow. He promised that if my team wins this competition, he'll get me something better. Something that will cure me for good."

"Do you believe him?"

She tucked the box back inside her backpack and carefully covered it with her mountain of items, shifting the ropes a little, adjusting the balled-up jacket. Stalling. Finally her hands stilled, and she looked up, her eyes wide and vulnerable. "I don't know," she whispered. "And I'm scared, Caden. I'm so, so scared. I don't know what to do." She wrapped her arms around herself and started crying.

When Caden was in elementary school, he'd learned that other kids didn't like the way he seemed to know what they were feeling. They'd called him creepy, a mind reader, ghoul boy. So he had turned himself inward. If they didn't want anything to do with him, then fine. He didn't need them, either. He had his family, his drawing, and his mom's business. He didn't need friends.

And then Aiden had vanished, his parents had started drifting apart, and he'd been banned from helping with Paranormal Price. He hadn't recognized how alone he'd felt until Rae moved to Whispering Pines. Rae, who seemed to understand him.

Now Rae was his friend. And so, he realized, was Vivienne. He couldn't close his heart to her, and her outpouring of pain surrounded him like a hurricane.

This was the downside of his gift, the thing his brother had once warned him about. If he let people get in too close, their pain became his.

Caden pressed a hand against his chest. He knew he could put up his shields, imagine himself in a ball of white light, and shut Vivienne out. Let her deal with her own pain. It's what his brother had always recommended. Instead, he scooted over and clumsily put an arm around her shaking shoulders.

"I'll help you," he said, holding her. "We'll find a solution together. I promise."

"Thanks," Vivienne sniffled, her tears slowing.

They sat there in silence for several minutes, as Caden increasingly noticed how close they were, the way her hip was against his, how he still had his arm around her. Should he move it? Or wait until she moved? He had no idea what to do in this situation.

"Well, this is awkward," Vivienne said at last.

"You know, you're not the first girl to say that to me recently," Caden admitted.

"I'm not surprised."

"Should I move my arm?"

"I think so," she said.

Caden carefully lifted his arm like he was taking off a coat.

Vivienne laughed. "You don't hug many people, do you?"

"Not often, no."

"We'll have to work on that." She twisted to smile at him, her eyes still glossy with tears. "Thank you." She hesitated. "Can you maybe not tell Rae yet? I'll tell her eventually. I will. But not yet."

Caden was good at secrets. He'd had plenty of practice keeping them. But the thought of keeping one from Rae made him uncomfortable. Still, it was Vivienne's secret to keep or share as she wished. "Okay," he said at last. He got a glimpse of emotion. A sort of embarrassed worry. "But Rae isn't going to hold this against you," he said, slowly understanding her reluctance. "You know that, right?"

Vivienne shrugged. "I ate a rabbit."

"Yeah, well, we all make mistakes."

She snorted. "Thanks, ghoul boy."

Caden stood and offered her a hand up. "Anytime, ghoul girl," he said. "Anytime."

29.

RAE

Rae trudged inside her house, kicked off her shoes, and headed immediately to the kitchen. She dropped her backpack on the floor with a dramatic thump, then slumped into a chair next to it.

"Someone's not looking perky," Ava said. She had taken over the kitchen table, her calculus book lying open next to a notebook full of what looked like alien chicken scratch.

"Not looking perky?" Rae repeated. "What are you, seventy?"

Ava grinned and took a big sip from her mug.

Rae opened her bag and tugged a large library book out of it, dropping it on the table in front of her. The cover read: BUGGING OUT: A GUIDE TO ALL THINGS CREEPY-CRAWLY. It seemed like a good place to start. "Does Mom know you've been pilfering her coffee?"

"Pilfering, huh? Now who's old-fashioned?"

"It was a vocab word. I'm trying it out." Rae flipped open her book. "I can't imagine 'perky' was your English class's word of the day."

Ava snorted. "No, it wasn't. Which is too bad, really. Not enough people use it. And no, Mom doesn't know. And you're not going to tell her either." She pointed her pen at Rae, who put her hands up. "Wait, it's Thursday! Aren't you supposed to be at cross-country practice?"

Rae checked the index of her book. "Today's practice was canceled."

"Canceled? Really? I thought that as long as the world wasn't coming to some horrible apocalyptic end or the field hadn't been swallowed by a sinkhole, then practice went on."

Rae found the section on Myriapoda, "the many-legged ones," and flipped to it. The first page had a close-up photo of a large millipede. "Coach Briggs was sick today," she said. Which, according to Alyssa, was weird. She said their coach never got sick. Rae had wanted to ask Vivienne about it too, but she hadn't been able to find her after school.

Rae frowned. In her mind she replayed that awful scene from yesterday, Vivienne's eyes as she licked blood off her fingers, the smears of red on her chin . . .

"You okay?" Ava asked.

Rae forced a smile. Caden had promised to look into it. She had to trust him. It was hard; trust wasn't something that came easy to her these days. "Yeah," she said. "Just . . ." She shuddered.

"I know what you mean. I keep thinking there's something crawling on me."

"Me too." Rae felt it now, even. The echoing sensation of hundreds of tiny legs whispering across her skin. She slapped at her arms and legs, even though she knew it was just her imagination. She tried ignoring it and went back to her reading. "Did you know centipedes are venomous?"

"Isn't that delightful information." Ava glanced at the book. "Bit of light reading?"

"Researching the things we saw. I figured this huge book"—Rae tapped it with one finger—"ought to be a good place to start."

Ava shook her head. "You know there's this thing called the internet."

"You know, I don't care."

"So do bugs normally lay their eggs inside goats? Or is that an alien thing?"

"Some insects do," Rae said. "For instance, there's a type of spider that lays its eggs under a person's skin. Luckily, they live in another part of the world."

"Did you read that just now, or was that fact already stored away in that disturbing brain of yours?"

Rae grinned. "What can I say? Bugs are fascinating. Like, there's also a desert wasp that stings its prey to paralyze it, then lays its eggs on top, so that when they hatch—"

"Stop! I don't want to hear it."

"Hey, you asked the question. Besides, aren't you planning to major in biology or something?"

"Astrobiology. It's completely different," Ava said.

Rae stared down at the photograph of the centipede in her book and thought of another photo. One she'd never shown Ava before.

She'd wanted to. After their dad disappeared and she'd discovered it hidden in his office, she'd gone to Ava intending to tell her everything. But her sister had been so scornful, right from the start. *You're being a child. There's no such thing as aliens, and no one* took *Dad. Grow up, Rae. Lots of people's dads run off*... After that little lecture, Rae had kept the photo tucked away, and she and Ava had slowly drifted apart. If Ava wanted to pretend that everything was normal when Rae knew it wasn't, then fine. But Rae wasn't about to pretend with her.

But recently everything between them had changed.

Ava had admitted that she did believe Rae, that she was still searching for their dad too. And the two of them had made a deal: they would share their info, and search for him together.

It was time for Rae to start upholding her end. "There's something I need to show you," she said. "I'll be right back."

She used to keep all of her top-secret articles pinned to a corkboard hidden behind a decoy board on her desk. But then the Unseeing had somehow snuck into her room and put his own photo there, and suddenly her hiding spot hadn't seemed so secure. So she'd moved all of her papers and photos and articles into a folder that she kept hidden at the bottom of her underwear drawer. It wasn't the safest place, but for now it worked.

She slipped a photo out from the back of that stack and hurried downstairs, her heart hammering with every step. "I found this in

Dad's office," she told Ava, laying it on the table in front of her. In the photo an alien peered out from between the bars of a cage, its eyes large, dark ovals sunk deep inside the gray skin of its face. It had no hair and no discernible mouth, but there was something almost humanlike in its expression.

Rae felt oddly exposed as her sister stared down at that picture. It reminded her of the way she felt when Caden really studied her, like her soul was on display.

"And you're sure this is real?" Ava said at last. "No Photoshop?"

"Remember those men who were tearing up Dad's study? I think they were looking for this. So yeah, I'm pretty sure it's real."

"It's awful." Ava's eyes watered. "Look. They have the poor thing tagged like some kind of animal."

Rae peered down at the photo. She hadn't noticed the small green tag before, sticking out from the alien's neck, almost blending into the bars of the cage. "Hmm. I wonder why they—"

"Look at the two of you doing homework together," their mom said as she walked into the kitchen. She was already wearing her sea-green scrubs, her damp hair pulled back in a tight braid.

Rae nudged the photo underneath a stack of papers while Ava made a show of attempting to hide her coffee mug. "You're down early," Ava said.

"I saw that, Ava." Their mom snagged the mug and took a large gulp.

"Hey!"

"You shouldn't be drinking this stuff. It'll stunt your growth."

"I'm almost eighteen," Ava grumbled. "I doubt I'll be growing much more." She eyed their mom. "You just didn't want to bother with making your own coffee."

"Is that really what you think of me?" Their mom made an exaggerated sad face.

Ava laughed. "Nice try, Mom."

"Fine, you got me. But only because I'm running out of time."

Rae watched the two of them, her heart a stone in her chest. She used to have easy interactions with her mom, but now it felt like every exchange was weighted. Her mom was either distant or hypercritical ever since her dad was taken. Or maybe her mom had always been like that with her, but she hadn't noticed because her dad had been there to cushion it.

". . . heading in early today," her mom was saying. "I'll be pulling a double shift, so you're on your own tonight. And also tomorrow."

"We know the drill," Ava said.

"Okay. Love you." She kissed Ava on the top of the head, then turned to Rae. For a second their eyes met, and Rae felt the stone around her heart cracking. But instead of kissing her, her mom frowned at the open book on the table. "You know, I saw something that looked like that in the bathroom just now. Creepy." She grabbed her purse and her keys and headed for the door. "Call me if there are any problems!" The door slammed shut.

Rae stared at Ava, who stared back. Then they both looked at the centipede photograph in Rae's book, the antennae in front, the hundreds of legs splayed out to the sides.

"You don't think . . ." Rae couldn't even finish the thought. It was too horrible.

"Coincidence." Ava scratched her neck. She froze. "Um, Rae?"

"Yeah?"

"Is there something on my back?"

"Not funny," Rae said.

"I'm not joking."

The fear in Ava's voice convinced Rae that her sister was serious. Rae stood and, heart pounding, inched around Ava.

A pale yellowish bug, as long as her index finger and about the same width, was crawling down the back of Ava's sweater.

Rae yelped and leaped back, her hands clasped over her mouth.

Ava's eyes went wide. "Don't just stand there! Get it off!"

"I don't want to touch it!"

"Well, I don't want to wear it!"

"Take off your sweater."

"I'm scared I'll accidentally knock it into my shirt."

Rae shuddered. "Okay. Okay, wait. I'll get something." She turned and rummaged in the drawers.

"Hurry," Ava said through gritted teeth. "I can feel it crawling."

Rae found a spatula and came back, brandishing it in front of her like a weapon.

"Seriously?" Ava said.

Rae raised it up over her head, focusing on that creepy-crawly.

"Wait, Rae—"

Whack! Rae slapped the bug off her sister and onto the tiled floor, then grabbed her book off the table and dropped it on it.

"Effective," Ava said. She crouched and lifted up the book so they could look at the smashed bug underneath it.

"See? Could the internet have done that?"

Ava laughed, and it only sounded a little strained, but then it stopped abruptly. "No," she whispered, horrified.

"What?" Rae whipped around but didn't see anything. *"What?"*

"I saw something moving. On the love seat." Ava swallowed.

"Maybe it was a spider?" Rae knew it was not a good day when she was hoping for a spider.

"Maybe . . ." Ava stood. "I'm going to see if we have Raid anywhere."

Ava returned a moment later with a can of citrus cleaner and a metal-handled mop. "No Raid. Instead they will get death by lemon spray." She passed Rae the can. "Now, let's go check out this bug."

They crept toward the couch, Rae clutching her can of Super Citrus, Ava brandishing her mop ahead of her. Ava pointed at the love seat, then at Rae, making a little lifting gesture.

Rae shook her head. No way was she going to move the cushions.

"This is ridiculous," Ava said. "Why are we trying to sneak up on them? It's not like they can hear us coming."

"Actually, a lot of bugs are quite sensitive to noise vibrations, more so than most other animals," Rae explained, feeling oddly like Nate in that moment. It was a good thing Vivienne wasn't there to witness it.

"Did you get that from the bug book you're reading?"

"No, that fact *was* from the internet."

"Oh, good. Now quit stalling and lift those cushions."

"*You* lift," Rae said.

"Isn't this whole bug mystery part of your internship project?"

Ava had a point. Rae hated when that happened. "Fine," she grumbled. She eyed the couch, with its two overstuffed cushions. She didn't like it, but she'd have to risk her fingers to its darkened underbelly. She put down her can of citrus and rubbed her hands together. "Ready?"

Ava clenched the mop. "Ready."

Rae lunged for the bottom edge of the closest cushion and hoisted it up. Immediately, two many-legged, milky-white bugs uncurled from the shadows. They skittered rapidly out of the couch and onto the floor. One of them went straight for Rae's feet.

Rae squealed and dropped the cushion, leaping on top of it, while Ava beat the first bug into oblivion with the cheap mop.

"Ava, quick, toss me the Super Citrus!"

Ava tossed the can one-handed, and Rae snatched it out of the air. She flicked the nozzle open and doused the second bug. The aroma of citrus was thick and sickening. And completely ineffective. The bug twitched, and then resumed scurrying.

"Argh! Mop!"

Ava smacked her mop into the insect, smashing it. "So much for the Super Citrus," she said, panting slightly.

"I guess it should really be 'Not-So-Super Citrus.'" Rae frowned at the can.

"At least they squash easy."

"Yeah." Rae looked at the dead bug on the carpet. It was a little smaller than the one she'd found on Ava's back, but just as creepy, all of its legs splayed out. "Do you think there are any more in our house?"

"I don't know. But there's no way I'll be able to sleep until we find out for sure."

Rae remembered the bugs she'd found in the Town Square, their bodies stained pink with blood. Now that she'd found the same kind of bugs in her own home, she wasn't sure she'd be able to sleep tonight no matter what. "Are you thinking what I'm thinking?" she asked her sister.

"It's time for some serious cleaning." Ava hoisted her mop.

Rae nodded grimly. "Let's do this."

30.
CADEN

"Are you sure your mom won't mind dropping me off?" Caden asked Vivienne as they waited in front of the school.

"You only live a few minutes away. Of course she won't mind." Vivienne pulled on the straps of her backpack and shuffled her feet back and forth, not making any eye contact. It was like she wasn't sure how to act around him now.

He felt the same way. He kept picturing how her face looked wet with tears, and it made him feel strangely off-balance. It was a whole different side to Vivienne, a side he hadn't even suspected existed. He'd always assumed her life was great since she was popular, smart, athletic . . . he'd thought she was happy. And this whole year, she'd been carrying around a fear so dark and terrifying even *he* didn't want to think about it too hard.

He knew what it felt like to be afraid of yourself. Of what you might become. But at least he had control over himself. She had nothing—nothing except a magic amulet and an unreliable promise from Patrick.

Caden thought of his own promise to her and hoped he'd be able to keep it.

"There she is," Vivienne said as a sleek gray car pulled up. "Finally."

Caden noticed a dent in the front bumper. It seemed strangely out of character, considering what he knew of Mrs. Matsuoka. It was like walking into a beautifully maintained house and then discovering a hole in the kitchen wall. "What happened to your car?"

"Oh, Mom swerved to avoid a deer last weekend and ended up kissing a tree. She's okay," Vivienne hurriedly added. "She was a little shaken up when she got home that night, but she said the damage is just cosmetic, not structural. She's been really busy since then, and my dad is still out of town, so . . ." Vivienne shrugged. "It'll get fixed eventually."

Mrs. Matsuoka opened her door and stood, her eyes meeting Caden's. Terror sliced through her, sharp and sudden. "What are you doing?" She stepped back, her gaze flicking between him and Vivienne. "I did what you asked!"

"What?" Caden didn't understand, and her anguish felt like a million little knives slashing at him, making it hard to focus.

"Uh, Mom?" Vivienne said gently. "This is my friend Caden. I was hoping we could give him a ride home?"

"Caden?" Mrs. Matsuoka peered at him, then forced a laugh. "I'm so sorry. I thought you were someone else."

"Who?" Vivienne asked.

Her mom rubbed her eyes. "Oh, no one. I'm having one of those days."

"I think you need a vacation."

"Wouldn't that be nice?" Mrs. Matsuoka pasted a wide smile on her face. It looked about as sincere as one of Patrick's promises. "I'd be happy to give you a ride, Caden."

"Thank you." Caden slipped into the back. Vivienne followed him, setting her backpack between them.

On the drive Mrs. Matsuoka kept sneaking glances at Caden through the rearview mirror. Now that her panic had ebbed, he sensed something beneath it. An emotion almost as strong, pulsing in sluggish green-brown waves like a moss-choked pond. Guilt, or shame, maybe? It was hard to tell between the two.

He tried picturing Mrs. Matsuoka visiting his mom and then, abruptly, he remembered Aiden's story. How someone at Green On! had helped him escape. He caught her gaze in the mirror, holding it for a second before she looked away. And he knew. He wasn't sure how, but he did.

She was the one who'd helped Aiden get away from the lab.

He wondered how she had known about his brother's kidnapping; he didn't get the impression that her department worked much with Patrick's. But maybe she'd been involved somehow, possibly as part of the deal she'd made with Patrick for Vivienne's elixir. And maybe she'd felt guilty about her role, and that was why she'd freed Aiden.

And maybe that was the real reason Patrick had stopped giving Vivienne her elixir.

It was a lot of maybes. Caden wished he could ask her about it, but he wasn't even sure where he'd begin.

She pulled up in front of his house without needing his address. But then, of course she knew where he lived. He was the son of the resident ghost hunter. "Thanks for the ride." He glanced at Vivienne. "See you tomorrow?"

"I sure hope so." She grinned at him, and it was almost normal between them again. Only the lightest touch of awkwardness.

Caden got out and waited until the car pulled away again before he started walking up his driveway.

His dad's car was still gone.

Caden frowned. His parents had to be back by now. Maybe his dad had gone out somewhere again? He fished out his key and unlocked the front door, then walked inside, stopping just in the doorway.

The energy in the house felt all wrong, as musty and unmoving as if no one had lived here for years. He knew immediately that something was wrong.

His mom had taught him it was dangerous to stand in a doorway for too long, so he made himself take a step inside, and another, quietly shutting the door behind him. He slipped off his shoes and his backpack, leaving them in the landing area before walking into the kitchen. Empty. He glanced at the table where his mom usually left notes. Nothing.

But then he noticed that the table seemed different. Like it had been moved a few inches, the chairs scattered. He turned slowly. Two of the cupboards hung open slightly, like someone had gone through all of the shelves.

Caden went cold all over. He took the stairs two at a time. "Aiden?" He couldn't tell if his brother was there or not. *That company owns this town. They can do anything they like with impunity. What if they change their minds about Aiden and demand we give him back?* His dad had been worried about Green On!, despite Aiden's and Patrick's supposed "understanding." Maybe it was for good reason.

Aiden had only been home a few days. And Caden had spent all of that time avoiding him as much as possible. What if he was gone again, this time for good? Caden pictured the fortress that was Green On!, with its security detail and cameras and cement outer walls. If they decided to take Aiden back, there would be no way to fight them. Who would believe the Prices if it was their word against the people of Green On!, the largest employer in Whispering Pines, the company that funded the local schools, contributed to the chief of police's reelection campaign, provided free energy to those who opted into their programs?

"Aiden!"

Sick with worry, Caden yanked open his brother's door. Empty. Reluctantly Caden did a quick check of his own room—also empty—and his parents' room. No one there at all. He closed their door and leaned against it, trying to calm himself down, the panic expanding in his chest like a soap bubble.

He pulled out his phone and called his mom. It went straight to voicemail. Again. He dialed his dad next. Same thing. He even tried Aiden's new phone. Voicemail.

Caden shoved his phone into his back pocket with shaky fingers. He wasn't sure what to do.

He could try Rae. She always seemed to have a plan. Not necessarily a good plan, like the time she'd suggested they break into a therapist's house, but right now he needed something. Anything.

He slowly crossed the hall and walked down the stairs, a small niggling doubt poking into his bubble of worry.

Maybe Aiden hadn't been taken at all.

His brother had been strangely accepting of the loss of his powers, yet still eager to learn more about the safeguards that kept some great evil imprisoned in the rift. Plus he'd been reading books on the history of Whispering Pines ever since he got back. Clearly, he was looking for something. A way to get his magic back.

Maybe he'd found it.

Caden slowly walked down the hall and opened the door to his mom's study, bracing himself for what he'd see. At first, it looked as untouched as the bedrooms upstairs. But as he wandered through, he noticed that there were several things missing. His mom's large silver ritual bowl, all her tea candles, some incense, and chalk.

Caden sank onto the end of the bed, the dread he'd been ignoring for days rising up to choke him. And for the first time, he wondered if his parents were really at a relationship workshop or if their absence was due to something far more sinister.

31.

RAE

Rae sagged against the wall, exhausted and sweaty and dirty and yuck. "I feel like the business end of a mop."

"I know what you mean." Ava leaned next to her. "I could take a thousand showers and still be dirty, I just know it."

"At least the house is clean."

"Cleanest house ever."

"Mom is gonna be surprised."

"Yep." Ava glanced at the clock. "It's almost midnight. We should probably finish up and get to bed."

"I call shower first."

Ava sighed. "Fine. But only if you check on *them*."

Rae knew exactly what her sister meant by "them." They'd managed to catch three of the centipedes alive, trapping them inside a large glass bowl turned upside down and placed on top of a cookie sheet. Ava had fetched a heavy rock from outside and put it on top of the bowl to hold it in place. "Why?" Rae whined. "They're fine!"

She'd seen enough of the ugly little things to last a lifetime; in addition to the three they'd trapped, they'd killed another five. The citrus spray hadn't done anything but make the house smell nice, so Ava had gone searching in the garage and found some Raid. They'd thought that would do the trick, but it had as much effect as the other sprays, barely slowing the bugs down. So they'd resorted to physical violence, squashing the bugs with a mop, a shoe, and, in one horrifyingly disgusting case, the bottom of Rae's foot; she put boots on after that. She just hoped that was all of them. They'd been thorough in their cleaning efforts, but those creepy-crawlies were fast and sneaky.

"What if they eat through the bowl? Didn't that happen with your friend Vivienne?"

"Yeah, but that was a water bottle with a plastic lid. This is glass."

"Just check, okay? I'll sleep better."

Rae pushed herself to her feet, still grumbling, and stomped over to the kitchen. She peered in at the glass, then frowned. "Ava? You might want to see this."

"Oh no!" Ava rushed in. "Did they get out?"

"No. I think . . . I think they died." One of the insects had curled into a little ball. The other was stretched out on its back, legs sticking up. And the third . . . the third was in oozing pieces. As if the first two had ripped it apart.

Rae tapped the glass with her nail. Nothing happened. "Do

you think they suffocated?" It made her feel strangely guilty. Even if they were flesh-eating insects.

"No," Ava said. "There's enough air in there for them."

"Starved?"

"Same thing. Shouldn't have been so fast."

"Hmm." Rae had no other ideas. Nate might know more. He'd stayed behind yesterday to study at the lab, and he'd skipped school today to do more research. She collected her cell phone and punched in his number.

Nate picked up on the third ring. "What happened?" he demanded, his voice high and anxious.

"I had a question about the bugs."

"A question?" Nate said slowly.

"Yeah. A research question."

"Nothing life or death?"

"Not yet, at any rate," Rae said.

Silence. Then, "Do you have any idea what time it is?"

Rae checked her phone. "Eleven fifty-eight p.m."

"So you do know."

"Uh, yeah . . ."

"Then why, oh why, would you call me at this hour for a research question? You almost gave me a heart attack! I thought those bugs had eaten Vivienne or something."

"Not as far as I know."

"I'm hanging up."

"Wait, Nate. Sorry, you're right, I should have waited until tomorrow. It's just, I found some of those bugs in my house. And I started worrying that maybe they've already spread all over."

"I found a few in my house too," Nate said quietly. "But before you panic, I believe the ones currently skittering through our respective houses are merely hitchhikers, thanks to our trek through the tunnels."

"Panicking anyhow," Rae muttered.

"I'm calling these small pale ones the workers. Their job, as far as Doctor Nguyen and I have been able to determine, is to modify the makeup of their environment."

"To do what now?"

Nate sighed, loudly and deeply. "They are transforming the soil to make it friendlier for their kind."

Rae still wasn't sure exactly what that meant, but clearly Nate was already on edge. "Okay," she said. "I guess."

"And they require a specific kind of organic material to do this."

Rae thought of the dead animals she'd found. "Flesh."

"Exactly. Plant matter doesn't seem to cut it."

"Well, that's horrifying."

"However, much like the common fruit fly, these smaller workers seem to die within a day or two."

"Oh! That's good!"

"Yeah, *that's* good."

Rae really didn't like the way he'd said that. "What's the not-good part, then?"

Nate sighed. "I was going to give you and Vivienne the full report tomorrow."

"Want to just give me the highlights now? I won't be able to sleep otherwise."

"Fine. You remember the one we caught in the lab?"

"No, I've forgotten," Rae muttered.

"If you're going to be sarcastic, I'm leaving."

"Sorry, sorry. Please continue."

"As I was saying. Those bugs weren't queens at all, but rather males, as far as we could determine. Their job appears to be incapacitating larger prey and then dragging it off to the nest, where the queen will shove her eggs inside to produce more males that will continue repeating that gruesome process."

Rae wrinkled her nose, trying not to imagine how she had almost been "incapacitated" by one of them.

"These males will continue growing until they're killed. The one we caught in the lab is already twice as big as it was, and I haven't seen it eat anything."

Rae slowly sank down onto the floor, the phone pressed to her ear.

"I could be wrong on this—I'm presenting my findings to Patrick tomorrow at school—but I believe at this time there is only one queen. She probably stays very near the nest. However, I think that these bugs are preparing to swarm soon."

"Swarm?"

"Like a honeybee hive. Once it gets large enough, it produces a second queen. That queen takes half the hive and sets up base somewhere else, and the cycle continues."

"Oh, great."

"Like I said, I could be totally wrong. But . . . I don't think I am." He yawned. "I need to get some sleep. We can talk about it in the morning, okay? Patrick called a meeting for first period after homeroom."

"Okay."

"And you owe me for the emergency call."

"I owe you," Rae agreed.

"I mean, honestly you're lucky I even picked up."

"I know, I know. And I promise if you ever call me, even if it's in the middle of the night, I'll pick up too, okay?"

"You'd better." And he hung up.

Rae stared at the upside-down bowl and the dead bugs and thought of the noises she had heard, deep down in the tunnels. The sound of something very large crashing after them. Had that been the queen?

From above she heard water running. Ava had totally snaked the shower. "Hey! Cheater!" she yelled, all thoughts of bugs vanishing as she sprang to her feet and dashed up the stairs.

32.

CADEN

Caden didn't think he'd be able to sleep, but as soon as he closed his eyes, the dread that had been bubbling in his stomach seemed to expand and suck him under. And the dream began.

He was in the Watchful Woods, slices of moonlight hitting his face through the branches, the smell of damp earth and moss and the sharp, sweet scent of pine filling his nostrils. Just ahead, the trees opened up to reveal that old, rotting cabin, paint curling down the sides in long, messy strips, the front porch sagging as if crushed beneath an invisible weight.

Caden was drawn to the cabin like a fish on a line, pulled inexorably forward, the door bursting open before he touched it. Inside, at first all he could see was dark. But slowly his eyes adjusted to the lighting, picking out details. There was the couch, pushed all the way to the side to leave the room bare. There was the fireplace, lying cold and empty, the mantel above it where the Unseeing had kept its jar of stolen eyes.

A whimper from the back corner, where the darkest shadows collected. Caden turned, the movement slow and drawn out in the way of dreams. He already knew what he would see.

Rae, her back to the wall, her hands up defensively. He couldn't see her face well in the gloom, but he recognized those large doe eyes now full of terror. And standing over her, the Unseeing, its silhouette taller than Caden remembered, more humanlike.

He could hear Aiden's voice, just like he'd heard it the night he confronted the Unseeing. *"The rift! You need to open it now! It's her best chance."*

Caden began reaching for the energies of the house, then stopped. Why was he having this dream now? Rae was safe, the Unseeing sealed back inside the Other Place where it belonged. But this didn't feel like a memory.

It felt like a prophetic dream. Only . . . not quite. Something was off.

The Unseeing turned and looked at him, and it was wearing Aiden's face and Aiden's smile. *"I knew you'd figure it out,"* it said with Aiden's voice. *"Better hurry if you want to save her."*

"Save her?" Caden frowned. "From what? You're gone."

"Am I?"

And Caden realized it wasn't the Unseeing at all. It never had been.

Aiden grinned. Then he pulled a familiar long, white bone-handled knife out of his pocket and lunged at Rae.

Caden sat up in bed, panting. His shirt clung to his sweaty back like the spiderwebs in the woods. It took him several long moments to get his heart rate and breathing under control. He kept seeing Rae's panicked face as Aiden lunged for her with their mother's knife . . .

Better hurry if you want to save her.

Caden went cold all over. That had felt like a message. A threat from his missing brother.

There was one way to know for sure.

Caden kicked off his blankets and raced out of the room, taking the stairs down two at a time. It was later than he'd thought, the morning light already trickling over the horizon, sliding warm fingers through the windows in the kitchen as he ran past.

He barely slowed when he reached his mom's study, shoving open the door and leaping over the barrier of her protective chalk line, and going straight to the small bedside dresser. When he threw open the top drawer, he froze.

The bone-handled knife was gone. Instead, a card sat there, covered in his brother's looping purple script:

Meet me in the woods.
You know the place.

—A

33.
RAE

Rae's phone vibrated angrily from her nightstand. Still half asleep, she fumbled for it, her muscles groaning in protest after the events of the last few days. Between the tunnel climbing and the housecleaning, she was sore all over.

"Hello," she mumbled.

"Rae? Are you okay? What's going on?"

The voice sounded so panicky that Rae had to glance at the name on her phone. "Caden?" He never sounded like that. "I'm fine. Why?"

Silence.

"Is there a reason I shouldn't be?" she asked cautiously.

"Oh, no, not at all." Now he sounded too casual. It made Rae extra nervous.

"Caden—" she began.

"Hey, I'm not going to be at school today. But I don't want you to worry. Everything's fine."

She frowned at her phone. "Obviously everything isn't, or . . ." She finally noticed the time and practically fell out of bed. "Oh no! My alarm didn't go off!" Patrick had called a meeting after homeroom. She could *not* be late to school today. Still. "Are you sure you don't need my help with anything?" The internship was important, but Caden was her friend. If he was in trouble, that took priority.

"No, I'm okay. I'll call you later, all right?" He hung up.

Rae stared at her phone for a second, troubled. But she really didn't have time to worry about him now. She pulled on the first clothes she could find, yelling for Ava.

No answer.

"Ava! I need a ride! Please, please, pretty please?" She banged on Ava's door. Still no response. "Ava?" Rae pushed the door open. Her sister wasn't there. But then Rae remembered that their mom had the car today. The high school bus came earlier; Ava must have caught that. She'd left all her school papers scattered, though, several pages blowing across her desk from the open window.

Rae dashed inside and shoved the window shut, locking it, then ran to the bathroom to finish getting ready. She managed to jab herself in the throat with her toothbrush and didn't have time to brush her hair, just grabbed her bag and sprinted for the door.

She barely caught the bus in time, sliding in next to Vivienne as it rolled away.

"Where's Caden?" Vivienne asked.

"He's not coming today. Also, good morning to you, too."

Vivienne laughed. "Sorry. Nice look, by the way. I like the hair."

Rae's hand went to her tangled locks. "I slept through my alarm," she admitted. If Caden hadn't called, she might've missed the bus entirely. "Pretty sure this is not going to be my best day ever."

"Especially not when Alyssa sees you."

Rae groaned. "I don't suppose you carry a brush in that monstrosity?" She poked Vivienne's backpack, wedged between them.

Vivienne grinned. "It's your lucky day."

Rae seriously doubted that, but she took the brush and hoped it would be true. She had a feeling she was going to need a little luck before this day was through. As she brushed her hair, she surreptitiously studied her friend.

It was hard not to remember what Vivienne had looked like at Green On!, standing over Priceless Art. Rae opened her mouth to ask her about it, then stopped. What would she say? *Uh, so I noticed you were drinking goat blood. What's up with that, by the way?* Even by Whispering Pines standards, that sounded too insane. Sitting here, on a bus surrounded by people, it just didn't seem like something she could ask.

Besides, Caden had promised to look into it. Maybe she should wait until she talked to him first.

Rae worked the remaining tangles out of her hair and stayed quiet. For now.

As Rae sat through the morning's announcements in homeroom, she couldn't stop thinking about Caden. He'd sounded so scared when he called her. She should have insisted on finding out why, instead of worrying about catching the bus.

"And finally, Dana S. students, some terrible news," Ms. Lockett said over the loudspeaker. "I have just been informed that we have another code yellow. Curfew will be enforced. All after-school activities will be temporarily postponed."

It felt like a terrible omen. Rae glanced at Vivienne, who looked as worried as she felt. "You don't think Caden—"

"No," Rae said quickly. "I talked to him this morning."

But code yellow meant *someone* was missing.

Alyssa leaned in close to Rae and Vivienne. "My mom told me Coach Briggs didn't show up for work yesterday," she said quietly. "And no one knows where she is today."

"Oh no!" Vivienne said.

Several kids turned to look at them.

"Shh," Alyssa hissed. "No one's supposed to know about it yet."

"Why not?" Rae asked. "Isn't that the point of a code yellow?"

"Code yellow is only for students," Vivienne said. "Missing teachers get a different code."

"Shouldn't that alert be going out, then? If Coach Briggs is . . ." Rae couldn't bring herself to say it.

"Like I said, no one's supposed to know yet," Alyssa said firmly. "We don't want a panic."

The bell rang, and Rae gathered up her stuff, her stomach twisting. Another student had gone missing. It felt like a repeat of her first day at school, when kids were vanishing only to be discovered later with their eyes torn out. And a teacher had vanished too? She thought Alyssa was wrong; a panic was definitely in order.

She, Vivienne, and Alyssa were the first ones in the old science room, but Becka and Matt soon joined them.

"How's your assignment going?" Becka asked.

"Oh, really good. Amazingly," Vivienne said. "We have this in the bag."

Becka smirked. "That's not what I heard."

Rae and Vivienne looked at Alyssa, who went pink. "What? I didn't say anything!"

"You must have heard from an unreliable source," Vivienne told Becka.

"I guess we'll see," Becka said. "Rumor has it Patrick is choosing the winners today."

Rae shot Vivienne a questioning look as Becka, Alyssa, and Matt took their places at the other table.

"News to me," Vivienne whispered.

The door swung open, and Nate staggered in and flopped into the seat next to Vivienne, clearly exhausted.

"Wow, you look terrible," Rae said.

"Yeah, well, you have toothpaste on your shirt."

Rae glanced down. "Dang it."

"Sorry, I didn't have the heart to tell you," Vivienne said.

"And neither did Alyssa. Very unlike her." Rae glanced at the other girl, who was anxiously whispering with Becka and Matt. Had they really discovered the secret behind Whispering Pines's stone wall?

"*Someone*," Nate continued, "decided to give me a midnight wake-up call. I couldn't go back to sleep after that."

"Oh. Sorry, Nate. Didn't mean to *bug* you."

Nate sighed. "That was terrible."

"Hey, I've been thinking about the spaceship," Vivienne said. "Would bugs be able to fly that thing?"

"Of course not," Nate said.

"Then what did?"

Rae frowned, realizing what Vivienne meant. It was so obvious, she couldn't believe she hadn't wondered the same thing. "What else is on that ship?" Something else must have come to their planet with the centipedes. Something that Green On!, and Patrick, were keeping secret and possibly hidden away in one of their underground labs. She pictured the alien her dad had photographed.

"One mystery at a time, folks," Nate said. "Let's focus on the bugs first, okay?"

"Hello, interns," Patrick announced, striding into the room, his suit crisp, his hair perfect. "I see we're missing someone."

Rae glanced around and realized Blake wasn't there, his usual chair between Alyssa and Matt sitting empty.

"Blake is checking on his uncle," Becka said. "Apparently no one has seen him in a few days?"

"Hmm. That's unfortunate," Patrick said, but he didn't sound too bothered by it.

Rae exchanged a worried look with Vivienne and Nate and was sure they were thinking of that empty yurt, that open goat pen. What if Gary hadn't just moved away?

Patrick's phone went off, the soft nondescript ringtone filling the science room. He picked it up and listened a moment without saying a word, then hung up.

"Wrong number?" Nate asked.

"Something like that." Patrick smiled around the room. "I have been very impressed by all of your efforts this week, both in this classroom, learning how to take proper samples and work in a hazmat suit, and in your chosen tasks. Our initial training phase will be coming to an end soon, as I plan to choose my winning team . . . today."

Becka shot Rae and Vivienne a small, triumphant look.

"Whatever," Vivienne muttered.

"You will each have one final task," Patrick said. "Whoever completes theirs first wins. Simple, right?"

Rae very much doubted that.

"Ms. Wilson, Ms. Lockett, Mr. Garcia. Please wait outside while I speak with the other team first." Patrick waited until they were gone, his arms crossed, one foot tapping slowly and methodically, like a clock. When they were alone, he said, "Mr. Cliff has done some truly remarkable work in the lab these last few days, studying our specimen, taking soil samples, creating a solid hypothesis."

"Nice job, Nate," Vivienne whispered.

"Not just nice," Rae said. "Truly remarkable."

"Thanks." Nate beamed.

"If you're quite done?" Patrick raised his eyebrows.

"Sorry," they all muttered, grinning.

"After perusing Mr. Cliff's work, I must agree with his conclusion that Whispering Pines is in the midst of an infestation. One that could become deadly, if not dealt with immediately. But I am also convinced that there is an easy solution."

"And what's that?" Nate asked.

"Isn't it obvious? Kill the queen."

"What about the males?" Nate frowned.

"I believe—and Doctor Nguyen does as well—that, like the smaller worker versions, they will die soon once the queen is dead."

"How are you going to kill the queen?" Nate asked.

"Me?" Patrick laughed. "Mr. Cliff, this is *your* task. It will be up to your group to take care of this."

There was a moment of shocked silence. "You want *us* . . . to go into the tunnels and kill the queen?" Vivienne asked slowly.

"And destroy her nest, too, if you can."

Nate exploded up from his seat. "No," he said. "No way!"

"Mr. Cliff—"

"I can't . . . I can't go down there again." Nate was shaking all over.

"Yeah, this seems a little extreme for a middle school internship," Rae said.

"Ms. Carter, what if I were to tell you that I've discovered the answer to your question?"

Rae blinked. "My dad?" she whispered, ignoring Vivienne's quizzical look. She had never told Vivienne about her missing father. "You know where he is?"

"I do."

Rae's vision went blurry with unshed tears. Her dad. "Is he alive? Is he safe?"

"I will tell you everything I know. *After* this current problem is dealt with." His expression softened. "But yes, he's alive, and safe."

"Then where—"

"After, Ms. Carter. You have my word."

Rae felt her face going hot, her eyes threatening to spill over. She blinked rapidly. Her dad was alive and safe. She had to believe Patrick was telling her the truth.

"And Ms. Matsuoka. I have a solution to your problem, too."

"A cure? A real cure?"

Now it was Rae's turn to stare at Vivienne's profile. A cure for what?

"I don't believe in fake cures." Patrick chuckled.

"And what about me?" Nate demanded, crossing his arms. "What could you possibly offer me that would get me to go back into that dark underground hellhole filled with killer bugs?"

Patrick spread his hands wide. "Exactly what you have been looking for from this internship. A full-ride scholarship to the university of your choice. And it would be *your* choice, Mr. Cliff. I am very well connected. Just say the word, and you will be accepted anywhere."

Nate stared at him. And then he shook his head. "No school is worth dying over. And no amount of money is either." He looked at Rae and Vivienne, almost like he was willing them to rise in protest with him.

But Rae knew she couldn't. She had to do whatever it took to find her dad. And Vivienne wasn't standing either.

"Fine." Nate backed away. "You'll have to do this without me."

"I thought you hated social loafers," Vivienne said.

"This is not just some group science project anymore. This is insanity!" He turned on Patrick, desperate. "Why us? Why not a team of highly trained adults?"

"Because, Mr. Cliff, I believe in all of you. As I've said before, you children are the ones who will save this world. You see things that others just walk on past. You noticed these bugs first, and I have every faith in your abilities to handle them."

Those words spread through Rae's chest, warm and validating. Until Patrick added, "Also, the tunnels are a little narrow for adults."

34.
CADEN

Caden had watched Rae board the bus, comforting himself with the knowledge that she should at least be safe for now, but that did nothing to quench the gnawing feeling in the pit of his stomach. He had to get to the cabin. Whatever his brother was up to, Caden was sure it would be bad news for everyone else.

He grabbed extra purification salt, a flashlight, and two granola bars. At the last minute he also took the rose quartz his mom had been using in their training sessions together, tucking it safely into his pocket before heading for the waiting trees of the Watchful Woods.

The woods didn't seem nearly so scary with sunlight streaming all around him, and his hike was pretty uneventful, other than getting turned around twice. The stone wall had shifted again, and it took Caden a bit to figure out where he needed to go. But eventually the trees opened up, revealing the cabin from his dream.

He never thought he'd see it again. It looked just as he remembered it from his first—and only—time opening a rift into the Other Place. He'd been successful then. He wasn't sure he would be as lucky this time.

He left the false safety of the trees and walked across the overgrown yard to the porch. The rotting boards moaned and shrieked under his feet, but when he tried the front door, it swung open easily.

"Hello?" Caden called. "Aiden?"

He thought he could hear something moving inside, but no one answered. Tentatively he let his awareness float gently outward like a dandelion seed on the wind.

Immediately he sensed that deep, consuming nothing that marked his brother. Only it seemed larger now, as if it had expanded to fill the entire house.

Caden pulled the flashlight out of his backpack and turned it on, the cheerful glow oozing into the dark. He stepped forward, leaving the door open behind him. In the living room, the old battered couch had been pushed to the side, just like in his dream, its hulking shape hidden in the shadows, and the fireplace was cold and bare. But on the mantel above it, in the place where he'd once seen a jar full of eyes, sat a few candles.

He recognized them. His mother's good ones, the ones she only used for her biggest spells.

Something on the couch whimpered, and he turned back, shining his light on it.

Three people sat huddled together on the cushions, their mouths hanging loose—and the holes where their eyes should be huge and black and empty.

The flashlight toppled from Caden's numb fingers and rolled across the uneven floor, its beam illuminating slices of the room, other faces, other empty eyes.

Gasping, he dove for the light, clutching it in shaky hands. "B-Brandi? Jeremy?" He recognized them as two of the victims of the Unseeing. Neither of them responded. He swept his light around the whole room, counting the others.

Eight. All of the kids the Unseeing had attacked.

Slowly they all turned toward him, the caverns of their gaping eye sockets drinking in the light. The one closest to him—a girl with long blond hair—stood. "Eyes," she said, her voice a low, deep growl. She took a lurching step forward, her hands extending.

Caden inched back toward the door, horror gripping his heart in icy claws.

Jeremy stumbled to his feet, his own empty eyes fixing on Caden. "Lovely eyes," he mumbled, shuffling closer.

"Lovely, lovely eyes," the others echoed, all of them swaying in unison, taking small, uneven steps toward Caden, their hands reaching.

Caden tried keeping the light on all of them at once as he backed up, his other hand clutching his pendant protectively.

"Hello, little brother," Aiden said from behind him.

Caden spun.

Aiden stood framed in the doorway, blocking him in.

"What are you—" Caden began, just as Aiden flung his hands up.

A wave of darkness slammed into Caden, and he fell backward, pinned beneath it. Just as consciousness slipped away, Caden heard the sound of a phone ringing. *Huh,* he thought. *A working phone in the Watchful Woods.* Despite everything, it seemed the most surprising development of the day. Aiden's voice said, "Everything is in place," as the darkness seeped behind Caden's eyes and soaked into his mind, turning it the peaceful black of an ocean at night.

35.

RAE

Rae wanted to ask Vivienne about Patrick's cure, and her blood drinking, and if they were related. But she was afraid she'd then have to tell Vivienne about her dad. She'd gotten so used to keeping that a secret that it was hard to picture sharing it now.

She'd told Caden, though. And he'd believed her.

Rae glanced sidelong at Vivienne, who was flipping through pages in the bug book, trying to come up with a battle plan. What they were about to do was very dangerous. Maybe it was time to take all their secrets out of their hiding places and put them in the open. "Vivi—"

"Your phone is ringing," Vivienne said.

"What?" Rae listened, and heard the faint vibration now too. She dug it out of her backpack and flipped it open. "Hello?"

"Do you ever pick up your phone?" Nate sounded halfway to

panic mode, so Rae resisted any sarcasm. "You and Vivienne need to get here fast."

"I thought he quit," Vivienne said.

"I didn't quit, I just . . . protested."

"I think he can hear you," Rae said in a stage whisper.

"Of course I can hear her. It's not like Vivienne talks quietly."

"Ouch!" Vivienne said. "You wound me, Mr. I-quit-but-don't-want-to-admit-it."

"Tell Vivienne that that name is ridiculous!"

"Nate says that name is ridiculous," Rae said.

"Yeah. I heard. He's loud too." Vivienne smirked. "Tell him I said so."

"Vivienne says you're—"

"Stop," Nate said. "Just stop."

Rae was pretty sure she could hear him grinding his teeth, and grinned. It felt good after all the stress of the day to annoy Nate. "So what do you want?" she asked.

"Is Caden with you?"

Rae's grin slipped away. "No." She'd tried calling him the moment she got out of school, but it went straight to voicemail, and the windows of his house were all shuttered and dark. "It's just me and Vivi."

"I always suspected that Caden was smarter than he let on." Nate took a deep, noisy breath. "You know how I live near the Town Square?"

"Yeah . . ."

"Well, Blake is my neighbor. Technically not my actual neighbor; he's a few streets down. But close."

"Okay . . ." Rae felt like Nate was stalling. It made her nervous.

"I thought I'd check on him when I got home. You know, because it's a code yellow, and last time he vanished he ended up living in a yurt in the woods with his curmudgeonly uncle. I wouldn't wish that fate on anyone."

"Get to the point, Nate."

"He's gone."

"Gone?" Rae said. "Like . . . missing?"

"Well . . . not exactly, no. Because I think I know where he is."

Rae was afraid she might know where Blake was too. She swallowed. "So, you've figured out where the nest is?"

Nate was silent for a long moment. Then, "Yeah," he whispered. "I think so. Meet me over here?"

"We'll be right there." Rae hung up. "We need to get to the townhomes by the mall."

"Will your sister take us again?"

Rae frowned. "You know, it's weird she hasn't gotten home yet. She doesn't usually stay late at school. But she wouldn't have the car anyhow. My mom took it to work."

"Bike?"

"I think that's our best option. I'm sure Ava won't mind if you borrow hers. I'll just leave her a note." Rae thought of her sister and how mad she'd be if she knew they were chasing after another alien bug. "You know, maybe I won't," Rae decided. She didn't want her sister to worry. "Let me grab a few things, and let's go."

They biked fast and hard, Rae following Vivienne down side roads and over hills. By the time they approached the Town Square, Rae was hot and sweaty. They slowed down, circling around to the nearby townhouses. Nate was already waiting for them at the bottom of one of the driveways.

"Finally!" he exploded.

"Easy there, Nate." Vivienne hopped off her bike and stood next to it, casual and not at all tired. Rae got off her own bike more slowly. "We're here now."

"Yeah, but I wanted you here thirty-five minutes ago."

Rae glanced at her phone. "You only called me twenty minutes ago."

"Actually it was twenty-eight."

Vivienne rolled her eyes. "The point still stands. How could we have been here thirty-five minutes ago, if you only called us in the last half hour?"

Nate adjusted his glasses. "Twenty-eight minutes. And I said I wanted you here, not that I expected you here."

Vivienne sighed deeply. "Are you sure you don't want to quit again?"

"I told you, I was just protesting. This, what they have us doing, is not normal. You do see that, right? They want us to go into a tunnel and fight a giant alien bug. And we're twelve."

"I'm thirteen," Vivienne said.

"Oh, well, I guess it's okay then," Nate muttered.

"What did you want to show us?" Rae asked. She knew Nate was right. There was something about this town that almost made her forget what normal really was, but regardless, she had accepted this mission. Not just so Patrick would tell her where to find her dad, but also because, if there was a chance that she could help Blake, she had to take it. She'd been too late to save her neighbor or Jeremy Bentley from the Unseeing, but she had to believe that this time she'd succeed.

"Follow me." Nate led them past all the blue-gray townhouses, their pointed roofs and fake-shutter windows all alike, until they reached a small cul-de-sac lined with a final row of townhouses. Beyond them stood a copse of trees.

"The Town Square is through those." Nate pointed at the trees.

"So that's where the ground caved in?" Rae asked.

"Yes," Nate said.

Rae was beginning to get a terrible feeling about all this.

"Did you call Patrick?" Vivienne asked.

"I texted Doctor Nguyen," Nate said.

Vivienne nodded. "Almost as good."

Rae thought Doctor Nguyen might actually be a lot better. She seemed like she wanted to protect her young interns, while Patrick was content to use them like playing pieces on some warped game of life.

"Blake lives in this one." Nate pointed to the townhouse that stood closest to those trees. He led them up its paved driveway and then around the side to a small fenced-in yard. Just past the little fence, inside the yard, there was a mound of loose dirt. "I spoke with his parents when I got here. That"—he pointed at the dirt—"is where they buried Waffles."

Rae stared at him. "Okay, I know this town has some weird customs, but I'm really not following how that's relevant."

Nate sighed. "Not the food. Waffles the goat. A few days ago, a 'wild animal' attacked him. Or at least, that's what they thought." He gave her a pointed look.

She got it. "Because the goat's stomach was ripped open."

"Exactly."

Rae felt sick as she imagined the scene. The bugs bursting forth, hiding nearby, coming back for Blake. If they were taking kids now, then all of Whispering Pines was in trouble.

"Alyssa told us that Blake was looking for his uncle, who went missing," Vivienne said.

"That's what his parents said too. He went out last evening and then never came back." Nate turned his back on the house. "There's something else you need to see." He led them across the grass and into the trees, stopping a few feet in and pointing at the largest bug skin Rae had ever seen. It had to be six feet long. And it was different from the others. Where the little ones had been a milky yellow-white, and the larger males had been a night-washed green, this one was almost the same color as the grass and dirt around it. Like it was camouflaged. "I think *that* might be from our queen."

Rae pictured something that size scuttling through the darkened tunnels beneath their feet. "So she does come above ground," she whispered.

"Probably has to, when it's time to molt."

Rae tried to remember what she had read about bugs and molting. Something about how they couldn't breathe while shedding their skin, and how that was a moment of weakness. Seemed like they'd missed an opportunity there. She ran a hand over her face, thinking hard. "If the queen came up above ground to molt, then her nest must be near here. Right?"

"That is the conclusion I reached," Nate said.

Rae had the sudden urge to climb a tree and never come down. Nate shuffled, looking like he had the same idea.

"And . . . if she's molting, does that mean she's getting ready to swarm?" Vivienne asked.

"Also probably accurate. Although technically I believe she would remain here, as the older queen, and the new one would swarm."

"No, actually, it's the old one that swarms, if they behave like bees," Rae said. "The younger one remains with the original nest."

Nate and Vivienne stared at her.

"You just out-Nated Nate," Vivienne said, holding her hand up for a high-five.

Rae gave it to her, grinning. But her grin fell away quickly as she gazed across the trees. She could just make out the spot where the ground was broken, the tunnel partially collapsed. Someone had cordoned off the area with orange cones and a bit of rope. Otherwise, it stood open and unguarded. "What did Doctor Nguyen say when you texted her?"

"She said Patrick was on his way." Nate sighed. "We're going to go in there, aren't we?"

Rae knew that if a second queen was born, and she started a new colony somewhere else, this infestation would double, and then quadruple, and pretty soon it would be unstoppable.

And then not just Blake but all of Whispering Pines would be in trouble. Maybe even the country. Maybe even the *world*.

"I think we have to," she said.

36.

CADEN

Caden woke slowly, his head throbbing. For one confused moment he thought he was home. But the light was wrong; he never slept by candlelight. It was too unreliable. And he wasn't in his bed, either. Instead, there was a cold hard surface beneath him. And someone was chanting.

Caden sat bolt upright, those last few moments before he fell unconscious catching up to him in a rush: the note, the eyeless horrors, Aiden, the crushing dark.

"So glad you've returned to the land of the living, little brother," Aiden said.

Caden blinked, warily taking in his surroundings. Aiden had drawn a pentagram—a five-pointed star—in the middle of a circle using some of their mom's thick chalk. The design created eleven spaces, all of them outlined in rows of small tea-light candles.

Caden was in the uppermost point of the star, while Aiden sat in the space between its two bottom legs. In every other space sat one of the Unseeing victims, silent and motionless as dolls, their legs crossed, hands in their laps, reflected candlelight flickering in their gaping eye sockets. And in the center, the spot reserved for the spell's focus—

Ava Carter, bound and gagged, her eyes wide with terror.

For half a second Caden could only stare at her. He'd thought it was *Rae* in danger. He'd never even considered . . .

Ava whimpered around her gag, and Caden burst to his feet, reaching for her.

A wall of fire erupted between them, the flames licking hungrily toward his skin. Ava cried out on the other side of it, and he stepped back, dropping his hands. The flames immediately ebbed.

"Uh-uh, Caden. If you want to rescue her, you'll have to do better than that," Aiden said.

Caden's fear uncurled like candle smoke. He looked past Ava at his brother, who sat calmly, cross-legged and relaxed. "What do you want?"

Aiden tilted his head, the light filling in the hollows of his cheeks, glinting in the dark of his eyes. "Why, I just want to live. Isn't that what anyone wants?"

"Then what's stopping you? Why do all this?" Caden indicated the pentagram, the eyeless ones, Ava.

"You asked me before how I survived." Aiden twirled that strange ring on his thumb. "Nine long months, trapped in a world filled with monsters that fed on my blood, that knew how to find me whenever they wanted. There was no escape. I would run until I couldn't anymore, and they would wait, and then they would find me, and they would feast. I couldn't die. They wouldn't let me. I couldn't live, because there is no life in that place. Not really. I could only . . . exist." His mouth twisted into a bitter curl. "I thought I was strong. But that place broke me."

Caden felt the tiniest surge of pity. But then he let his gaze shift from Aiden to Ava, and the pity was gone. "So how did you survive, then?" he asked coldly.

"I struck a deal."

Caden remembered the conversation he'd had with his mother, just before Aiden reappeared. When she'd explained the Other Place was meant to be a prison for something evil and indestructible. And Caden knew exactly who his brother had struck a deal with.

"And now . . ." Aiden slid their mother's knife out from behind him, its long slender blade catching the light. Their mom used it for her most dangerous and important rituals, so she kept it clean and very, very sharp. "It's time for me to fulfill my end."

"Why Ava?" Caden asked desperately. "What do you need her for?"

"She's here to ensure your good behavior, brother dear. You see, I realized that my own safety might not be enough to inspire you to act. Then I thought, maybe even our parents' safety wouldn't be enough. But a hostage? Right here in front of you? With your tender heart, that would do the trick." Aiden smiled and reached into Ava's space, stroking her cheek.

She flinched back, her eyes narrowing, and growled at him through her gag.

Aiden laughed. He hefted his knife, turning it so the candlelight gleamed along the edge of the metal. It looked like he was holding a blade of fire.

Ava made a small noise. She was bound so securely all she could do was twitch in place.

"If I cooperate with you, you'll let Ava go?" Caden asked.

"I will."

"Where are our parents?"

"Somewhere safe."

"Why don't I believe you?"

"I don't know. I've never lied to you."

"You said you didn't have your powers anymore."

"That wasn't a lie. This power here isn't mine. It's borrowed. Otherwise I would open the rift myself. Now. You know what I need you to do."

Caden's dream hadn't really been a message, but a trap. And he'd stumbled right into it. He thought of some way to stall, to save Ava, to escape. But he recognized the sealing spell his brother had done and knew there would be no way out until Aiden released him.

"Open the rift, little brother."

"And then what? Will this evil escape?" He made himself look at Ava. At her eyes, so similar to Rae's. At her trembling lips. He had his own shields up tight, but even so, he could feel her terror battering against them.

Rae had lost her father. If she lost her sister, it would destroy her. But . . . if saving her meant unleashing a terrible evil on the world, an evil that his family was bound to keep imprisoned, could he really live with himself? What if it murdered everyone he loved?

"I see your resolve is shaking," Aiden said. "Maybe I'd better inspire you." He lunged forward, grabbing Ava by the throat and dragging her closer, his knife point digging into the skin under her left eye.

"Don't!" Caden yelped. "I'll do it!"

It was the wrong choice. He was certain of it. But Aiden knew him well. He *was* too tenderhearted.

Aiden's grin was as sharp and wicked as the blade in his hand. "Excellent, little brother. Begin, if you would."

Caden let out a breath, ignoring Ava thrashing next to him, ignoring the screaming of his own consciousness, the feeling of strangeness in the air, the smell of smoke and incense and blood. He pushed it all from his mind. And let himself sink into the spell.

37.

RAE

Rae turned on her newly acquired headlamp, and its beam sliced through the darkness of the tunnel in front of her like a laser. "Whoa."

"Pretty cool, right?" Patrick said from above. She turned, and he immediately put a hand in front of his eyes. "Watch it!"

"Oh, sorry." Rae turned her headlamp off again. "It's a surprisingly hard habit to break."

"I'll just wait to turn mine on, then," Vivienne said. She stood next to Rae, all suited up and obviously eager to get to work.

Rae wished she had even half of Vivienne's confidence and enthusiasm. Rae's own stomach had gone right past knots and straight into the world's largest tangle, and she hoped she didn't throw up all over her fancy Green On! suit. It was a modified version of the hazmat suit Patrick had issued to them on their first day. Sleek and new, it hugged her body like some sort of futuristic wet suit and had apparently been equipped with technology that would allow Patrick to monitor her location in the caves and keep track of her heart rate and breathing.

Patrick had also included a more mundane survival kit in the front zippered pocket of each suit: bandages, gauze, a lighter, iodine pills for water treatment, a small emergency blanket, and a very loud whistle, like the kind lifeboats carried on the ocean. "Just in case" was all he had said about those items. Rae had stuffed her inhaler into the pocket with them and tried not to imagine being trapped down here in the dark, huddled under a foil blanket and attempting to purify cave water.

The only thing Rae liked about her new attire was the long, straight knife strapped to her left leg inside a faux-leather sheath, which made her feel like an action hero.

On her back she wore a slim plastic case like a pack. It connected to a nozzle that was fastened over her chest. Vivienne wore an identical version. It was the first time Rae had ever seen her friend without her giant backpack, not counting cross-country practices. "You were going to tell us about these," Rae called up to Patrick, tapping the nozzle.

"Oh, those are flamethrowers."

"Really?" Vivienne asked, all excited.

"No. I wanted to give you flamethrowers for this, but Doctor Nguyen vetoed that idea," Patrick said. "And what's the point of having a right-hand woman if you don't take her advice?"

Rae couldn't tell if he were joking or not. A flamethrower

probably would have worked on the bugs—she remembered the corpse they'd found in Gary the Goatman's old clearing, all burnt to a crisp—but it also probably would have killed them, too.

"Luckily, Green On! has been working on a new high-powered bug spray for the town. Nontoxic, naturally. As are all our products." He flashed a wide grin, as if he were performing an infomercial on live television. "We haven't had a chance to test it on these particular bugs yet, but I feel confident that it will work."

"I notice you're not coming down here with us," Rae said.

Vivienne elbowed her.

"What? It's true."

"Only because I have even more confidence in your abilities, Ms. Carter."

"It's just, I haven't had the best of luck with bug spray lately. Not with these things." Rae thought of her marathon cleaning session with Ava. All those bugs had seemed oddly resistant.

"Oh, but this is a special kind. Try it."

"Do I have a choice?"

Patrick gave her a wide smile. "That's the right attitude."

"Are you sure I shouldn't go too?" Nate asked. He stood above the tunnel next to Patrick, looking miserable.

Rae's heart surged with a rush of gratitude. She knew how much Nate did not want to go. The fact that he was willing to offer meant a lot.

"Unfortunately, we only have two of these suits ready. No, Mr. Cliff, I have another important task for you. Something more befitting your unique talents."

"Is that a nice way of saying I'm too much of a coward?" Nate asked.

"Not at all," Patrick said, but Nate's shoulders had slumped, his face red and mouth grim.

"Hey, Nate?" Vivienne called.

"Yeah?"

"Ergo."

"Ergo," Rae agreed.

Nate blinked. And then he laughed. "Ergo." His laugh hitched a little, and he added, "Be safe, okay?"

"We'll try," Rae said.

"You'd better get going," Patrick said. "You won't want to be in there when night falls."

"You'll help if we need it, though, right?" Rae asked, suddenly terrified that he might just leave them there.

"Oh, of course, of course. Don't worry, Ms. Carter. You're in good hands."

Rae was beginning to seriously doubt that, but she took a deep breath and stepped into the mouth of the tunnel anyhow.

She and Vivienne hadn't walked long before the light from above faded away behind them, leaving them trapped in darkness. Only their twin beams lit the path ahead, reflecting off yellowed bones wedged into the walls and ceiling and floor. A thigh bone here, a hand there. The occasional super-creepy skull.

The tunnel slowly slanted downward, the temperature dropping. Rae's nostrils filled with the smell of damp soil and the sickly sweet scent of decay. She was very conscious of the sound of her own breathing, and of Vivienne right behind her, their footsteps crunching softly, the gentle trickle of dirt disturbed by their passing.

At least she didn't have to worry about her headlamp burning out this time. Green On! would have taken care of that detail.

"Did you notice that all the dead animals were removed?" Vivienne asked.

Rae frowned. "I didn't, but you're right. Did Green On! do that?"

"I don't know. I hope it was them."

"I do too." Rae lapsed into silence, trying not to think about that giant bug exoskeleton, or the speed and ferocity of the centipede that had burst out of the goat. She kept hearing Nate's voice in her mind: *This, what they have us doing, is not normal.* Why, oh why, had she been willing to come down here herself? Ava would kill her if she knew.

After the whole incident in the cabin with the Unseeing, Rae had promised herself she would stop diving headfirst into things, and here she was anyhow. But if Patrick really knew where her dad was, then all of this would be worth it.

"Oh, actually, there's an animal," Vivienne said.

Rae spotted the large furry shape up ahead. It looked like a rat, but as they got closer, Rae noticed the bushy tail. "Is that a squirrel? It's huge! Like, the size of a skunk."

"I told you the squirrels around here are no joke." Vivienne grinned, the light from Rae's headlamp gleaming in her wide, excited eyes. And Rae was suddenly reminded of a time she went hiking with her dad back in California. They had miscalculated how long a loop would take and had ended up finishing after sunset. As they booked it to their car, they caught a glimpse of cat eyes staring down at them from the rocks overhead, intense and predatory, and Rae had suddenly realized how small and vulnerable she was.

She and her dad had never hiked so late in the day again.

And now she was trapped in a tunnel with someone who gave her that same uneasy feeling. It made her wonder how well she really knew Vivienne. She kept her hands at her sides, willing them not to shake. She didn't want to be afraid of her best friend. "Vivi, can I ask you something? About . . . about Emmett, and what really happened to him?"

Vivienne's smile fell away. "Did Caden tell you?"

"What?" Rae said. "No . . . should he have?"

Vivienne shook her head. "He promised he wouldn't. I just . . . I wasn't sure if he'd keep that promise."

"Caden?" Rae blinked. "Of course he'd keep it." She took a deep breath. "And if you don't want to tell me anything, I won't push. But, you know, I saw you drinking blood. And I've got to be honest, it's kind of freaking me out that you're pretending that was a normal thing and we're not talking about it."

Vivienne sighed. "Yeah, it's really not normal." She looked down at the mangled squirrel. "Let's walk, and I'll tell you everything, okay?"

"And Patrick was giving me an elixir that helped, until that day we were touring the lab and there was the false alarm," Vivienne said.

"And after that, nothing. I've been dealing with all the symptoms on my own."

"Wow." Rae swept her beam along the walls and across the floor as they walked. "That's pretty messed up."

"Which part?"

Rae thought about Vivienne's story. Cursed columns and bloodthirsty urges and Patrick's elixir. "All of it, really," she decided. "But especially Patrick. He just stopped helping you 'cause he was mad at your mom?"

"I'm not sure if that's it," Vivienne mumbled. "He said he wanted to make something better."

"Maybe he just wanted to see what would happen." Rae glanced at Vivienne. A girl who she now knew had superhuman speed and strength . . . and a taste for blood.

"This is why I didn't want to tell you," Vivienne said quietly.

"Why? Because it made me more critical of Patrick?"

"No. Because now you're afraid of me."

Rae was silent. She knew Vivienne was right, and it made her feel terrible. Was she really scared of Vivienne? Friendly, brave, funny Vivienne? Did knowing this secret about her really change anything?

She had her own secret too. It had cost her a friendship. Actually, all of her friendships. Even though she was still the same person, everyone at her last school had viewed her differently after word got out.

"I get it," Vivienne said. "I'd be freaked out about me too. After we get rid of these bugs, if you'd prefer not to hang out, then—"

"It's not like that," Rae said quickly. "Vivi, I'm . . . well, I'm a little scared. But not *of* you. Not really. I'm scared *for* you." She stopped walking, careful this time not to shine her light in Vivienne's eyes. "I'm sorry that happened. But you're my friend, and I trust you. This doesn't change that."

"It should. I ate a rabbit. Who knows what I'll eat next time." She swallowed. "Or w-who."

Rae suddenly felt a little too hot in her suit. "Do you, um, feel any bitey urges right now?"

"Bitey urges?" Vivienne managed a weak grin. "No."

"Okay, good. Just warn me if you do." Rae smiled and squeezed Vivienne's shoulder. "My dad was abducted by the government, by the way. If we're sharing secrets."

"*What?* Why?"

"Because he found an alien."

They resumed walking in the dark, and Rae told her the story. It felt . . . *good*, finally sharing this part of her life. And when she was finished, Vivienne didn't look weirded out.

"Thank you for telling me," she said.

Rae shrugged, already feeling lighter. Her dad might still be missing, but she had a lead, and she wasn't alone. She had Ava, and Caden, and now Vivienne. "I guess we're best friends for real now." Then she felt awkward. What if Vivienne didn't see it that way?

But Vivienne grinned. "I guess we are."

And even though they were heading down a dark tunnel to destroy giant alien centipede monsters with untested equipment, Rae was feeling pretty good about everything. Until she heard the noises.

Scraaaaaape. Click. Click. Click. Scrape.

Rae froze, her hand convulsing around the nozzle of her spray gun.

"I heard it too," Vivienne whispered, stopping next to her. "See the way the tunnel bends up ahead? I think it's just past that."

Of course it would be around a bend. Rae figured she should just be thankful that she didn't have to go through a crawl space to get to the nest.

Vivienne unhitched the nozzle to her bug spray. She looked a little like a Ghostbuster clutching it, and if Rae hadn't been so terrified, she might have laughed.

"Go around the corner shooting?" Vivienne asked.

"I think we should see what we're up against first," Rae said, thinking of Blake. She really hoped he'd just run off again and was hanging out with his uncle in a new yurt somewhere. But just in case . . .

"Go around the corner slowly and methodically and *then* start shooting?" Vivienne suggested.

Rae nodded. "Let's do it."

They eased around the corner.

The tunnel opened up into a large cavern. Stalactites dripped down from the ceiling, some so long their points almost brushed the ground, while towering stalagmites thrust up to meet them like giant broken teeth. And in between, the bones and half-decayed bodies of at least a dozen animals littered the floor.

It smelled awful—rotting flesh and damp earth and, underneath that, a strange acrid scent like fermented gasoline. Rae tried breathing shallowly as she stepped into the cavern, carefully avoiding a carcass. She swept her beam around.

It caught on something hanging from the ceiling. A large, yellowy something, throbbing and pulsing like an infected wound. A giant egg sac, Rae realized, tangled around a lanky boy, his eyes half closed, his red hair gleaming in her headlamp.

Blake. Alive, but already part of the nest.

Rae stared at him for so long that at first she didn't notice all the giant centipedes crawling down from the ceiling and along the walls, moving rapidly toward her.

38.

CADEN

Caden could feel every single one of the Unseeing's victims as if he were them. For brief seconds, he was Jeremy Bentley kissing Alyssa Lockett, his hand in her silky ponytail. And he was Brandi Jenson sitting on the floor of her room, watching her pet ferret run through a tube. And he was Jake Green kicking a soccer ball with his sister. And all the others, the images blurring and folding together until Caden didn't know where they ended and he began.

It was terrible, his mind unraveling out, becoming all these other kids. And the whole time he could sense their knowledge of what had happened to them, could feel their horror in those last few seconds.

It was like the echo of a scream, going on forever. They weren't really there anymore, but they weren't really gone, either. They were caught in between. And they were cold, and frightened, and everything was dark, so very, very dark, and they didn't want to be alone anymore. They clutched at Caden, pulling him to them, holding him tightly.

He didn't want to hurt them, didn't want to leave them behind. But he couldn't save them. He didn't even know if they *could* be saved. They might have been nothing but ghostly imprints left behind when Ivan devoured their souls. Nothing more than a memory.

But Caden didn't completely believe that, either. They felt too real. Too alive. Was it possible their souls weren't gone but *trapped* in another dimension like the Other Place?

I'll come back for you, he promised, although he didn't know how. But he wouldn't forget them. Somehow, he would find a way to help them. He owed it to them for his part in setting the Unseeing free.

Don't leave us! they howled. *It hurts!* She *hurts us.*

But Caden had no choice. He built up a barrier in his mind, enclosing himself and blocking them out.

"Mom was right about you," Aiden whispered.

Caden twisted around. He didn't see anything but the golden white walls of his bubble.

"You really need to expand your repertoire. This little trick? It's gotten predictable. And predictable is dangerous in our line of work."

Caden felt the walls of his bubble crumpling, as if they were made of paper and Aiden had them in his fist. Pain lanced through Caden's mind as the light surrounding him vanished, and he cried out, wrapping his hands over his head.

"I did try to leave you out of this. But Mom wouldn't help me. So you were my only option. I won't hurt you, though."

Caden opened his eyes, and the world wavered around him. For a second he could see the Other Place, the landscape barren and alien and stretching endlessly in all directions. Overhead loomed a giant sphere the yellow-green color of an old bruise. It beat down relentlessly like a diseased sun, filling the air with a moist, dirty heat. Something with long, hungry tentacles slithered toward him.

Caden blinked, and he was in the cabin again, with the neat little rows of candles, the kids with their gaping eye sockets. In front of him, Ava lay on her back in the center of Aiden's pentagram, palms turned upward, eyes open and unseeing.

Caden's heart lurched.

He tore his gaze from her, meeting Aiden's eyes. "What have you done?"

"What I had to do."

"You didn't have to do *any* of this!"

"Oh, but I did. She was devouring my soul, Caden. And she would have gone on feeding until I fulfilled my end of the deal and helped set her freedom in motion."

"*We* could have helped you."

"No, you couldn't have. There is no escape from her." Aiden shivered. "You'll understand that soon enough."

Everything shifted again, becoming now the Other Place, and then the cabin, flickering rapidly like a candle in a high wind. Caden felt like he was standing with one foot in each world, the anchor point for both, the only real thing in either. Both places tugged at him, the pressure building in his head, pulling at his thoughts. It was getting harder to focus. He wasn't sure how long he could keep this up before he was ripped in half.

He didn't know how to end it.

Cool hands touched his face, and he became aware of Aiden kneeling in front of him. "Nine outside to break the lock," Aiden whispered. "Seven within to create the key."

"What?" Caden tried to concentrate. "What does that mean?"

"She has three already. Four more are on their way."

Three? Four? It didn't make any sense. Caden clutched at his brother. "I don't understand."

"I know. But you will." Aiden smiled, a real smile. It had been so long since Caden had seen anything like it on his brother's face. It made him think of their last conversation.

What happened to us? We used to be close. It was us against the rest of the world . . .

And Caden remembered his brother teaching him how to shoot baskets behind the house. How he didn't like reading until Aiden made it his mission to find the right book, the one that would get him hooked. The time he had come home crying from school, when everyone decided he was too freaky to play with, and Aiden had dried his tears and told him he didn't need any of them. *You've got me. You don't need anyone else.*

But you have so many friends, Caden had said.

And Aiden had smiled and ruffled his hair. *None of them matter to me. Only you. Brothers till the end.*

Caden blinked, the memories over in a flash. And despite

everything, despite the horror and the blood, the guilt and the fear, he realized that he still loved his older brother.

"I'm sorry." Aiden said it like he meant it. A real apology to go with his real smile. He put his hand on Caden's forehead, and pressed.

Pain seared Caden like a brand, fire coursing through his nerves, filling his muscles, his vision turning red. He tasted blood, his world nothing but agony that went on and on until, abruptly, it was over.

39.

RAE

"Rae!" Vivienne shrieked. "Look out!"

Rae blinked, tearing her gaze away from Blake's pale, agonized face.

The walls of the cavern were moving. Everywhere she looked, it all shifted and oozed and scuttled as dozens of centipedes poured toward her. They ranged in size from as long as her hand to as long as her leg, all of them gleaming that hard, oily color in the light of her headlamp.

The nearest one launched itself at her, hissing.

Rae squeezed the nozzle of the Green On! spray and hit it full on. It staggered, then fell over onto its back, its many legs twitching in the air. Rae let out a breath. Patrick was right about this spray: it *was* very effective, like it had been designed specifically for these bugs. Rae caught movement in the beam of her light and sprayed just as another centipede charged her.

"Get Blake!" she told Vivienne, spraying the next centipede, and the next. As much as she wanted to be the rescuer, she knew Vivienne was faster and had a better chance of saving him than she did. "I'll keep our exit open."

Rae's world narrowed to the thin strip of light from her headlamp illuminating the centipedes boiling out of hidden holes in the walls. She kept her finger on the nozzle, spraying each bug just as it charged, aiming for their creepy underside faces.

How much spray did she have?

Rae risked a quick glance over at Vivienne. Her friend had climbed one of the stalactites in order to reach the ceiling and was cutting away at the egg sac with her knife, her teeth bared in a silent snarl. She moved fast, slicing and then whipping around to spray a bug in midair before going back to Blake, her balance on that slender column of rock perfect.

And then Rae realized Vivienne wasn't snarling at all. She was laughing.

Something hit Rae in the back of the knees, and she tumbled forward, catching herself on one hand. Immediately a horde of bugs surged forward. She could hear the awful clicking of their feet against the rock, her vision full of millions of legs.

Rae scrambled up, spraying all around her, no longer aiming, just squeezing the handle of the nozzle and hitting whatever she hit. She couldn't breathe, couldn't see. They were all around her!

Another bug hit her legs, and she stumbled, then kicked it away. She soaked it in spray, spinning to take out a few more, her breath wheezing in her ears, the smell of fake orange cleaner filling her nostrils.

It reminded her of Ava and the Super Citrus. And that helped her calm down a little. But it was still several more seconds before she could make herself ease up on the trigger, and by then the pressure of the spray had gone from a firehose to the gentler trickle of a shower.

Rae finally took her finger off the trigger. Nothing moved, the cavern still and quiet, only the sound of her breath wheezing in her ears. She turned slowly, her headlamp illuminating a circle of corpses around her. The bugs lay crumpled on their backs with legs curled inward, a few of them still twitching. She felt sick.

So much death.

"I've got him!" Vivienne yelled. She dropped from the ceiling and did a forward roll, coming up just in time to catch Blake in her arms as tiny bugs poured down around them from the slit egg sac above. Blake groaned and clutched at her shoulders with one arm, his other clamped around his stomach.

"The bug," he moaned. "It—"

"Shh," Vivienne said, carrying him toward Rae and the entrance. "I've got you. Don't talk." She had to walk over a couple of dead bugs, their bodies crunching under her feet. "Ready to go?"

Rae swept her headlamp around the cavern, still searching. "The queen."

"What?" Vivienne asked.

"We haven't seen her. We're destroying her whole nest, and she isn't here, protecting it. Why?"

"I have no idea."

Rae frowned, turning, her headlamp creating a ribbon of light. But nothing moved in it.

Something was wrong.

"Rae, we need to get Blake back now," Vivienne said. "Remember Priceless Art?"

Rae did remember. It was too easy to imagine the same thing happening to Blake, his stomach bursting as the eggs inside him matured, the bugs exploding their way out. Still. "If we don't kill the queen, then this"—Rae indicated the cavern, the bugs, Blake—"won't end."

"I understand that. But if we don't save Blake—"

He whimpered.

"Shh, shh, we've got you." Vivienne dropped her voice, even though Blake was right there, so that hardly helped. "If he dies like that, there will be so much blood. So much." Vivienne swallowed. "And then it might not be the bugs you'd have to worry about."

Rae frowned, confused.

"I am barely keeping it together as it is," Vivienne whispered. She was trembling violently, her eyes wide, teeth gritted.

Sudden understanding hit Rae, faster and more terrible even than a killer alien insect. And she knew she couldn't put Vivienne in that situation, mission or no. "We'll come back later," she decided.

Vivienne relaxed. "Thank you." She hoisted Blake up a little higher and started for the tunnel entrance.

She never made it.

A huge shape erupted from the shadows, slamming into Vivienne in a fury of legs. She cried out and dropped Blake as she fell back. The thing thrashed on top of her, its body rippling while it trampled her into the dirt.

Rae slid her knife out from her thigh sheath and lunged forward, stabbing at the creature's back. Her knife crunched through its outer skin, and it whipped around, its upper half lifting, the face beneath clearly visible. Multiple rows of eyes, black and cruel, a slit of a nose, and in the mouth, two sets of mandibles. It hissed, those mandibles clicking.

Rae shot a blast of chemicals straight to its clicking head. The queen lurched back, and Rae pushed the trigger again.

Nothing. Her spray was all used up.

Rae stared into those rows of eyes and swore she could see triumph in them.

Vivienne reared up and thrust her own knife straight into the queen's mouth, stabbing deep and then twisting.

The queen shrieked, legs flailing as it jerked hard . . . and then finally went still.

Vivienne met Rae's eyes above the dead bug's head.

Rae froze, her breath hitching. Something stared out at her from her friend's face. Something cruel and inhuman. This wasn't the same as gazing into the eyes of a mountain lion after all. It was more like staring into the eyes of a hooded cobra. Rae couldn't look away.

Vampire. The word sprang into Rae's mind and stuck there.

Vivienne didn't have her magic sealing stone with her now. She didn't have any special elixir. There was nothing keeping her curse under control, nothing to prevent it from taking her over.

Nothing to stop her from leaping on Rae and tearing her throat wide open.

40.

CADEN

Caden blinked.

He was lying on the floor of the cabin. The candles had all sputtered out, but the front door was open, filling the room with enough light to make out the dim shapes of the couch, the fireplace, the discarded knife.

And Ava, lying motionless in front of him.

"No," Caden whispered, scrambling over to her. The other Unseeing victims were gone now, and so was Aiden. "Ava?" Caden knelt, feeling for her pulse.

It was there, but faint.

"Ava!" He shook her gently. Her head rolled back and forth, but she didn't wake up. Didn't react at all.

He checked her over quickly, carefully, and there weren't any obvious wounds. No blood. Until he checked her hands. Across each palm spread a thin slice, already starting to heal. Tentatively he opened his senses, feeling for her.

She felt like Aiden had felt. Like there was no one there at all.

He didn't know what he should do now. He had no experience with this kind of thing. He should have paid more attention to his mom's lessons.

Caden ran fingers through his hair, thinking furiously, his brother's last warning echoing in his head. *Nine outside to break the lock. Seven within to create the key.* It sounded like one of the rituals his mom might have scribbled in her Book of Shadows.

Caden sat back on his heels, studying the smeared remains of chalk on the floor, barely visible in the dim lighting. There had been eight victims of the Unseeing . . .

And Ava.

He went cold all over as he looked at her lifeless face, felt her empty soul. Was she meant to be the ninth victim on the outside?

Seven within to create the key.

Aiden told him there had been three in already. Caden thought of the three Green On! employees that Aiden had said were dead now—or as good as—after pulling him out of the rift. Were they like Ava was now, empty vessels of flesh? Was that what Aiden had meant? If so, then the evil inside the Other Place just needed four more victims to wander into her prison.

Caden scrubbed a hand over his face. He'd worry about all of that later. Right now, he had to focus on Ava.

41.

RAE

Rae slowly, carefully raised her arms, putting her hands up protectively. Vivienne's eyes narrowed, tracking the movement. "Vivi." Rae made her voice gentle. "It's me. Your friend. Rae-Rae." She backed up a step. It was a mistake; she knew it the moment she moved.

Vivienne's lips pulled back in a silent snarl, her body tensing.

Rae froze, not even breathing.

Vivienne blinked, then blinked again, and life flowed back into her face. Her body relaxed, and she was herself again.

Rae sagged and she put a hand to her chest, pressing on her heart.

Vivienne's expression crumpled. "I'm so, so sorry. I—"

Blake screamed, his whole body arching, hands scrabbling in the dirt.

Vivienne rushed to his side. "Hang on, Blake."

"I . . . can feel . . . them," he gasped, clutching at his stomach. His freckles stood out like chicken pox against the ghostly white of his face, and his red hair was matted with sweat and some sort of goo from the egg sac.

"Get him outside to Patrick quick," Rae said. "I'll do a quick final sweep, and then I'll be right behind you." Blake had gone missing only to turn up here. Rae wanted to make sure she wasn't leaving anyone else behind.

"Here." Vivienne shrugged out of her pack and tossed it to Rae. "Just in case."

"Thank you." Rae dropped her empty pack and pulled on Vivienne's, clipping her bug spray nozzle in front.

Vivienne slung Blake over her shoulders like he was a goat. "Don't stay too long."

"I won't," Rae promised.

Vivienne nodded, and then left. Rae watched her light moving down the tunnel and around the bend. Then it was just her inside the cavern. Just her, and a mountain of the dead.

Rae shivered as she walked the perimeter of the cavern, sweeping her headlamp back and forth along the ground and the walls, checking the milky-white egg sac that spread across the ceiling like a giant web, purposefully not thinking about Vivienne and what had almost happened between them.

Her light caught on a shape near the farthest corner of the cavern.

Rae hesitated. Without Vivienne, her fear of the dark tunnels had started to eat away at her. The walls closed in, the shadows growing longer and hungrier. Rae squeezed her eyes shut and took a deep breath.

It stank like rotting meat and decay.

Rae opened her eyes, gagging. Before she could totally panic, she moved toward that corner, trying not to think too hard about what she might find. The sooner she checked, the sooner she could get out of here. Above her, the egg sac no longer crawled with bugs. All of the ones she passed were dead.

She reached the corner, and the shape.

It was a man, his upper half stretched out across the cavern floor, his feet still tangled in the webbing above. His torso was ripped open the same way Priceless Art had been.

Rae staggered back, her hand over her mouth. She did not need to see more. She didn't want to see his last agonizing moments stamped across his face; she already had enough nightmares.

Click. Click. Clickity-click.

Rae whipped around, frantically searching the dark for any movement. Her headlamp highlighted a bulge of gooey white just ahead, tucked behind a stalagnate. And sticking out of that bulge, a familiar leg clothed in neon orange and ending in a well-worn sneaker.

"Oh no." Rae eased herself around the pillar, her whole body trembling. Maybe she wasn't too late. Maybe, just maybe, she could save one more person. "Coach Briggs?" She carefully slid her knife into the webbing and sliced it open, and her running coach tumbled out. A couple of tiny bugs burst from the egg sac to skitter around her, but Rae ignored them.

Her coach's mouth hung open, her glossy eyes gazing at nothing. She was dead.

Rae backed away, shaking her head, like she could somehow will it not to be true. Her pack bumped up against the natural pillar.

Click, click . . .

Rae turned, but too slowly. A large, dark shadow slammed into her with the force of a tidal wave. She fell, the knife skidding from her hand, the bug looming over her. It was much larger than the queen Vivienne had killed. At least eight feet long, and wide, its legs spread on either side as its front half lifted.

Rae stared up into its furious face. Rows of eyes, cruel and black, stared back at her. Its mandibles opened wide, exposing a second, smaller set behind them. Rae barely got her hands up before it shot a thick stream of yellowish-white goo at her face.

It oozed around her fingers, splattering against her skin and into her mouth and eyes, all warm and sticky, smelling like battery fluid and sticking to her like rancid mozzarella.

Rae retched and flailed backward, searching blindly for her lost knife. Her fingers found the handle, and she jabbed it upward just as the queen lunged. Her knife slid into the space between the queen's head segment and the rest of its body, and stuck in deep.

The queen screeched, long and terrible, before turning and scurrying into the shadows.

Rae rolled over to her side. Everything hurt, her whole body battered. She spat the goo out of her mouth and scrubbed at her face with her sleeve, getting rid of as much as she could while she searched the dark for the queen. Her knife was gone, but she still had Vivienne's bug spray. She unclipped the nozzle and held it ready, her hand trembling violently, fingers pressing into the metal so hard they went numb.

Click. Click. Click.

Rae couldn't tell where the noise was coming from. Sound echoed strangely in the cavern. It almost sounded like . . . it was right above her!

She threw herself to the side as the queen dropped from the ceiling and slammed into the ground.

Rae lurched to her feet and pointed the nozzle, then pulled the trigger, prepared for the gush of spray.

The queen paused, waiting.

There was a loud hiss of air, and then a few tiny drops squirted out.

Rae stared at it, then at the queen. "That's not good," she whispered, inching backward.

The queen's mandibles clicked together, sounding almost like laughter. The knife jammed into its body quivered, and just below its hilt, Rae spotted something strange. A small green tag, very similar to the one Ava had pointed out on the alien in her dad's photograph.

Shock rippled through Rae like a lake on a windy day.

The queen charged, and Rae thrust her questions aside and ran as fast as she could.

The bug was much faster. It knocked into her from behind, sending her flying. She skidded across the ground and crashed into a stalagmite. The queen scurried up her body, its weight crushing her legs, pinning her to the ground as it moved relentlessly up until its face loomed just above her own. Rae thought of stomachs bursting and imagined what it would feel like. Her hands were icy with fear, one of them still wrapped around the nozzle, the other pushing uselessly at the slick exoskeleton of the queen.

She'd never get it off her that way.

She had a sudden desperate idea and slid her hand into the front of her suit, pulling out the lighter. Patrick hadn't given her a flamethrower, so she would make her own.

As the queen's mandibles extended, the second pair sliding forward, already dripping with goo, Rae flicked the switch of her lighter and held it in front of the nozzle of her chemical gun. She looked the queen straight in the face. "Eat this," she said, and pressed the trigger. The chemicals spurted out, hitting the flame and shooting out blue fire.

The queen shrieked and fell back. Rae rolled away from it and pushed herself to her feet, watching as the bug writhed on the ground, the flames spreading as they touched on the corpses of dead bugs around it, leaping to engulf the remaining egg sacs. Heat rose up in a searing wall, pressing Rae back, until she turned and sprinted through the cavern and into the tunnel, leaving the nest to burn behind her.

She wanted to feel victorious, but she kept seeing that shape rolling on the ground, unable to put out the flames, kept hearing that awful scream. And she didn't feel good about any of it.

It had to be done. Rae knew that. Those things had already killed plenty of animals and at least two people. But as she ran, she could feel the guilt keeping pace with her. She remembered what Patrick had said, that those bugs were just obeying their biological imperative.

So did they deserve to die?

Rae knew they could never coexist on this planet. Someone would have had to take out their nest eventually. But she began wondering *why* she and Vivienne had been the ones forced to do it. Because Nate was right; they were kids. They shouldn't be the only ones standing between Whispering Pines and a serious infestation of alien bugs.

And that tag . . . it was a Green On! tag, Rae was sure of it. Which meant the company must have known where the queen was the whole time and hadn't done anything about it. If Rae hadn't killed it, those bugs would have spread until all of Whispering Pines was crawling with them.

Patrick said he had faith in them. But Rae knew that wasn't the whole truth. He was up to something, using his interns like they were a part of one of his experiments, all in the pursuit of some unknown goal.

She was sure of only two things now: First, that Green On! *had* been involved with the alien her dad discovered. Which meant they must have had something to do with his disappearance too. So Patrick really might know where he was.

But the second thing she knew for sure was that Patrick was not to be trusted.

42.
CADEN

Caden tripped over a root and dropped Ava. She fell like a sack of potatoes, all boneless weight and no grace. He scrambled to her side. "I'm so sorry," he said, even though he knew she couldn't hear him. She had a scrape on her cheek now, and dirt caked into her T-shirt. He winced. "So very sorry."

She didn't move. And for one heart-stopping second, he worried that she was well and truly dead. But then he noticed her chest rise and fall. Relief surged through him, and he pressed a hand against his own chest, his heart aching. He wasn't sure what to do.

His mom would know.

He wished he knew where she was. Part of him had thought his parents would be in the cabin with Aiden. Or that they'd be in the Other Place. Now he didn't know where to look for them.

A bird called in the distance. One of Whispering Pines's infamous whippoorwills, welcoming the coming of night. Caden shivered and pushed himself to his feet, then bent and hauled Ava up, slinging her over his left shoulder like the sack of potatoes he'd imagined.

He flinched at his own callousness, then continued his slow, steady progress through the woods. It was a warm evening, the air heavy with moisture. He ignored the mosquitoes, occasionally stopping to pull his phone out of his back pocket and check the cell reception. Always, there was nothing.

He wasn't even sure he was going the right way. The Watchful Woods was a confusing place even in the best of situations. Now, with panic eating him from the inside out, his head throbbing, and the branches closing around him like the clasping hands of some gnarled creature, he could be walking in a giant circle.

It was a terrible thought.

Caden wasn't sure what, exactly, Aiden had done to Ava, but he suspected he had somehow severed the connection between her spirit and her body. Which meant if there were any chance at all of restoring that connection, Caden would have to do it quickly, before her spirit moved too far away. He couldn't waste all his time wandering in the woods.

He stopped walking, leaned against a tree, and closed his eyes, Ava still slung over his shoulder. He did his grounding exercises, the ones his mom had drilled him on ever since he could remember. He imagined roots bursting from his feet, digging deep into the soil, wrapping around rocks and sending tendrils out in all directions.

Above the ground, he pictured a bubble of white light forming delicately around him, reflecting that light back into him.

You really need to expand your repertoire.

It was the same thing his mom had been telling him. She'd insisted he had other abilities, and Caden had pretended not to believe her. But the truth was that he knew he could do more. He was just afraid to try. Afraid of what it would do to him.

Afraid fully using his powers would turn him into his brother.

He pushed those worries away and focused on his mom, picturing the way she'd looked that afternoon just before Aiden showed up, with her long black braid and the amethyst earrings, the smell of her favorite sandalwood incense clinging to her shirt. He painted the colors of her aura in his mind, a soft lavender ringed with green . . . and felt something. A gentle tug, similar to the sensation he got from the warding circle around his house when something moved through it. His mother was searching for him too.

He opened his eyes and resumed walking, letting the pull of his mother's aura carry him forward.

The trees thinned out, opening up on a slice of familiar street. And rushing toward him—

"Mom! Dad!" Caden ran. Despite the heavy weight of Ava on his numb shoulder, his sore legs, his exhaustion, he ran. For a second he felt like he were five years old again and secure in the knowledge that whatever was out there, his parents could take care of it. They would protect him.

His dad reached him first. He lifted Ava down, then threw his other arm around Caden and hugged him hard. Then his mom was there, hugging him too.

". . . trapped at Green On!" his dad was saying. "We couldn't leave!"

". . . Patrick tricked us," his mom babbled at the same time. "I knew he was up to something—"

"—Audrey eventually let us out. Even dropped us off at home. I think she feels terrible. Poor woman is under a tremendous amount of stress," his dad finished.

Caden kept his arms around his parents for a few more seconds, and then he pulled back. "Aiden is trying to set *her* free." Caden looked at his mom and saw that she understood who he meant. "He convinced me to open the rift, or he was going to hurt Ava."

His mom cupped Ava's face in her hands, frowning.

"Can you help her?"

"I . . . don't know." She rubbed her temple. "I'll try."

"I'll call Rae, see if she can help."

"Is that wise?"

Caden nodded. "Blood calls to blood." He'd been mulling it over on his hike through the woods. "I think we'll need her."

"It will be a dangerous ritual. Do you trust her?"

Caden didn't hesitate. "With my life."

43.

RAE

Rae climbed out of the tunnel just in time to see a Green On! van taking off down the street, green lights flashing. Vivienne stood watching it go.

"Did Patrick take Blake?" Rae asked.

Vivienne turned. "Rae-Rae!" She rushed over, her arms wide, and Rae remembered the cavern and her certainty that her friend was about to attack her. She flinched. She didn't mean to, but Vivienne immediately dropped her arms and stepped back, looking crushed.

Rae angrily shoved that fear away. This was her friend. "Vivi." She gave Vivienne a quick hug and was rewarded by her relieved smile.

"I was so worried about you!" Vivienne said. "I smelled the smoke."

"The queen is dead. Pretty sure everything else in there is too," Rae said grimly. "The infestation is over."

They both looked down at the open mouth of the tunnel.

"Patrick didn't take Blake," Vivienne said at last. "I called an ambulance, and Green On! sent a van out here for him instead." She sighed. "Patrick was actually gone when I got out here."

"What?"

"Nate too. I tried calling him, and he didn't answer." Vivienne scowled. "I can't believe they just left. This mission was important!"

"I'm beginning to wonder if Patrick wanted us to succeed."

"Why would you wonder that?"

Rae debated about pushing it. She knew how Vivienne felt about Patrick and Green On!. "It's just," she started, feeling her way. "This bug spray. It was so effective."

"Good thing, too."

"Yeah, good thing. But . . . how long does it take to invent a new kind of bug spray?"

"I have no clue."

"I think it would take longer than a few days. And we only told Patrick about the bugs on Wednesday. Yet"—she gestured at her discarded pack—"here we are."

"What are you trying to say?" Vivienne crossed her arms.

"I don't know. Just that something doesn't line up. He sends us—*kids*, like Nate said—into a tunnel to clear out a deadly infestation and doesn't even stick around to make sure we're successful. Like it doesn't matter to him. Because . . . because if we fail, and the bugs spread all over town, then at least Green On! has their fancy new spray. A spray that everyone will need. I mean, these bugs are taking pets and children, and now even adults, too. People will pay anything for protection."

Vivienne's eyes narrowed. "You sound a lot like Caden, you know that?"

"Thank you."

"*Not* a compliment."

Rae winced.

Then Vivienne sighed. "Actually, I quite like Caden. And . . . I think you're wrong. But I can understand why you might be suspicious. It *is* weird that Patrick left while we were still in there."

Rae wasn't sure "weird" was the word she would use for that. "A terrible act of betrayal" would be more accurate. "I guess I'd better call Ava, let her know where I am." She thought of the bike ride home, and her sore body. "Maybe she'll give us a ride."

"I thought your mom had the car."

"Dang it. Maybe your mom will give us a ride?"

"I already tried her," Vivienne said. "Went to voicemail."

Rae pulled her phone out and dialed Ava. Her sister didn't pick up. "Apparently no one answers their phone anymore," she grumbled.

Her phone rang.

Rae almost dropped it, she was so startled.

"Who is it?" Vivienne asked.

Rae glanced at the name. "Caden." A sudden heavy sense of foreboding enveloped her. It was like seeing that shape in the darkness of the cavern all over again and knowing it would be a body. Hesitantly, she answered her phone. "Is everything okay?"

"I'm sorry, Rae." Caden took a breath. "It's Ava."

44.

CADEN

Caden finished drawing the final line of chalk, then sat back on his heels to study the design.

A pentagram inside a circle, each point marked with an unlit tea candle. It looked just like the one Aiden had drawn out, minus the maimed kids. A Summoning ritual.

"Are you sure about this?" his mom asked him quietly.

Caden felt a brief surge of anger. She wouldn't be questioning Aiden. She would trust him to know what he was doing. Caden took a deep breath, trying to bury those emotions, but he could feel their sharp edges pressing against his layer of calm. It reminded him of the bug corpse Gary had hidden under a rug. "I'm sure," he said.

"Because you don't have to be the caster."

"I have the best chance," Caden said. "You were the one who

told me that." Since he had been included in the original spell that had severed Ava from her spirit, he still had a small tie to her. A sort of magical echo that he could call upon to help her two selves reunite.

His mom studied him, her expression unreadable. "You have the best chance at succeeding, true, but this spell will require a lot of magic. And it will be very dangerous. All of us will be tied to the outcome. Do you understand that?"

"I do."

"It means if this goes wrong, Ava will not be the only lifeless husk—"

"I said I understand!" Caden snapped. "You don't trust me, do you? You don't think I can do this?"

Her eyes widened. "Oh, I'm sure you can." She put a hand on his cheek. "I trust you more than anyone. It's why I want you to take over Paranormal Price."

Caden's smile was small and twisted as he pulled away from her touch. "I'm your only option now that Aiden's gone . . . well. Wherever he went."

She sighed. "You were my first choice all along, Caden."

Caden snorted. He couldn't help himself. It was just so ridiculous. Obviously he was the runner-up.

"You have always looked up to your brother. Even when you were afraid of him, he's been the yardstick you use to measure your own success. You are both my sons, and I love you both. But you have been given very different paths to walk." She took his hands in her own, her fingers icy. "Because you spend your life comparing yourself to Aiden, you believe everyone else is too. But we're not. I hope someday you'll understand this." She squeezed his fingers, then let go.

Caden wasn't sure what to think of that. "Aiden is much stronger than I am."

"Not true. Aiden's magic comes from here." She tapped her forehead. "Yours comes from here." She laid a hand on his chest. "That can be very powerful indeed, when fully harnessed. Use it. But be careful."

"I thought you said you didn't compare us."

She laughed. "I said I didn't always compare you. Now, stop being insecure. We have a major spell to perform."

Caden smiled weakly, then went to get the others.

Caden sat cross-legged at the top point of the star, his parents across from him in each of the legs, Rae and Vivienne across from each other in the arms. And Ava in the center, lying flat on her back, palms turned up. Caden closed his eyes and grounded himself, then started chanting the mantra of summoning.

The emotions of everyone in the room swirled around him in one interconnected haze. Rae's love, Vivienne's concern, his mom's pride, and his dad's resignation. And below those emotions, he felt their power.

He was tapped directly into it. He could take whatever he wanted.

Caden tugged at the magic nestled deep inside his mom and used it to light the candles placed at each intersection of his pentagram. It was as easy as flicking a switch; the candles burst into flame.

Why just candles? He let those flames spill over, dripping along the lines of chalk, felt the alarm growing around him. Fear was powerful, giving him even more energy, and he drank it in. For once in his life, he felt strong and competent. Unstoppable. He could do anything he wanted.

Was this what Aiden felt like when he was in the middle of a powerful spell? Was this why he loved it so much?

Caden hesitated. He felt like he were going down a steep slide, trying to grip the sides with greased fingers. All the power in the room flooding through him made it hard to concentrate, to remember who he was, why he was doing this.

Rae.

He was doing this for Rae. To save her sister.

He focused on her, sensing her terror as the flames in the room crept higher, and abruptly he felt sick. He pulled back some of the power in the spell, allowing the flames to trickle down lower.

He centered his attention on Ava next, using the emotions of the others to build a tower that could slice into the spirit realm and send out a beacon.

This was the tricky part. Too narrow a beacon, and you risked it going unheard. Too wide, and anything might pick it up, and take it as an invitation.

Ava Jan Carter, he called, gentle but commanding. *Return to us.*

He felt an answering call almost immediately. And then a rushing feeling, as if something were coming at him very fast and—

"Watch out!" Caden flung his hands up, yanking all the power he could from everyone in the room and throwing it out in an invisible net.

The candles sputtered, went dark.

Something laughed, high-pitched and girlish. Caden felt a wave of pure terror, as black as the deepest night, colder than anything, and knew he was in the presence of true evil. It crawled down his skin, tore icy claws through his heart, and whispered, gently, insistently, into his ear: *You are mine.*

And then it was gone, and the candles were lit, and everyone was staring at him.

"—den?" Rae said. "Caden? Are you okay?"

He blinked. "Did it work?" he croaked.

"Shouldn't you be the one telling us?" Vivienne asked.

"I . . ." He stopped, stared at Ava. Her fingers twitched. Then her leg trembled. And suddenly her eyes flew open and she sat up and screamed.

Caden clapped his hands over his ears.

"Ava!" Rae lurched forward, but fire erupted between them, sending her flinching back. "Ava!"

Cursing, Caden began taking down the protections.

"Wait!" his mom said. "Caden, be cautious."

"I need to see my sister!" Rae yelled. "Let me see her!"

And through it all, Ava was still screaming, screaming, and Caden couldn't think, couldn't concentrate, but he knew his mom was right. He couldn't rush this part. He had to make sure it was really Ava who had returned.

"Ava Jan Carter," he intoned.

She fell silent, only tiny gasps escaping.

"Ava?" Rae said.

"It's me," Ava sobbed. "It's me. Oh, God . . . I saw her. She said . . . she said she wanted me to give a message to the Prices."

"Who?" Caden asked.

"She said you'd know."

And of course they did.

"What's the message?" Caden's mom asked.

Ava swallowed. "She said . . . she's coming for you." And she put her face in her hands and sobbed.

Tentatively Caden reached out his awareness, brushing it against Ava. It was definitely her. He allowed the protections to flow away. "You can go to her now," he told Rae. "It's safe."

Rae threw herself across the chalk line and put her arms around her sister, both of them hugging each other and crying.

Caden sank back. He was suddenly completely exhausted. His mom and dad both hurried over. "Oh, Caden, you were so good!" His mom hugged him. "See, Vincent? He can handle it."

"You were very brave," his dad said, putting his own arm around him. He hesitated, then put his other arm around Caden's mom, the three of them forming a small huddle. Caden relaxed into their embrace and let his worries drift away. There would be time enough for them tomorrow.

45.

RAE

Rae wrapped her hands around her mug, enjoying the warmth. She was so tired, and still gross from the tunnels, all covered in bug goo and dirt. But it felt nice to sit here at Caden's kitchen table and drink his dad's fancy tea.

"The secret is plenty of honey," his dad told her. "If you think you have too much, you're wrong."

Rae took another sip, enjoying the sweetness of it.

"See what I mean?"

"It's really good, Mr. Price. Thank you." Rae turned to Mrs. Price. "Is Ava going to be okay?"

"She's going to be fine, darling. She just needs plenty of rest. And she'll probably have nightmares for the next several nights."

Rae nodded. She was pretty sure she'd have her own share of those as well.

"I can go check on her, if you'd like?" Mrs. Price suggested.

"Thank you," Rae said.

Mrs. Price looked a lot like Caden when she smiled, the expression softening her face. "You're very welcome. Vincent? Care to join me?"

"That's okay," he said, leaning against the kitchen counter.

Mrs. Price narrowed her eyes. "I would really appreciate your assistance."

He blinked at her, and she shot a not-so-subtle look at Rae and then Caden sitting across from her.

"Oh! I see what you mean." He put his mug down and gave Rae and Caden a wide grin. "I suppose the two of you could use a little alone time, eh?"

"Dad," Caden hissed. "Seriously."

His mom sighed. "Sorry, honey. I tried to be subtle, but you know your father." She grinned, and his dad grinned back, and then the two of them walked down the hall to the study where Ava was resting in a "restorative meditative state."

"Sorry about that," Caden muttered, his face red.

Rae laughed. "Your parents are cute." It made her a little sad, remembering the way her own parents would tease each other.

"I'm actually pretty happy to see them like that. They haven't been . . . well. Let's just say they were having some relationship problems. I guess getting locked together in an underground lab for a few days is good for a marriage."

Rae wasn't sure about that, but she let it go. "So," she said.

"So," Caden agreed.

"We saved Whispering Pines again."

Caden nodded. "For now, at least."

"It seems to be a regular occurrence for us." Rae paused, her heart hammering. She had a plan, something that had slowly come together in her mind in the hour since her sister had recovered. She remembered the terror she'd felt back when she'd faced Ivan in the basement of the forest cabin, and then tonight, how afraid she'd been in the alien bug nest. It was the fear of knowing that the monsters under her bed were real, and they were coming for her.

But real monsters could be dealt with more easily than the monsters that lurked in the shadows of her imagination. Especially if she had help.

"I was thinking," she said slowly, watching Caden's face carefully. "Maybe we should form, I don't know, a team, or something? Like, officially?"

"You mean like your Green On! teams?" Caden frowned.

Rae bit her lip. This wasn't quite going how she wanted. "I guess that did give me the idea a little," she admitted. "But our team would be different."

"How so?"

"Well, first of all, it would only have people we trust in it. No Patrick, no Green On!, no way."

Caden smiled at that. A good sign. "Who would you suggest?"

"Aside from the two of us?" Rae tapped her mug. "Vivienne."

"I figured. Anyone else?"

"Nate. If he ever bothers to return my calls. Social loafer." She shook her head. "And . . . and Alyssa, I think."

Caden's eyebrows shot up. "Really?"

Rae nodded. Her arrival in Whispering Pines had driven a wedge between Vivienne and Alyssa. Maybe it was time, now, to fix that. Plus, she kept thinking of how determined Alyssa was to win the competition so she could help save Jeremy. She was smart and loyal and brave. She would be a good addition.

And maybe inviting her would help soften the blow on Monday when she found out that Rae's team had won.

Caden rubbed his chin. "And we'd, what? Solve mysteries? Fight crime? Break the occasional school rule?"

"Something like that." Rae pressed her hands against her mug so Caden wouldn't be able to tell they were shaking. If he said no, this whole thing was off. She didn't want to do it without him. She'd never admit that out loud, but she needed him. It had been a long time since she'd really needed anyone, and it was a scary feeling, as terrifying as anything else she'd dealt with tonight. But it was also kind of wonderful.

Because she had a feeling that he needed her, too.

Caden nodded. "Okay, I'll join."

"Really?" Rae sat up straighter. "You will?"

"On one condition."

She waited, nervous all over again.

"I refuse to wear matching T-shirts with anyone."

Rae grinned. "I'll give you a uniform exception."

"Then it's a deal." He held out his hand.

Rae stared at the rings glinting on his fingers and remembered how strange he had seemed on her first day in Whispering Pines.

It was amazing how much had changed in the short time she had lived here.

She put her hand in Caden's, her fingers entwining with his.

Maybe it had taken her dad's disappearance to bring her to the place she'd belonged all along.

EPILOGUE

{ MEANWHILE, BACK AT THE LAB . . . }

Nate did not like this, not one bit. He had been shut in a very strange room—no furniture, two walls of plain concrete, and two walls of floor-to-ceiling mirrors—with the other team, all of them wearing modified hazmat suits, the material sleek and snug. They reminded Nate of high-tech space suits and looked very similar to the ones Rae and Vivienne had been given at the mouth of the tunnel. Their helmets were lined up on the ground nearby. Nate already felt too hot and wasn't looking forward to cramming that fishbowl over his head.

No, he didn't want to be here at all. Especially not with these kids. Matt was all right, but Becka and Alyssa kept giving him that look, the one that told him that he didn't belong here.

Which was true. He belonged with Rae and Vivienne, who he'd

abandoned below ground. For all he knew, they were being turned into bug food this very moment.

He paced, wishing he could go back in time and change things, hating how he felt about all of it. Relieved that he wasn't in the tunnels with them, guilty that he felt relieved, and so worried about them. He didn't have many friends. Probably because he always corrected people. Vivienne told him that was an annoying trait, and he was sure she was right, just as he was sure he couldn't help it.

But he'd started to feel as if Vivienne and Rae and even Caden really *were* his friends. Like maybe once this whole thing was done, they'd still want to hang out once in a while.

Probably not now, though. Not after his betrayal.

He paced faster, angry with himself for listening to Patrick, angry with Patrick for forcing him to leave the others behind and come to the lab, angry with his mom for insisting he take on this internship in the first place. So much anger, it felt like he might explode with it.

"Hey, can you quit pacing already?" Alyssa said. "It's incredibly irritating."

Nate turned on her. "It's called thinking, though I know the concept might be foreign to you."

Matt snorted but turned it into a cough when Alyssa glared at him.

"Whoa," Becka said, putting her hands out in a soothing gesture. "Remember, we're a team now. We need to work together, okay?"

"Sorry, Nate," Alyssa muttered.

“It’s okay.” Nate hesitated, then added something true. “I’m scared too.”

It earned him a small smile.

He stopped pacing and leaned against the far wall, his Green On! hazmat suit cushioning him from the hard concrete. He glanced at the mirror in the back of the room. He was pretty sure it was a one-way screen, like an interrogation room. Behind that reflective surface there were probably a whole bunch of scientists monitoring them, tracking their heart rates, their breathing, noting their interactions. How long were they planning on keeping them trapped in here?

Nate couldn’t decide if he wanted to get this over with now or if he would prefer more time to pace and worry and feel awful about everything. Scratch that, he knew what he wanted. “What are we waiting for?” he demanded.

As if in answer, the mirrors on the other side shimmered.

“Helmets, everyone,” a voice said through the speakers in the corner.

Nate’s mouth went dry. He changed his mind; he wasn’t ready to go yet. But there wasn’t any choice. Becka had already tried the door once and found that they were all locked in here. So Nate lined up with the others, putting his helmet on with trembling fingers.

He remembered what it had felt like when he’d leaped into that dark hole in the earth. At least then he’d been with people he trusted. He barely knew these kids.

“Portal opening in one minute,” chimed a mechanical voice through his helmet speaker. *“Make sure your cameras are turned on.”*

Nate reached up, and with a shaky hand, clicked on the camera on the front of his helmet.

Was a scholarship really worth this?

He squeezed his hands into fists, wishing he knew how Rae and Vivienne were. Wishing he could tell them he hadn't abandoned them on purpose. Wishing—

"Thirty seconds."

The glass rippled like the water of a pond, and then a picture formed on its surface. It seemed a little blurry, the details concealed behind a hazy yellowish-green glow.

"Remember, this is merely a short exploratory mission," another voice said in Nate's helmet. A familiar voice. Patrick. "Go in, collect samples of soil, organic matter, or anything else you see. Plant the weather station somewhere a few feet from the gate so we can continue to collect readings, and then return."

Becka picked up the so-called weather station, which looked a lot like a small satellite dish and had been devised to read temperature, rainfall, wind, and who knew what else. Originally it had been Matt's job to take it, but on the way to the room, Matt had tripped and somehow chipped his helmet, so Green On! asked Becka to carry it instead.

"We will keep the gate open for precisely thirty minutes. Make sure to return within that time frame."

"Can we return earlier?" Nate asked.

"Now, Mr. Cliff, you can return whenever you need to. Naturally. As long as you have collected the necessary samples."

"Portal is now open."

Nate really, *really* didn't want to do this.

Alyssa nudged him forward, and he stumbled, putting his hands up to the place the mirrored wall should have been. Instead of cool glass, it felt like a wall of gelatin. He fell against it, barely keeping his balance as it swallowed him, sticky even through the helmet and suit.

He broke out onto the other side, the resistance abruptly gone. "Huh," he said, turning in a slow circle. Everything still looked hazy. He turned back as Alyssa pushed her way in, followed by Becka and then Matt.

"Control," Becka said, putting the weather station down. "We are on the other side, and it looks . . ." She took a breath. "What's the technical term for 'super creepy'?"

"Menacing?" Alyssa suggested.

"Disturbing?" said Matt.

Nate looked up at the yellow-green orb of the sun, the nearby plants with their long waving tentacles, the mist that oozed sluggishly around them. "Sinister," he said quietly.

Becka nodded. "I think that's the winner." She turned, spouting out a list of other readings. Temperature, oxygen density, moisture. Nate wasn't listening anymore, his eyes fixed on the nearest plant.

It had moved.

He rubbed at his eyes. This strange mist made it hard to see, giving everything a really bizarre shadow. But no, that plant was definitely closer. It was a deep, dark purple, like an eggplant, and stood almost as tall as he was, the tentacle-like leaves drifting toward them. It rocked a little, and its roots pulled out of the dry soil with a long *sluuuuurp*.

"Um, guys," Nate said.

"Control, can you hear me?" Becka asked.

A burst of static shot through Nate's speaker, and he yelped, instinctively trying to cover his ears. The others all did the same. It went quiet, and then more static, softer this time, like an endless whisper.

"Control? *Control?*"

Nate glanced over his shoulder. The portal flickered like the screen of an old television. "No!" He lunged at it just as it winked out of existence.

Nate fell, skidding across the dirt. He pushed himself up immediately, scanning the horizon.

The portal was gone completely.

He exchanged terrified looks with the others and knew the truth: they were trapped here in this alien place.

"One, two, three, four," chanted a girlish voice. Nate whirled but didn't see anyone. The voice seemed to float all around them, not belonging to any one thing.

A woman stepped out of the hazy yellow mist. She was tiny, under five feet, with the sweet old face of a kindly grandmother. Her long white hair hung loose down her back, and she wore a green polka-dotted dress.

"Hello?" Nate called.

As the woman shuffled closer, Nate noticed other details. Disturbing details. Her dress was made of vines, and those polka dots were really eyes, hundreds of them, all staring at him. Her bare, veiny feet made no sound as she walked toward them, yellow toenails curling into the soil.

“My, oh my. What has stumbled right onto my front doorstep?” She stopped a few feet away and put her hands on her hips. “You poor little things. You must be scared.”

“We’re not scared,” Becka said, stepping forward, her chin up. Nate was impressed with her bravery; he wanted to turn and run screaming across the sand. But if she could be brave, then so could he. After all, he couldn’t imagine either Rae or Vivienne fleeing.

“Not scared?” The woman’s wrinkled face stretched in a wide grin. She was missing all of her teeth, except for two long, sharp fangs. “Don’t worry, sweetheart. You will be.”

A nameless dread wrapped itself around Nate, weighing him down, pinning him to the spot as ghostly fingers plucked the helmet from his head and crushed it into a thousand shattered pieces. He had only a few seconds of complete terror before everything went black, as in the distance someone laughed and laughed.

Acknowledgments

Our thanks to everyone working behind the scenes at McElderry Books to make this book a success, including Justin Chanda, Karen Wojtyla, Anne Zafian, Bridget Madsen, Tiara Iandiorio, Chrissy Noh, Devin MacDonald, Karen Masnica, Cassandra Fernandez, Brian Murray, Anna Jarzab, Emily Ritter, Annika Voss, Lauren Hoffman, Lisa Morelda, Lauren Carr, Christina Pecorale and her sales team, and Michelle Leo and her education/library team. Also a huge thank-you to our cover illustrator, Xavier Collette, who drew the world's most terrifying alien insect—we love it!

Writing a book in the middle of a pandemic was challenging. It would have been impossible without the help of these people:

Our editor, Sarah McCabe, who is a true plot wizard, always helping us find the best possible version of each story.

Our agent, Jennifer Azantian, who continually keeps us focused and inspired.

Our writing community, full of supportive, amazingly talented people, all willing to spend time beta-reading chapters and talking us through plot tangles. A special shout-out to Alan Wehrman for initial brainstorming help, and to the Kidliterati: Suzi Guina, Katie Nelson, Jennifer Camiccia, Kaitlin Hundscheid, Liz Edelbrock, Taylor Gardner, and Tara Creel, who all read and critiqued parts of this story.

Our families, including our parents and in-laws Rich, Rose, Lyn, and Bruce, and siblings Rosi, Ed, Jesse, and Ashley, who give us constant encouragement. Ember and Evelyn, who provide the ultimate motivation to keep working hard, as well as giving us excellent time management skill training. And our partners Nick and Sean, who have been a part of this journey from the beginning.

And to everyone who read and loved the first Whispering Pines book, we appreciate you more than you can know and hope you enjoy reading this next installment of Rae's and Caden's adventure as much as we enjoyed writing it.

HEIDI LANG & KATI BARTKOWSKI

are a writing team of two sisters. Heidi is afraid of all things that go bump in the night but watches shows like *The X-Files* and *Stranger Things* anyhow. Kati enjoys reading about serial killers and the apocalypse but secretly sleeps with a night-light. They believe that the best way to conquer fear is to share it with as many people as possible, so between the two of them, they love creating stories full of all the things that scare them most. They are the coauthors of the Mystic Cooking Chronicles trilogy.